THE COLOR OF THE SOUL

D1057319

The COLOR of the SOUL

TRACEY BATEMAN

BARBOUR
PUBLISHING

For more information about Tracey Bateman, please access the author's Web site at the following Internet address: www.traceybateman.com

Cover image by Oak Alley Plantation, Vacherie, Louisiana
        www.OakAlleyPlantation.com
Cover design by Müllerhaus Publishing Arts, Inc.

Published by Barbour Publishing, Inc., P.O. Box 719, Uhrichsville, OH 44683, www.barbourbooks.com

Our mission is to publish and distribute inspirational products offering exceptional value and biblical encouragement to the masses.

 Member of the
Evangelical Christian
Publishers Association

Printed in the United States of America
5 4 3 2 1

- Dedication -

To Aunt Edith and my cousin Vivian. You've forgotten more about history than I'll ever know. Thank you for scraping and digging and finding such rich information about our family history. I wouldn't be surprised if someday your research takes us all the way back to the Flood (the big one). You amaze me. This book could only have been dedicated to you.

- Acknowledgments -

Special thanks to my editor, Rebecca Germany, for believing in this story.
Thanks to Tracie Peterson for so many reasons.
I'll always be more grateful than I can express.

Nancy Toback—the first person I shared this idea with.
If you hadn't been so excited about Andy and Cat,
I might never have had the nerve to share the idea with my editor.

Once again to Chris Lynxwiler, without whom I could never write a book.
Your friendship means more to me than you'll ever comprehend.
Thanks for making me a better writer with your honest critiques
and a better person with your honest friendship.

Susie Warren—thanks for making me look deep into the souls of my characters
and for challenging me to get to the gut of what makes each one tick.
For asking me what God wants to say through each and every page. Y
ou've taught me so much. Thanks for loving me enough to know when I need
prayer or a phone call. I think we might have been separated at birth.

And to the rest of the Pinkies—I love each one of you.

~ Part One: Shame ~

My confusion is continually before me,
and the shame of my face hath covered me.

Psalm 44:15

CHAPTER ONE
~ 1 9 4 8

Rain pelted Andy's face beneath the brim of his brown felt fedora, the stinging drops doing nothing to improve his foul mood. Hundreds of miles of riding in the back of a bus had grated on him. No, not grated. Downright stabbed at his pride like a pirate's dagger.

He adjusted his suitcase to the other hand and turned up his collar. Education, a swift mind, talent. Those things caused a man to think he might make something of himself one day. Andy Carmichael had been given benefit of all three. But the farther south the bus had driven, the more his sense of self-worth had waned. What good were those things in the South? For a black man, anyhow.

A hot wind carried the stink of the river to his nostrils. Sharp teeth of anger clamped tighter on his already-raw emotions as the red dirt beneath his feet softened to miry mud.

His wingtips were getting ruined.

He swiped at his brow and glared at the rain. He hated the South. The sooner he finished his business and got back to Chicago, the better.

A motor roared down the road, coming louder, closer. Andy jerked his head toward the sound and swallowed a rush of panic. A black Ford sped toward him, then slowed to a crawl as it approached. Andy kept his focus ahead, his heart beating a rapid rhythm against his chest. Anxiety clutched at him, squeezing tighter with every forward step.

"What do you think you're doing on our road, boy?"

Andy sucked in the inside of his cheek and halted his steps. He slowly turned toward the car. Three young men, white boys of probably no more than eighteen years, hung out of open windows, grinning with wicked intention.

Andy knew he couldn't give in to the instinct to drag the loudmouthed idiots out of that car one by one and stuff them in the trunk. Everything within him screamed for one thing: survival. He racked his brain, trying to remember the proper stance and facial expression to show respect.

"You deaf?" A fat, red-haired mongrel stuck his head out farther and shoved Andy's chest with his fingertips. "Or just too blasted ignorant to answer?"

Andy went with the shove and stepped back. *Don't fight.* Fighting back had dire consequences. No matter who was right, he would lose.

"I asked you a question, nigger." The young man's ruddy face grew redder. "You lookin' for trouble?"

"No, suh. I ain't lookin' fo' no trouble." Andy dummied up his articulation, knowing the repercussions for educated blacks. "Just headed up the road there." He nodded in the direction he'd been walking.

"We know that, you ignorant fool. Where are you headed? I ain't never seen you around these parts before."

"No, suh. I ain't never been in these here parts befo'." At least not that they had any need to know.

The "sir" served its intended purpose and seemed to

mollify the aggressive youth. Andy sensed the tension inside the car relax. But he kept up his guard.

From the corner of his eye, he spotted movement and heard the telltale rattle of a wagon coming closer.

"Hey, Gabe," said the driver of the car. "Looks like we got company."

"Move it, you cockeyed mules," muttered the old man in the wagon. His disgruntled voice gave the boys a good laugh.

Andy kept his attention focused on the boys in the car, despite his curiosity over the expletives coming from the wagon.

The redhead scowled and turned back to Andy.

"Come on, Gabe," the driver groused. "Roll up the dadgum window. I'm getting wet. Besides, I don't want to miss the matinee over some colored. Just let him be."

The redheaded boy sneered, his lip curling to reveal a wad of chewing tobacco.

Andy had a split second of premonition. Nevertheless, he stood his ground as the young man spat a stream of tobacco juice on his pant leg.

The engine revved amid shouts of laughter. The wheels spun and mud whipped up, dousing Andy's clothes.

Lord, he hated the South.

He yanked a handkerchief from his front pocket and wiped the rain from his face, then turned his attention toward the wagon.

The old-timer tugged the mules to a stop. "This ain't no kinda day to be walkin'. Get up in this here wagon, and I'll take ya wherever ya need to go, young fella."

Andy nodded his thanks to the old man, tossed his suitcase into the back, and climbed onto the wagon seat. "I hadn't anticipated rain when I started out."

"There ain't no anticipatin' to be done this time o' year."

"I suppose."

The wagon lurched forward as the animals strained against their bits. Andy hadn't stared at the backside of a mule since he left Georgia twenty-six years earlier. And he wasn't crazy about the view now.

Returning to the rural county of his birth had been like going back in time a hundred years. At least from a Negro perspective. The whites still owned all the cars. Blacks either walked or took the bus. Or in the case of old-timers, hitched a wagon to a pair of mules.

"You ain't from around here, is ya?"

Well, he was and he wasn't, but no sense in starting a story he had no intention of sharing to its conclusion. He shook his head. "Chicago."

"Oo-ee. That far? Ain't every day you see a stranger from Chi-ca-gy walkin' down this here road. Can't help but think on jus' why a fella'd do that."

"I'm on my way to Penbrook House. You know the place?"

A toothless grin split the old man's face. "Sure do." He nodded toward the two gray mules slogging through the red mud. "Ol' Pru and Pete'll have us there in a jiffy."

"I'm obliged."

"You hirin' on to help old Miss Penbrook with the harvest?"

"Hardly." Andy cringed at the sarcasm in his own voice. But did he really look like a field hand?

"You got somethin' agin honest work?" The old man gave him a look of hard scrutiny.

Heat rushed to Andy's ears. "I'm a writer. Miss Penbrook has enlisted my services to write her memoirs."

His face scrunched. "What's that?"

"Her biography."

"That right?" He pulled against the reins, yanking the mule on the left to counteract its tendency to pull toward the right side of the road. "This bi–og—. . .What'd you call it?"

"Biography. Her life story, in other words."

His face lit with a smile of understanding. "Why didn't ya jus' say so, 'stead of usin' that fancy talk?"

"Sorry."

The old man turned the wagon onto the long lane heading up to Penbrook House. Mammoth oaks lined each side of the road as if watching over them, escorting them in. The mules seemed to feel safer and pulled in the same direction for a change.

A canopy of leafy branches hovered over the road and offered a respite from the rain. Andy looked down at his wet, muddy suit and mud-caked shoes and grimaced. So much for making a good first impression. Under other circumstances, he'd dry off and change his clothes before meeting the woman. But he hadn't thought to find a rooming house or a hotel before setting out for Penbrook. Now he had no choice but to face the famous author in disgrace. Then again, the woman was more than a hundred years old. Maybe she had poor eyesight.

He lifted his gaze and took in the impressive sight of Penbrook House. The 150 year-old mansion stood before him in regal splendor, a monument to all that was beautiful about north Georgia, past and present.

His memory of the old place didn't do it justice.

The old man pulled the mules to a stop in front of the house. "There ya be."

"Thanks for the ride." He climbed down and grabbed his suitcase from the back of the wagon.

"I was pleasured to do it. Like me to wait and drive ya back to town?"

Andy hesitated a moment, then shook his head. The rain had stopped, and the skies seemed to be clearing. "I hate to impose on your generosity. Besides, no telling how long I'll be."

The old-timer nodded. "Ya take care now. An' don't git yerself in trouble with them white fellas. They'll likely be lookin' fer ya when they ain't got nothin' better to do." Without waiting for an answer, he flapped the reins and fought the mules to get them turned back to the oak-lined lane.

Andy moved toward the mansion. Towering columns graced the wraparound porch. Above him, a balcony spread across the front and wound its way around the two sides of the house. He climbed the stone steps leading to an ornately carved wooden door and rang the bell.

While he waited, he turned to watch the old man and his mules slog away from Penbrook House.

Andy shuddered at the thought of what his future might have been if his mother hadn't sent him away. His heart clenched at the painful memory. Emotions that belonged to the ten-year-old boy he'd been when he boarded the train headed for Chicago sliced at his heart.

With his attention diverted, he jumped at the sound of the mammoth door creaking open. Feeling like a fool for being so easily distracted, he straightened his tie and flashed his best winning smile at the stern face of the Negro woman standing before him.

She gave him a suspicious once-over, then frowned as her gaze settled on his suitcase. "We ain't takin' in no strays."

"I have an appointment with Miss Penbrook."

Her brow rose dubiously.

Heat warmed Andy's neck. "I can imagine how I must look, ma'am, but I can explain."

She folded her arms and waited.

"I walked from town in the rain, and some boys drove by in their car and splashed me. That's why I'm covered with mud."

"What's your name?"

"Andy Carmichael."

The housekeeper nodded and stepped aside, swinging the door wide open. "Don't take all day gettin' in here. We don't need no more flies."

"Sorry, ma'am." Chills slid down Andy's spine as he stepped inside. "This is quite a house. Not as big as I remember. But then, I haven't seen it in twenty-six years." Small talk really wasn't his strong suit, but tight nerves always made him ramble.

She ignored his observation anyway. "Set down that bag and follow me. Miz Penbrook's ailin' and can't get out of bed. You'll have to go to her."

Andy felt like a ten-year-old boy again, wide-eyed and overwhelmed by the enormity of his surroundings. The housekeeper led him through the expansive foyer and up a winding, plush-carpeted stairway. A crystal chandelier sparkled in the sunlight peeking through floor-to-ceiling windows. Andy allowed his fingertips to trail along the

smooth mahogany rail, his gaze taking in the richness surrounding him.

At the top of the stairs, the housekeeper turned and
led him down a long hallway. Andy tried to keep his gaze
straight ahead, but curiosity got the better of him, and he
couldn't help but twist around to take in the beauty.

Paintings lined the corridor—faces from the past. One
black woman stood out among the sea of white. Andy
stopped and stared into her eyes. She bore the telltale light-
ness of a slave of mixed blood. He shook his head, faintly
recognizing the deep set of her eyes. Unsettled by the sense
of familiarity, Andy turned away.

The housekeeper stopped before a half-open door at the
end of the hall and pounded on the door frame. "He's here,
Miz Penbrook." She turned back to Andy and glared. "You
comin'?"

Her sharp tone yanked Andy from his pensiveness. He
hid a smirk. Nothing like a bona fide Southern black woman to make a man feel like he was about to get a whippin'.
Even at thirty-six years old. Some things never changed.
"Sorry."

She pushed out her bottom lip and harrumphed. "You're
gonna have to talk loud. She cain't hear much. And her
mind gets addled when she's tired, so don't ask too many
questions."

"Yes, ma'am."

"Are you going to show the gentleman in, Delta, or must I
walk to the door myself?" The voice was crisp and clear, not at
all the crackling, frail voice Andy would have expected from a
woman over one hundred years old.

The housekeeper rolled her eyes. "Go on in."

Gripping his hat between his hands, Andy stepped across the threshold. He tried to shake off the feeling that the house was filled with ghosts from the past. But there was an eeriness to the dimly lit room that only added to his anxiety. Vague shadows of memories fell across his mind. Images veiled by darkness and hoarse whispers. The moisture of his mama's tears soaking his neck. A dream?

"Come in, Mr. Carmichael." The voice came from the four-poster bed pressed against the wall straight ahead. "I'm afraid I cannot get up to welcome you properly. But you may come and sit next to me."

He strode across the room, the *click-clack, click-clack* of his shoes resonating off the hardwood floor. The dimness slowly receded to unveil a tiny, wrinkled woman huddled under a thick, rose-colored comforter.

He stopped next to the bed and reached out in greeting. "Thank you for seeing me, Miss Penbrook. It's a great honor."

Her veined hand slipped into his, and she snared his gaze, rendering him incapable of looking away. "You don't speak like any colored man from around here. I swear, if I closed my eyes, I couldn't tell you from a lily-white gentleman of the South—except perhaps you have better grammar." She cackled at her own joke.

Indignation beat a cold, hard rhythm in his breast. Did she honestly think that was a compliment? Was he supposed to kiss her skeletal hand and thank her?

He couldn't do this. Why in God's name had he come back here? The entire state of Georgia reeked with the sweat and blood of his brethren. Bile rose to his throat, and he swallowed hard to keep from retching all over the old belle's clean floor.

The witch turned loose of his hand and waved him to an emerald green wing chair. He sat down, set his briefcase on his lap and clicked it open, then removed pen and paper to take notes of the interview. "I'm from Chicago. But then, you already knew that."

She gave a loud snort—the kind only a woman who had become such an icon that nothing she did could possibly jeopardize her position among polite society could get away with. "You're an uppity colored, aren't you?"

Andy's defenses rose, and he had to remind himself that this woman was very, very old. "I beg your pardon?"

"You beg my pardon?" She scowled, making her wrinkles run together in her scrunched-up face. "Fancy talk in a colored man might work up north, but no one appreciates it in the South. So don't act uppity with me. That skin of yours might be lighter than Delta's, but you would do well to remember who you are and where you came from if you want to get along down here. We don't spoil our coloreds the way the Yankees do."

"Yes, ma'am. I'm sure you don't." Andy fought the urge to laugh at her assumption that just because he lived in the North, his light skin made any difference. He was still a colored man, and most white people thought he wasn't quite as good as even the dumbest and poorest among them. His own kind automatically assumed he considered himself a higher class of Negro, and sometimes that made life in the ghetto difficult. But they didn't know him. No one really knew him. All he wanted was peace. To live his life, raise a family, and make a good living for his wife—if she'd take him back. It's all he'd ever wanted.

He glared at Miss Penbrook. What did she know of being too white to be black and too black to be white?

"Made you good and mad, didn't I, boy?" The old hag cackled. "Good. Anger is an honest emotion. I can appreciate that."

Swallowing a retort, he cleared his throat and tried to remember that old people had the privilege of being rude to whomever they pleased.

"Miss Penbrook." He kept his voice deliberately calm, a difficult task when he was forced to yell in order for her to hear every word he said. "May I begin the interview?"

With a wave of her bony hand, she giggled like a schoolgirl. "You're trying to be polite, when you'd like to give me a good piece of your mind, isn't that right?"

"I assure you, Miss Penbrook, the last thing I want to do is give you a piece of my mind." Andy forced a smile. "You're much too important for me to offend you intentionally."

She gave him a look of scrutiny as though she knew he was only trying to placate her in order to get on with it. Andy held his breath and waited to see if she would challenge him.

Suddenly she spoke, "You want to know all about me?"

"If you please." Andy expelled a breath.

A smug smile showed toothless gums. "Maybe you do, maybe you don't. Sometimes knowledge is freedom, and sometimes it's nothing but a chain around your neck. You might not like my story."

What sort of game was the old debutante trying to play?

"I'm a writer. I don't have to like it. All I have to do is record it. Would you like to start?"

She scowled and waved again. "Young people are so impatient. But then, I suppose you have a story to write."

"Yes, ma'am." *Why else would I have left my wife at a time like this to travel down to this godforsaken wretch of a state?* He struggled to push away a sudden rush of memories. A shudder moved up his spine. The sooner he was out of Georgia, the sooner his stomach would unclench. This had better be worth it.

Miss Penbrook gave a sudden jerk of her head and eyed him with such intensity that Andy had to fight the urge to look away.

"Good," she said. "I'm ready to tell my story. I'm an old woman, and I've nothing to lose. Shall I begin my life with the beginning of my life?"

Andy nodded, recognizing her question as a line from *David Copperfield*. Did she think her story would become a classic piece of literature? Yes, she probably did. His stomach tightened with excitement. Maybe it would at that.

"I don't remember much of the beginning, to tell you the truth. I was very young. But the things I've heard. Oh, the things I've seen."

She fixed her gaze on a beam of light shining on the wall alongside the bed. The faraway look in her dark eyes sent a chill over every inch of Andy's skin. "I'm not sure of my exact age at the time, but I believe I was around four or five years old when my parents. . ."

GEORGIA, 1849
"For pity's sake, Henry, what on earth is the holdup?" Madeline Penbrook whipped out her pearl-handled fan and shook it furiously in an effort to provide her own personal breeze against the stifling Georgia sun. Much to her annoyance, the

carriage had come to a sudden stop on the cobblestone street.

After a long day of socializing with the wives of her husband's planter friends—ladies with whom she had little in common and for whom she had even less regard—Madeline's head ached and her stomach churned. She was in no mood for delays. All she wanted was to return home and relax out of the sun.

"Well?" she asked her husband, who was seated across from her, looking quite dashing in a pair of tan trousers and a matching coat.

"Dearest, you mustn't upset yourself." He studied her, his brow furrowed in concern.

"Fiddlesticks. Henry, if you do not immediately inform me of the reason for this delay, I shall stand up and turn around right here in this buggy and disgrace us both."

He released a heavy breath.

Looking into his clear blue eyes and deeply tanned face, Madeline softened her tone. "I am sorry to be so difficult. But I simply must know, and your hesitation only makes me all the more curious."

Henry craned his neck to see ahead of the buggy and frowned again. "It would appear a slave has run off from the auction."

Madeline shuddered and sank back against the seat. "I hope the poor creature gets away."

"Shh," Henry admonished. He darted a cautious glance at the four-year-old child lying across his lap, looking very much like an angel from heaven. She slept peacefully, her mop of beautiful chestnut curls splayed across her father's arm. "Do you want Camilla to hear you?"

The ear-shattering sound of a woman's wail cut off

Madeline's retort. She pushed to her feet before Henry could stop her and turned to see what the ruckus was all about. Her heart caught in her throat at what she saw. A young slave woman dressed in a neat calico gown, her hair bound by a red handkerchief, was struggling while a burly, barrel-chested man held on to her and another tried to wrestle a bundle from her arms.

"Don' take my chile! Please!" She broke loose and threw herself at the feet of the first man in the crowd of spectators. "Please," she begged, clutching her child tightly to her breast. "My little Catherina, she don' eat much. An' she kin already shine silver and brush young missies' hair. You be gettin' a real good bargain on da bof of us."

"What do I need with another pickaninny running about the place?" the man asked gruffly, tossing a cigar to the ground inches from where the woman knelt.

Her pursuers grabbed her while she desperately fought to hang on to her child. One of the men succeeded in snatching the child, a little girl of perhaps three or four, from the woman's arms. "Get back up there, gal."

"Ma!" Flailing her little body, the young girl struggled against her captor, clawing the air as she reached for her mother, who was being dragged back to the auction block. The little girl twisted. She reared back and belted the man squarely in the jaw.

"Why you little. . ." His hand came down hard.

Madeline winced.

The child stopped fighting.

Madeline's hand crept protectively to her rounded stomach, tears stinging her eyes.

Henry reached for her hand and pulled her gently back

to her seat. He motioned for the driver to move the carriage forward once more. "Don't cry, darlin'. We'll be back home soon, and you can forget all about this."

Madeline turned on him. "Forget about it?" she spat. "Do you think I shall ever forget the sight of that child being ripped from her mother's arms? It'll haunt me all my born days. And even into my grave."

The slave woman's cries, mingling with those of her child, seemed to grow louder as the carriage inched forward in the congested street.

"Don't look, dearest," Henry soothed.

"How can I not?" Her eyes scanned the yard of greedy landowners looking to purchase their pound of flesh. Bile rose to her throat. Anger shook her.

Unbidden, her gaze came to rest upon the young mother, now spent with tears. The slave woman had been stripped to the waist. She kept her chin down. Her arms were crossed over her breasts as she desperately tried to cover herself.

Suddenly the crestfallen woman straightened, as though lifted by some unseen force, and glanced over the crowd. Madeline caught her breath as the slave's dark gaze locked with hers, baring her soul and reading into Madeline's.

It was as though she were reaching out to Madeline, drawing her, calling to her. *Don' let dem take my baby from me. What if it was you? Your baby?*

The child within her chose this moment to make his presence felt. Tears burned her eyes, and she glanced at her sleeping Camilla. What if she were in this woman's place?

Once again, Madeline shot to her feet in the moving carriage, then grasped the seat to steady herself. "Stop the carriage, Toby," she ordered the driver.

Henry leaned forward, concern flashing in his eyes. "What's the matter? Is it the baby?"

"The baby is fine." Madeline quickly opened the carriage door and hopped out before Henry could set their child on the seat beside him and detain her.

She hurried through the crowd, which parted easily at the uncommon sight of a white woman in such a place. The bidding ceased as she strode to the front of the platform. "You, sir," she said, too overcome with indignation to be afraid. "Unhand that child this instant."

He turned his head and spit a stream of tobacco juice through the air, then wiped his mouth with the back of a hairy hand. He regarded her with a squinty-eyed gaze that made Madeline feel as undressed as the poor woman on the block. "I ain't unhandin' nothin'. This pickaninny is goin' up there right after the woman."

Swallowing back the nausea rising in her throat, Madeline stomped the ground. "Pickaninny, my foot." She glared at the uncouth man. "That darling child is as white as you are."

The little girl peeked up curiously at Madeline, her mouth open in wonder. Madeline smiled into the precious round face. A shy grin tipped the corners of rosebud lips, revealing perfectly straight white teeth, before the little girl ducked her head and stared at the ground.

Madeline glanced up at the slave woman who stood on the platform, hope shining in eyes luminous from tears.

Glaring at the slave trader, Madeline motioned toward the woman. "Allow her to cover herself this minute. You should be ashamed." Turning, she stared at the entire lot of onlookers. "You should all be ashamed. Now, I mean to buy this woman and her child. What is the bid?"

The bewildered slave trader named the price.

"That's fine. I'll take them both."

"Now, see here, lady. That ain't the way things are done." He looked over her shoulder. "This your wife, mister?"

"She is."

Madeline's heart hammered against her chest at the sound of Henry's cold voice behind her. She knew she was in for a stern lecture upon their arrival home, but for now she prayed God would give her husband the foresight to see this through with her.

"Well, get her outta here. This ain't no place for a woman."

Henry looked up at the slave, his eyes moving over her. Unease nipped at Madeline's stomach as she caught a flash of. . .something in his gaze. She shook off the disloyal thought. Henry had always been a good and faithful man.

When he spoke, she pushed the rest of her suspicion firmly to the back of her mind. "I believe my wife has expressed an interest in purchasing this female and her child." He turned to the crowd of men. "Any of you plan to do more bidding?"

The crowd shuffled, but no one spoke.

Digging her nails into her palms, Madeline held her breath and prayed. *Father, grant us mercy to save this one woman and her child. It's a small thing, Lord. Only two of Your precious children. But I beg of You, let it be.*

"Come, gentlemen," the slave trader appealed to the crowd. "Surely, you will not give up this fine female on the whim of a woman—lovely though she may be."

A tense moment of silence passed until a voice rose from the crowd. "Get them out of here and show the next one."

With helpless frustration, the trader glared at Henry.

"They're yours."

"Thank You, Lord," Madeline whispered.

Henry stepped toward his wife. "I will take care of the business. Get the woman and child to our carriage and wait for me."

"Yes, dear."

She eyed the unkempt man still holding on to the child. "I will thank you to turn loose of my property, sir." She nearly choked on the words but squared her shoulders and met his steely gaze head on.

Grudgingly, he pushed the little girl forward. She stumbled, then righted herself before crashing to the ground.

Madeline knelt before the child and smoothed back a tangled mop of hair, the same chestnut color as her own darling Camilla's. "What is your name?"

Popping a bony finger into her mouth, the girl dropped her gaze. "Catherina," she mumbled.

"A lovely name for a lovely little girl." Madeline straightened and reached out for Catherina's hand. "Would you like to come home with me?"

She tilted her head and regarded Madeline with a questioning look. "Mama, too?"

Through a veil of tears, Madeline nodded. The woman gave a glad cry and hopped off the platform, pulling her dress up and sliding her arms through the sleeves. She gathered her daughter into her arms, her body shaking with sobs. "Thank you, missus. Thank you."

Aware of the onlookers, Madeline leveled a gaze at the woman. "Follow me," she said with a curt nod. She remained silent until they reached the carriage, then she turned. "What is your name?"

"Naomi, missus."

"I'm very pleased to meet you and your lovely daughter."

Toby opened the carriage door, and Madeline stepped aside for Naomi and Catherina to precede her. The slave woman's eyes grew wide and she hung back. "Missus!"

Madeline felt heat creep to her face. She nodded. "Of course. How stupid of me," she said with a weary sigh. "Toby, help Naomi and little Catherina to the seat beside you, and please. . .watch for Henry for me, will you?"

Settled once more in the carriage, Madeline gathered her daughter, now wide-awake, into her arms. Feeling tears burn her eyes, she pressed Camilla close, hid her face in the little girl's soft curls, and longed for the sight of her Missouri home.

❧

"How could you have been so foolish, Madeline?"

Upon his return to the plantation, Henry had insisted Madeline retire to her bedroom. Now she lay on the four-poster bed she shared with her husband, taking a scolding as though she were a child. She kept her eyes fixed on the patchwork quilt she had made with her own hands during her confinement while carrying Camilla.

"I am sorry for embarrassing you, dearest, but I can't say I'm sorry for my actions." She met his hard stare, pleading with him to understand. "What if it had been Camilla and me on that auction block? It could have been, you know."

"Don't be foolish."

"Why is it foolish to try to put oneself in the shoes of another less fortunate? Just think, Henry. What if, God forbid, a race of foreigners invaded our shores and carried off the inhabitants to serve their own people, without a thought to the families being torn apart? Put yourself in Naomi's position, and tell me, how would you feel?"

With an irritated wave, he dismissed her entreaty. "What has that ridiculous thought to do with your actions this afternoon? Are a couple of slaves so important to you that you would risk the well-being of our own unborn child? What were you thinking?"

Madeline shrank from his wrath. Henry was a wonderful, indulgent husband, and she had never known his anger such as he displayed now.

That a Southern gentleman had even met, let alone married, the daughter of an outspoken abolitionist was a wonder she could only attribute to the hand and will of God. Henry had become friends with her brother at Harvard, the university both had attended, and Henry had come, on holiday, to their Missouri home. Love beyond reason was her only excuse for marrying a slave owner.

But after six years of living in Georgia, Madeline's heart still broke for the slaves, and she could hardly lift her head for the shame she felt every time her maids tended her.

She knew she had acted recklessly this afternoon, but she didn't regret it—nor would she confess to regretting her actions just to appease the man she'd once loved with reckless abandon. She stared now at her husband, who paced before her, red-faced with anger.

"Lord Almighty, Maddy," he muttered, his voice trembling with frustration. "You sound just like Jason. Sometimes I think you ought to have married that nigger-loving brother of mine instead of me."

"Why must you always bring Jason up whenever we

have a disagreement?"

He continued pacing as if he hadn't heard the question, though Maddy knew he'd heard just fine.

Henry's brother had not been content to cast his lot with the Southern planters. His heart led him to the West, away from slavery, away from his father's control. So Jason had received his inheritance early and left a couple of months ago to find his fortune in the West.

Maddy knew Henry was relieved. Otherwise, as the second son, he wouldn't have inherited the vast Penbrook lands when their father died.

But Madeline felt Jason's absence deeply. Each night she wrote her thoughts in the diary he had presented to her before he left. She wished he were still there to confide in. Jason had become her only friend in the South. She loved her husband but had realized soon after their marriage that his ideas were vastly different from her own.

"Henry, please calm down. As you can clearly see, I'm fine. It's done now, and I must say, I am sorely disappointed in you."

Henry halted his pacing mid-stride and glared at her. He opened his mouth to speak, then closed it again, drawing a deep, frustrated breath. He turned his back, clearly trying to gain control over raging emotions.

Encouraged by his silence, Madeline forged ahead, compelled to bring up a matter that had been heavy on her heart for several days. A subject she had been loath to broach thus far, for fear of shattering the peace between them.

"Henry, I must ask you about something I overheard you discussing with Father three days ago."

"Do not turn this around, Maddy," he said, silencing

her with an upraised hand, though he didn't face her. "I'll not allow it this time. We are discussing your inappropriate behavior. Not mine."

Madeline's temper flared. "Do not speak to me as though I'm a child, Henry. I must say, I find your attitude disconcerting, to say the least."

"You find my attitude disconcerting?" He swung about to face her. "I find your actions abominable! Mother has taken to her bed in shame after your conduct today. And my father is so angry. . . ."

Flinging the covers aside, Madeline shot from the bed and faced her husband, trembling with anger. "Do not speak to me of your father. He should be the one dying of shame, and not because of my actions."

"What are you implying?" he asked through gritted teeth.

"I—Yes, Henry, I will speak of this, though you do not wish to discuss your conduct." Unflinching before his anger, Madeline met his gaze head on. "I overheard your father and you discussing the selling of Abner and Jarvis."

His eyes widened, then an expression of shame flickered across his face. "I didn't intend for you to know until absolutely necessary."

"Then it is true?"

"I'm afraid we have no choice. Abner is insolent and unmanageable. We believe he is the reason Jarvis has tried to run away three times in the past year. Besides, with Jason taking his inheritance and moving west, we can't afford to hang on to slaves who aren't pulling their weight. We have no choice."

Lower lip quivering, Madeline blinked against a rush of

hot tears. "But, Henry, Jarvis has a wife and three children and another baby coming in the fall. How could your father sell him away from his family? And why did you not try to discourage such a thing? Wh–what if it was you who were being. . ."

"Do not bring that up again, Maddy." His tone, which had softened, now became hard-edged once more. "Jarvis has tried to run away three times. Was he thinking of his wife and children then?"

"Of course he was." Madeline gripped Henry's arm as a wave of dizziness swept her. She stepped back suddenly and sat hard on the bed.

In an instant, Henry knelt beside her, his face clouded with concern. "Are you all right, dearest? Should I call for the doctor?"

"I'm fine. Just a little dizzy. My head is clearing now." She searched Henry's tender face. How could he be so concerned for her and so unfeeling about another man's wife? Taking his hand between hers, she pressed it against her heart. "Don't you understand? Jarvis planned to do what he had to do to secure freedom. I am sure he would have returned, or arranged somehow for Lizzie and the children to follow. Would you have done less?"

"Come, lie down now. We'll discuss this no further."

A screech from Camilla's bedroom across the hall sent them both to their feet, running to see what was amiss.

Henry flung open the door and found Camilla and Catherina in a tug-of-war over a crocheted doll.

"It's mine," Camilla insisted.

"Missus tole me I could play wif it." Catherina kept a firm grip on the toy.

"Girls," Henry said firmly. "What's going on in here?"

Catherina gasped and relinquished the doll suddenly, sending Camilla backward. The child landed hard on her bottom. Her face contorted with rage, and she flung the doll at the cowering slave girl. Catherina clutched the doll tightly to her breast as though to protect it from Camilla.

"My gramps will whip the hide off you for that, girl!"

"Camilla Penbrook!"

Camilla shot a guilty glance toward Madeline. "Sh–she pushed me down, Mama." Tears glistened in her enormous blue eyes.

But Madeline refused to be moved. "She did no such thing. I saw what happened, and I insist you apologize to Catherina this minute."

"Really, Madeline." Henry's steady voice broke in. "Don't you think you're overreacting a bit?"

Recognizing a champion, Camilla bounded from the floor and raced into her father's arms. "I want my doll back, and she won't give it to me."

Madeline watched the exchange as if in a dream. To see her daughter acting in this manner without the slightest concern for Catherina's feelings was almost too heartbreaking to bear.

"Catherina," Henry asked, his voice stern but not gruff, "is it Camilla's doll?"

Madeline's temper rose again. How did he think a child of Catherina's circumstances would have gotten such a toy?

Trembling with fear, the slave child nodded.

"Well then, you must give it back. We don't take things that belong to others. Is that understood?"

"Yes, sir," she whispered, popping one thumb into her

rosebud mouth.

Camilla wiggled from her father's arms. She flounced to Catherina, jerked the doll from her hands, then tossed it onto her bed.

Henry's mouth dropped open at the display. He stared wide-eyed at Madeline.

"Now, may I deal with this?" she asked in a hoarse whisper, practically shaking with anger.

In stunned silence, he nodded.

Drawing a breath to steady herself, Madeline eyed her daughter, careful not to show her anger. "Camilla, darling, you have not played with that doll in months, so Mama gave Catherina permission to play with it. You were standing right there when I did so. Do you remember?"

"Yes. But I wanted it."

"Which of you two girls had it first?"

Camilla's gaze settled on the floor. "It's mine," she mumbled.

"Camilla Penbrook, I insist you look at me when I'm speaking to you. Who had the doll first?"

Sending Catherina a venomous look, she pointed. "She did."

Madeline swallowed hard and kept her words deliberately calm. "She has a name. Use it, please."

"Catherina did."

"I would like you to take the doll from your bed and hand it to Catherina so that she might play with it."

Madeline drew a sharp breath as a cramp tightened her abdomen. *Oh, dear Lord, please don't let me lose my baby.*

Camilla grabbed the doll from the bed and jutted her chin forward as she held it out for Catherina. The slave child took two steps forward. Just as she reached out for it, Camilla dropped the toy to the floor.

"Camilla Penbrook!"

"She can pick it up if she wants it."

Suddenly a spasm seized Madeline. "Henry." Her voice sounded strange to her own ears as she groped for her husband's steadying arm. Blackness invaded her senses, and she felt herself falling. . .floating. From far away she could hear the soft cries of her husband and child, then nothing-ness overcame her.

Andy glanced up as Miss Penbrook's voice trailed off. She stared in silence at the opposite wall, lost in her memories.

"I take it your mother lost the baby she was carrying?" he pressed, hoping to snap her back to the present. He waited until enough time had lapsed that it appeared she hadn't heard him. "Miss Penbrook?"

The elderly woman jerked her chin and stared at him, confusion clouding her eyes. "Yes?"

"Your mother. Did she lose the baby?"

"The baby went to heaven to be with Jesus." Tears sprang to the faded eyes. "It's all my fault. Now all she does is cry and cry. We're moving to Missouri so she'll be happy again."

Tears rolled down the weathered cheeks, and Andy felt his heart lurch. He glanced around, wondering if he should call for the housekeeper. Clearly, the elderly woman had lost her senses and thought herself a child.

He rose and walked to the open door. "Delta!"

The housekeeper appeared in a matter of seconds. "What

are you shoutin' about?"

"I'm sorry, ma'am, but something's wrong with Miss Penbrook."

A worried frown creased her brow. "I tole you she gets addled. The past always upsets her." Sending him an accusing glare as though it was his fault the old lady had lost her mind, she brushed past him.

She sat on the edge of the bed and took the weeping woman into her arms. "Shh. It's okay, Miz Penbrook. Delta's here."

"I'm sorry. I don't want the doll, really. She can have it."

"Shh," Delta soothed. "Don't go blamin' yourself, child. God needed that little baby in heaven. It weren't your fault."

Within moments, Miss Penbrook's sobs subsided, and her breathing slowed to a rhythmic rise and fall of her chest. Delta laid her gently back on her pillow. She arranged the comforter over her shoulders, then tiptoed toward the door, motioning for Andy to follow.

"She can't talk no more today. You got a room where I can call you when she's ready to go on?"

Andy shook his head. "I came straight here."

"It would be better for her to let it go. You see how guilty she gets to feelin' about her childhood." Delta shook her head and gave a low cluck of her tongue.

Disappointment swept through Andy. He had hoped to do the interview in one sitting and then go home, write his story, and claim the glory for a job well done. At the rate this woman was able to discuss her life, he would have to make multiple trips to Oak Junction to get the whole story. One hundred years was a lot of life to cover. It could take a year of traveling down to Georgia between other assignments to get enough information for a whole story about Miss Penbrook's life. And who knew how much longer the old lady would live?

"Delta, how long does her mind remain cloudy after one of these episodes?"

A shrug lifted the ample shoulders. "She'll probably wake up spry and clearheaded in the mornin' and be a-wonderin' how come you left in such an all-fired hurry." Her thick lips curved into a hint of an indulgent smile.

Andy rubbed his chin, drawing the inside of his cheek between his teeth. "Where's the nearest hotel?"

She gave him a quick once-over, amusement sparking her faded brown eyes. "Honey, if you go struttin' around town actin' like you's from the North, you gonna get yourself hurt. Where's the nearest hotel?" she mimicked. "What you should be askin' is where can a colored fella stay for the night without gettin' hisself lynched."

Andy frowned at the aging housekeeper, then nodded as clarity struck him. "Of course."

She gave him a quick pat on his arm, then moved to a small desk. In a moment, she handed him a sheet of paper with a name and address scribbled on it. "That's my nephew Buck's place. It's a roomin' house, not a hotel; but you just tell him Delta sent you, and he'll get you all fixed up."

"Thank you, Miss Delta. You will get in touch with me when Miss Penbrook is able to see me again?"

She nodded and showed him to the door. "I still think it's a bad idea. But you can't talk her outta something she gets into that head of hers. For some reason she thinks she needs to tell her story. And she won't tell it to no one but you."

"I wondered about that. Why do you think she wanted me?" Andy asked, standing in the foyer. He snatched his suitcase from the floor. "Has she read my work in the paper, or did she just pick my name out of a hat?"

Delta's stern gaze captured his. "You gonna have to ask Miz Penbrook that question if you really want to know the answer."

Andy flashed her a grin and moved toward the door. "I just might. Thanks for the address." He stepped aside and allowed Delta to open the door.

The old man's wagon stood just beyond the step, after all. He grinned when he saw Andy and lifted his hand.

"Looks like ole Jeb's waitin' to take you to town. Jus' tell him you be wantin' to go to Buck's place. He can git you there."

"Thank you." Plopping his hat on his head, he sent her another grin.

The housekeeper regarded him with a disapproving frown and closed the door.

CHAPTER TWO

After a fitful night's sleep, Andy rose early, washed his face, and wandered downstairs toward the heavenly smell of freshly boiled coffee and frying ham. Buck and Lottie Purdue proved to be a loving couple with a houseful of children and had welcomed Andy warmly. They'd even thrown in meals as part of the paltry sum he was paying for the use of a room.

"Good morning, Mr. Carmichael." Mrs. Purdue's cheerful smile greeted him as he entered the kitchen. "Coffee?"

"Yes, ma'am. And please, call me Andy."

"The children'll be down soon, but you might get to drink half a cup in peace."

Andy smiled. "Children don't bother me."

"You must have some of your own then. How many?" Mrs. Purdue set a mug in front of him on the table.

"No." A lump formed in Andy's throat. He swallowed it down with a gulp of burning coffee. "We lost two."

Unable to abide the sympathy in the woman's chocolate brown eyes, Andy turned away from his hostess and slid his finger around the edge of his cup.

"It's all right," she said softly, rinsing a dish under running water. "You don't have to talk about it. I lost three of Buck's babies before we got our first one. And look at how

God's blessed us since. A half a dozen and another one coming early next year."

"I don't think God's too inclined to bless me with anything. But congratulations on the new baby."

The dish clattered in the sink as she whipped around to face him. "Seems like you've been blessed with a good job, health, a wife. Wouldn't you call those blessings?"

Embarrassed and unwilling to argue with a woman he didn't really know, Andy shrugged. "If you say so."

The children began to filter in, a welcome relief to the awkward tension.

Directly after breakfast, a messenger arrived from Penbrook House announcing that Miss Penbrook regretted she would be unable to see Andy today. Perhaps tomorrow. In the meantime, she sent a box containing several books she hoped he would find interesting.

A heavy sigh escaped Andy's lips as he scooped up the box and headed back to his room.

He sat on his bed and fingered the books, his stomach a whirl of butterflies as he realized what he had at his disposal. Not only did the box contain Miss Penbrook's diary—in several volumes—but Madeline Penbrook's and Catherina's, as well. He rummaged until he found the diary containing Madeline's thoughts after her miscarriage.

Vaguely aware of the rumble of thunder outside, Andy stretched out on the bed and allowed Madeline Penbrook to take him into her world.

MARCH 1849

> *It is settled. Tomorrow Henry and I shall take Camilla and Catherina and move back to Missouri. I ache at the*

thought of taking the child from her mother. After all, why did I abase myself to barter for human flesh if all for naught? I am appalled that Henry would sell Naomi to his father without my consent. But he insists our financial situation is not good and moving to Missouri will burden him further. I believe he sold her to punish me, though whether the punishment is due to losing his son or for defying him in the first place, I cannot be certain. He has changed so much I scarcely know him at all anymore.

At any rate, I have promised my dear friend Naomi that I will look after her daughter as though she were my own. Henry has reluctantly agreed we should raise Cat as a white girl (for her skin is as white as my own), though I can see he is unhappy with the idea. I would like to raise her as our daughter, especially since, sadly, the doctor has advised it does not appear to be God's will that we have more children of our own. But Henry quite vehemently opposed my request. Indeed the suggestion enraged him, and I feared for a moment he might strike me. Thankfully, he did not.

He has decided that we should tell folks she is an orphan child we've taken in. I despise the deception, but if I do not comply, Henry will insist she serve us as a slave.

The past few months have caused a wedge between us. I only pray our move north will remind him of the lessons he learned about human equality before we were wed. That he is willing to make the move is a beginning.

Praise be to God.

Missouri, ten years later

"I've completed my lessons, Miss Maddy."

Madeline glanced up from her needlework and smiled at

fourteen-year-old Cat. "Already?"

"Yes, ma'am."

The child worked so hard to please. She far surpassed Camilla in lessons. And, as even Henry had to agree, Cat had a head for numbers.

"You've done very well, my dear. Come with me. I have a gift for you." Madeline set aside her sewing and stood.

"Have you a gift for me, too, Mother?" Camilla asked from her place at the table, where she had been doing her best to ignore her lessons.

Madeline hated to reward her daughter's laziness, but she found it difficult to refuse the lovely blue eyes staring at her, wide with pleading.

"Of course I have," she replied with an indulgent smile. "You may come along, as well."

The girls followed her to her bedroom, where Madeline removed a package for each from the bureau drawer.

Camilla squealed. "Oh, Mother, how lovely! A satchel— exactly like yours."

"Yes." Madeline smiled at the girl's enthusiasm. "And tablets so that you can keep account of your thoughts."

Camilla flung herself into Madeline's arms and rewarded her with an array of kisses. "Thank you, Mama. Thank you, thank you, thank you."

Madeline laughed. "I trust you find the gift pleasing, as well, Cat?"

Cat's eyes widened, then pooled as she cradled the tablets to her chest. Swallowing hard, she nodded.

Madeline gently set Camilla aside and reached for Cat. "May I have a hug from you, as well?"

Camilla huffed and stomped on the hardwood floor.

Cat darted a gaze at her and then back to Madeline. "Must I?"

Taken aback, Madeline frowned. "Why, no. I won't force affection from you. But may I ask what has brought about this sudden aversion? You've been hugging me all these years. Are you suddenly too grown up?" She kept her tone deliberately light to disguise her hurt.

"No," Cat replied hesitantly but still did not come forward. "It isn't proper behavior."

"Why, Cat," Madeline said, unable to hide the surprise in her tone. "What an utterly absurd thing for you to suggest."

"Oh, Mother, you know it's true. My goodness, have you ever seen one of Gram's slaves up and give her a hug?" Camilla jutted out her chin and gave a sniff. "I shudder to think what would happen."

Madeline's heart wrenched as Cat's cheeks reddened and she lowered her gaze to the tips of her shoes. "Camilla Penbrook, I don't know where you get such ideas. While it is true that your grandparents indulge in the institution of slavery, we do not. Cat is every bit as free as you are in this household and as dear to me as if she were my own child. I insist you apologize this minute."

Camilla's eyes sparked defiance, and for a moment, Madeline thought she might refuse. But, thankfully, she lowered her eyes in submission. "Sorry."

"Now, go finish your lessons."

Madeline turned back to Cat as Camilla flounced off to do as she had been instructed. "Now, what about that hug?"

A smile instantly covered the lovely, angelic face, and Cat rushed into Madeline's arms. "Thank you, Miss Maddy," she whispered.

Madeline pressed a kiss to the top of her chestnut curls. "You're welcome, my dear. I hope you will find that writing down your thoughts helps you sort through life's setbacks and joys, just as I have discovered for myself."

They returned to the front room, Madeline to her sewing and Cat to her tablets and inkwell. Madeline would have loved to peek over the girl's shoulder and read what was on her mind, but she determined to allow each of the girls her own thoughts without threat of invasion.

The door flung open, and Henry staggered in smelling of liquor. His bloodshot eyes made Madeline's heart race with disappointment. He had promised no more spirits after he lost his favorite horse during his last bout of drunken gambling.

"Bedtime, girls," she said quietly. "Run along, now. Quickly. I'll be in soon to hear your prayers."

"Let the girls stay," Henry said, slurring his words. He staggered to his chair and sat hard. "Come 'ere," he ordered Cat.

Madeline gasped. "Henry!"

Cat stood as though frozen in place, her face drained of color.

"I said, come 'ere!"

Cat shuffled cautiously across the room until she stood before Henry. He reached out and grabbed her arm roughly. "Where is he?"

"Wh—what?" Cat winced as his grip tightened.

A sneer curled his lips. "Don't play innocent with me. You darkies know everything that goes on behind our backs."

Madeline stepped forward and placed her hand over his. "Henry, for mercy's sake. What on earth are you talking about?"

He loosened his grip and leaned back in his chair,

though his gaze never left Cat's face.

Much to Madeline's dismay, living in Missouri had served the opposite effect of what she had hoped for. Though most who owned slaves held only one or two, a select few had acquired enough wealth to merit Henry's attention. He sought out these slaveholders for his companions and openly opposed the abolitionists. The past few years had been highly disappointing for Madeline, and distressing, if not a bit embarrassing, for her high-profile family. It broke her heart that she could only be loyal to either her family or her husband. But she had to think of the girls. So Henry received her outward support.

However, this accusation and manhandling she could not abide. "Henry, I believe you owe Cat an apology for your treatment of her. Gracious, I don't know what has gotten into you."

An unpleasant laugh rumbled from Henry's throat—a laugh not quite reaching his eyes. "You would have me apologize to this. . .this Negress? This slave?" he ground out between clenched teeth.

"Cat is not a slave."

"Yes, by heaven"—Henry rose unsteadily on his feet and stood inches from Madeline—"she is a slave."

At the venomous look in his bloodshot eyes, Madeline tightened her grip protectively around Cat's trembling shoulders and took a step back. Henry snatched the girl's tiny arm and jerked her forward as though she were a rag doll. "Where is the runaway?"

"Wh–what runaway, Mister Henry?"

"Don't play daft with me, girl." Henry's voice rose, and he shook with fury. "I have it on good authority you were seen going into Hanson's barn last night. And now his brother's slave, Horace, is missing. And just when they were getting ready to head back to Georgia in the morning. What do you know about it?"

Cat's mouth dropped open, her eyes wide with terror. "I—I swear, I don't know anything about a missing slave."

"For mercy's sake, Henry, you're hurting her."

Henry hesitated a moment, then dropped her arm. "Make her tell the truth, Maddy, or so help me, I won't apologize for what I do to her."

Fear caught in Madeline's throat. Gently she turned Cat from Henry's accusing glare. He dropped once more into his chair.

"Sweetheart," Madeline said to Cat, staying deliberately composed in the hope of restoring calm to the house. "Were you inside the Hansons' barn last evening?"

Tears glittered in Cat's soft brown eyes. She lowered her lashes. "Yes, ma'am."

Behind them, Camilla released a soft gasp. Madeline glanced up at her daughter. Alarm invaded her heart at the sight of the girl's pale face. "What is it, darling?"

"Nothing, Mother. I just cannot believe Cat would be so wicked as to sneak out at night." The look of utter hatred directed at Cat mirrored her father's.

Madeline shuddered. Henry influenced the girl far too much. "Camilla, it's time for bed."

The girl glared at Cat once more, then spun around and left the room.

Madeline turned back to Cat. "What were you doing in the Hansons' barn last night? Did you help a slave to freedom?"

Swallowing hard, Cat met Madeline's gaze. "No, ma'am."

"What then?"

"I—I. . ."

"It's all right. You can tell me."

Tears spilled from her eyes and slid down her cheeks. "I was meeting someone."

"You see?" Henry shouted. "Didn't I tell you they always stick with their own kind? Who were you meeting—one of those Quakers? Where did he take the slave?"

"Henry, please." A sudden pain pushed at Madeline's temples, draining some of her strength. If Cat had been caught helping a runaway, there was nothing Madeline could do for her. "Cat, whom did you go to meet?"

"Oh, Miss Maddy, I'm sorry." Cat hid her face in her palms and sobbed.

Cupping the girl's chin, Madeline pressed until she could observe all of the tearstained face. "Tell me."

"I went to meet Thomas Hanson. H–he and his parents are visiting from Atlanta."

Madeline's heartbeat increased. "How do you even know the boy, Cat?"

"I came upon him while I was walking one day. We've met several times since. He's ever so easy to talk to. He asked me to meet him last night because he was supposed to go home today. I've never snuck out at night before. I—I swear. We just wanted to say good-bye."

Henry sprang from his chair and slapped Cat hard, knocking her to the wooden floor. "What did you do with that white boy?"

Cat's round eyes filled with fear. "W–we just talked." Blood trickled from a cut on her bottom lip.

"Henry, for the love of God, leave her alone." Madeline knelt beside her. She removed the handkerchief from beneath her cuff at her wrist and dabbed at the child's lip.

"Don't lie to me," Henry screeched. "Did you lie down with that boy?"

Cat's gasp mingled with Madeline's. "No, sir!"

"Liar! Why else would you sneak off to meet him after dark?"

"Henry, Cat is a good Christian girl. She wouldn't do such a thing."

"She's a liar. They're all liars. And they have no morals. Why do you think there are so many yellow babies?"

Madeline felt her face burn. She knew only Henry's drunken condition could have induced such an indelicate remark. Still, she refused to let the statement go unchallenged. "I would say, Henry, that that unfortunate circumstance is due to immoral men, rather than women who have no choice."

He ignored the comment and addressed Cat. "Does the boy know what you are?"

Confusion clouded Cat's eyes. "I—I don't know what you mean."

"Henry, please." What sort of monster had her husband become?

He glowered at Cat. His eyes darkened, narrowed. "Does your lover know you're nothing but a darkie?"

"Henry!"

Cat's face blanched. "N–no." Her voice seemed to come from far away.

A sneer curled Henry's lips. "So you thought you'd snag a white man by pretending to be a white girl?"

"I—I never thought about it."

Madeline's heart nearly broke for the girl, and for the first time since moving to Missouri, she wondered if she had done the child a favor by allowing their neighbors to believe her to be white. In truth, marrying a white man was out of the question unless the girl fell in love with a man of broad ideas and they moved to Canada. Cat would probably never look at a Negro man as a suitable match any more than Camilla would.

Oh, Father, what have I done?

"Cat, darling. We've heard enough. I'll decide your punishment for sneaking out of the house and inform you in the morning. Run along to bed." She pulled the girl to her feet, careful to use her own body as a shield from Henry.

Henry spoke up. "She's not sleeping in Camilla's room any longer."

"What are you saying?"

An uneasy tension formed a knot in Madeline's stomach as Henry's drunken gaze slid up Cat's form. "She's not a child any longer. It's time she starts acting like a proper servant."

"Henry!"

"No arguments." He raised his hand to silence her. "As a servant, it isn't proper for her to sleep in our daughter's room."

Fury shook Madeline's shoulders, and she turned on her husband, meeting his gaze head on. "In the absence of slave quarters, where would you have her sleep?"

His eyes narrowed dangerously. "She can make up a pallet in the storeroom off the kitchen. If that isn't good enough, she can sleep in the barn with the rest of the stock."

Cat's head dipped in shame, and her lower lip trembled; but she didn't weep as Henry stumbled from the room.

Madeline gathered the girl into her arms and, for the first time in all the years she'd been caring for her, felt resistance in Cat's slight form.

"Oh, Cat. Perhaps Henry will be reasonable tomorrow after a good night's rest."

"Yes, ma'am." Her voice devoid of emotion, Cat patted Madeline's back. "Don't fret, Miss Maddy. I'll be all right."

Hot tears slid down Madeline's cheeks as Cat pulled away and regarded her through long, bristly lashes. "Don't cry," she said. "Please don't cry for me."

CHICAGO, 1948

"I'm back, Mama." The back screen door swung shut with a bang behind Lexie, and she struggled into the house carrying an armload of freshly dried clothing from the line.

Mama appeared in the doorway as Lexie deposited her burden onto the kitchen table with a heavy breath. "Gracious, Lex, you near gave me a heart attack."

"Sorry, Mama. I didn't mean to let it bang. My arms were full. It's starting to rain outside."

A smile showed Angel Kendall's strong, white teeth. She glided across the room, despite her two hundred pounds, and flapped her hands. "I'll live." She lit the stove and pulled the iron from the shelf over the burner. "How was work?"

With a shrug, Lexie dropped into a wooden kitchen chair and toed off her brown platform shoes. Bending forward, she rubbed her aching arches. "Mrs. Bell hollered at me again. I swear, Mama, I think that woman is losing her mind."

Angel's lip pushed out indignantly. "What'd she shout at you for?"

Lexie frowned, remembering the sixty-year-old woman's dark accusations. "I slipped on the freshly scrubbed foyer floor, and Mr. Bell. . .steadied me."

Mama nodded. "That woman knows her man likes the colored girls. I'm surprised she don't hire on poor whites."

A bitter snort left Lexie's throat. "They won't put up with as much meanness as we do. Whites know they can find other work. We got little choice but to work for some rich white woman and her handsy husband."

"You know Andy didn't want you workin' for that woman in the first place. He don't want you workin' period."

At the mention of her husband's name, Lexie's stomach dropped a foot. "A lot he really cares. He's as bad as Mr. Bell, chasing other women. It doesn't matter if he likes me working or not. I'm not taking him back this time, so I gotta have a job."

Angel opened a cabinet door and pulled down the ironing board. She licked her index finger and made a fast tap on the hot iron. Her saliva sizzled. With a satisfied nod, she snatched up Pop's white Sunday shirt—the only shirt he owned that wasn't looking worn in spots. "Jesus hates divorce, my girl. And your poppa and me, we didn't raise you to be gettin' no divorces."

"I know, Mama. But our marriage isn't like yours and Pop's. If Andy treated me the way Pop treats you, I'd be kissing the ground he walks on. But he doesn't."

"He's just still trying to prove he's a man, honey."

With a snort, Lexie eyed her mother critically. "Half the women in Chicago know he's a man. You'd think he'd have figured it out by now."

Angel cackled, then turned, her expression sobering.

"Honey, you can't expect a man who is bound by the prince of this world to think the same way your pop does. He don't know no better."

"I can expect him to love me like he promised."

"No, you can't. Only God is love. Outside of a walk with God, a person can't even begin to understand what it means to love."

Frustration shot through Lexie, loosening her tongue. "Mama, I mean the kind of love a man has for his wife. Not God's love."

"Husbands, love your wives as Christ loves the church." As though that settled the argument, Angel hung up the freshly ironed shirt and reached for the next.

Lexie stood and grabbed her shoes with one hand. "Do you want some help with the laundry?"

"No, baby, you're looking awfully tired. Go on upstairs and lie down for a while. I'll holler when supper's ready."

Lexie trudged up the steps, her stockinged feet making no sound as she padded down the hall and into her bedroom.

Tears formed in her eyes. She hadn't exactly been living like she knew any better herself. If she'd been serving God when she met Andy, he never would have looked at her twice.

She was only eighteen at the time and pushing against the confines of being a deacon's daughter. Sheila's Swing Club seemed like just the place to dust off a little energy. When Andy entered the noisy, smoke-filled room, everyone else ceased to exist. Seven years her senior, Andy already held a steady job. He seemed so sophisticated and suave. He'd swept her off her feet the instant their eyes met.

As much as she loved him, she'd managed to stay out of his bed until their wedding night. That was probably the only reason he'd married her.

Eleven years later, she regretted ever stepping foot inside that swing club. If only she'd never met him. If only she could stop hurting. If only she could stop loving him. If only she could stop crying.

Georgia, 1948
Please don't cry for me.

A rap on the door pulled Andy from his reading. Reluctantly he closed Madeline's journal and set it aside. He pulled his watch from his pocket and his eyes widened. It was nearly six o'clock. He'd been in his room reading all day.

The knock sounded again, more insistent.

"Coming." Andy sat up, buttoning his shirt. The metal headboard clanged against the wall as he stood, then strode across the room. He opened the door to find Buck scowling on the other side.

"'Bout time."

"Sorry," Andy muttered. "What can I do for you?"

"My missus says you should come down and take supper with us. It's rainin' cats and dogs out there. Ain't no sense you gettin' sick goin' out to get somethin' to eat when we got plenty."

A bright flash through the window punctuated his words. A clap of thunder shook the house. Andy raised his brow in surprise. He had been so absorbed in his reading, he hadn't even noticed the rain. "Tell your wife I appreciate her kindness," he said. "I'll wash up and be right down."

Fifteen minutes later, Andy sat at a table laden with fried okra, biscuits, and a mound of barbecued ribs. His mouth watered at the sight and smell of all that food. He glanced around, waiting for someone to offer him a platter of something. Instead, Buck eyed him for a moment, then bowed his head and closed his eyes.

Andy studied the top of his host's head. He couldn't remember the last time he'd prayed before a meal. He wasn't sure he cared to do it now, but in the spirit of courtesy, he bowed his head.

"Heavenly Father," Buck began, "we thank You for this bounty on our table. And for the guest You've sent our way. Lord, we pray You'll help him find whatever it is he's lookin' for. Bless his life and keep it from destruction."

Andy felt his ears burn at being the center of a prayer, and when he looked up, he expected to find everyone staring at him. At the very least, he anticipated an awkward silence. But the contrary proved to be true. Six children—ranging in ages from toddler to nine or ten, Andy guessed—all began speaking at once.

Chuckling, Buck held up his massive hands for silence. "Hold on, now. One at a time." He turned to a pigtailed girl to his left. "We'll start right here at the front of the table. Aletha, baby, what can your daddy do for you?"

Andy's insides twisted with longing for children of his own—the what-ifs that always accompanied thoughts of the two children he and Lexie had lost.

Buck's little girl grinned broadly and looked adoringly at her father. "Miss McGuffy says I have to have my science project in by tomorrow, and I need help."

Andy accepted the platter of ribs from Buck's wife, Lottie.

"Aletha, how long have you known about this?" Buck asked sternly.

The little girl shrugged. "I don't know."

Buck gave an exasperated sigh. "All right. Bring it to me after supper, and we'll see what we can do."

"Thank you, Daddy." Her face beamed with relief.

Andy's mind wandered back to the diaries as Buck moved to the next child in line. He needed at least a week in Oak Junction, maybe two, to finish reading the diaries, make his notes, and conduct another interview with Miss Penbrook.

Andy felt like there was much more at stake than a simple biography. This was about the heart and soul of three women and their different perspectives on the world that held them captive. Madeline and Cat's captivity were obvious. Madeline was chained to a man whose ideals were opposite her own. Cat was a slave—literally held in bondage. Miss Penbrook had to be Camilla. He couldn't figure her out just yet, but he would. Or he hoped he would, because the old lady obviously wouldn't be much help, other than perhaps to fill in some of the gaps. Thank God for the diaries.

He ate the last bite of his fluffy biscuit and pushed back his plate. "Thank you, Mrs. Purdue. Everything was delicious."

Lottie blushed under the praise. "I'm glad you enjoyed it. But you'll have to have a slice of lemon pie and a cup of coffee before you return to your room." She spoke with a quiet grace, her soft tones almost melodious. Unbidden, the gentle face of his mother flitted across Andy's mind, sending an ache across his heart. A longing for something familiar.

"No, thank you, ma'am." He wanted nothing more than to escape this gathering and retire to the solitude the small room upstairs afforded him.

She captured his gaze, regarding him with tender, almost

sympathetic brown eyes. "I'll save you a slice, and you can have it tomorrow."

Suddenly feeling very uncomfortable, Andy stood and cleared his throat. "Thank you. Good night."

By the time Andy took a hot bath, his watch read eight o'clock. Early enough to call Lexie at her parents' home.

He slid on his robe and tied it around his waist, then made his way downstairs.

The phone rang a dozen times before Andy released a disappointed sigh and hung up. He wandered back upstairs and took out the next diary. Stretched out on his bed, he was once again transported back in time—on the words of a fifteen-year-old slave girl.

Spring 1860

I've decided to stop praying altogether. After months of unanswered prayers, I took matters into my own hands and put an end to it tonight. At least I believe I did. I hope I did.

Henry Penbrook (I refuse to call him Master, Mister, or sir in my writings or my own thoughts) will not come to me in the dark again. I hid a very large, sharp kitchen knife under my bedding, and tonight, when he started to put his hands on me, I slid it out and pointed the tip at his chest. His eyes took on a look of fear that I must admit I relished.

I informed him that if he comes near me again, I will stab him through the heart, for I would rather hang than be forced to succumb to his disgusting desires ever again. He was angry. Angrier than I have ever seen him. But he left me alone.

Later I heard Miss Maddy crying, so I crept from the storeroom and listened outside their bedroom door. Henry informed her we are moving back to Georgia to live with his parents again on Penbrook plantation. Miss Maddy pleaded, but Henry insisted he has had enough of the North. He said that fool Lincoln will probably be elected president, and if that happens, the Southern states will secede from the Union. He will not live apart from his own countrymen.

Miss Maddy asked him what will become of me.

Henry said that perhaps in the South, I'll learn my place. But I will never believe I am less of a human being than he is just because I have a trace of Negro blood. As a matter of fact, I am more human than Henry Penbrook could ever hope to be.

My greatest hope is that I will be able to speak with Thomas again before we return to Georgia. Penbrook plantation sits only twenty miles from Thomas's home. If we move back there, he is bound to learn the truth about me, and he will no longer look at me with love in his eyes. I can't bear the thought of his hatred.

I tremble at what is to become of me back in the South. I want to run away and never come back. But who will look after Miss Maddy if I go?

Chapter Three
~December 1860

Cat tiptoed through the dark house, taking care not to disturb the loose board in front of the door. She felt sure Henry had purposely loosened the slat to alert him should she try to sneak out. But Cat was too clever for him. She knew where to step to avoid the creaky spot beneath the woven rug.

Besides, nothing would keep her from creeping out tonight. Thomas Hanson had returned to his uncle's home and would remain through the holidays. Three whole months.

Finally, an answered prayer. And she planned to get to him before Henry did. If Thomas was to learn about her bloodline, he would hear about it from her.

Perhaps she would give God another chance. After all, Henry hadn't touched her in months, and she would see Thomas one more time before Henry and Miss Maddy moved the family back to Georgia.

The familiar ache began in the pit of her stomach and rose to her chest at the thought of returning to Penbrook plantation. Impatiently, she pushed it away. Tonight wasn't the night to worry about that. Tonight she only cared about feeling Thomas's strong arms about her, listening to his wonderful stories and dreams for the future. Their future. She would allow herself to live the dream. One more time.

Please, let him be there. Please.

She stepped into the darkness and ran toward the woods that separated Henry's property from Mr. Hanson's.

Breathing heavily, she reached a small clearing in record time and smiled. Thomas paced in front of the barn. Her heart leaped as she recalled the last time they were together, six long months ago.

She pressed her fingertips to her lips and could almost feel his soft kisses.

"I'll be a planter, just like my pa," Thomas had said, passing along his excitement to Cat. "And you'll be my wife—the lady of my home."

He had pulled straw from her hair and gazed longingly into her eyes as she echoed his words of love. Now she understood the desire she had seen there. She'd seen a similar look in Henry's eyes countless times. Cat pushed aside the unsettling comparison and gathered air into her lungs to compose herself. She smoothed her trembling hand over her hair. It felt strange to be outside with her hair flowing down her back, but Thomas loved it that way, so she had loosened her braids and let them blow in the wind. Closing her eyes, she conjured the feeling that his hands running through her tresses had evoked in her.

"Thomas," she whispered into the darkness as her footfalls brought her within sight of him.

Without a word, he turned and quickly closed the distance between them, gathering her into his arms. He had filled out in the past six months, and Cat could feel the hardness of his chest, shoulders, and arms as he held her.

"Oh, I prayed you'd be here," she breathed against his ear.

He pulled away slightly and studied her face in the moonlight before grabbing her hand and leading her into the barn.

"Where else would I be?" He shut the door behind them. "I tried to get a message to you, but there was no opportunity. I hoped you'd feel my presence and come to me." He crushed her against his chest and sank his fingers into the thick mane down her back.

A soft sigh escaped Cat's lips as she relished his tenderness. "I missed you so much."

He released her for a moment—only long enough to pull her to a corner of the barn. When they were seated, he gathered her close once more. "I love you, Cat. I can't go back to Atlanta without you. I intend to speak to my pa about a betrothal."

Cat gasped and pulled away to stare up at him. "Oh, Thomas. Do you think they'll let us? I only just turned fifteen. And anyway, Henry sold the farm. We're going back to Georgia directly after Christmas."

Light shone in his eyes, and he grinned. "That's perfect. Do you know how close we'll be? Why, Penbrook is only twenty or so miles away. That's a mere two days' travel by horse and buggy. I could escort you to parties and court you properly."

Cat's heart leaped, and she couldn't help but catch some of his excitement as she envisioned the two of them dancing and sitting in the parlor. But reality penetrated her dreams with heart-wrenching clarity. Who knew how long she had before Henry revealed the truth to Thomas? Then she would lose him forever.

As if sensing her hesitation, he released a frustrated breath and pulled her close once more. "What is it? You still share my feelings, don't you?"

"Oh, Thomas, of course I do. Don't ever doubt it. Not ever. Even for one second. I'll love you until the day I die," she vowed.

"So I may speak to Henry about courting you once you return to Georgia?"

Again, Cat felt a sense of dread fill her. Henry would never allow it. He would tell Thomas the truth. Then Thomas would hate her. Tears welled in her eyes as she lifted her chin and pressed against him.

"Kiss me, Thomas. For now, let's not talk about it. Please? Just hold me."

With a moan, Thomas covered her mouth with his. Caught in the sensations spreading through her, Cat scarcely noticed when he lowered her to the soft hay. She hesitated only a moment. Then, because she loved him more than life, she allowed his caresses. She felt his love in each kiss. . .each caress. . .and she knew she would refuse this man nothing. He loved her as she loved him. Though they would never marry, she would allow herself this one night of his love. Then she would let him go.

Later, she lay in his arms and wept as he caressed her hair.

"I'm sorry, Cat," he whispered as her tears fell upon his bare chest. "I should have waited. I had no right. Forgive me. We'll run away and get married tonight. We won't even wait for permission. I'll make this right."

Unable to speak for the pain clogging her throat, Cat wept harder and buried her face in his shoulder.

"Darling, please. Calm down." Thomas's voice held a

tone of near panic, and his grip around her tightened. "I'll never forgive myself for taking advantage of your innocence." He reached into his trouser pocket and produced a handkerchief.

Cat raised up on her elbow and dried her eyes. "Thomas, there is something you must know. It will change everything, but before I tell you, promise me that you'll always believe I love you more than life itself."

"As I love you." He pressed her palm against his lips. A frown creased his flawless brow as she slipped her hand gently from his. "You can tell me anything, Cat. Especially now. Nothing will change how I feel about you."

Cat's heart ached, knowing the love in his eyes would soon change to contempt and anger and, in all likelihood, hatred.

She opened her mouth to speak, but her confession became a gasp as the barn door flung open, allowing frigid air to blow inside.

"Pa!" Still bare to the waist, Thomas shot to his feet. He stepped in front of Cat's unclothed body to shield her from two pairs of glaring eyes. Mr. Hanson stood in the doorway with Henry.

"What are you doing with my girl?" Henry demanded. Ignoring Thomas's effort to guard her, Henry stepped around the young man and grabbed Cat's upper arm roughly. In spite of herself, she cried out in startled pain. Standing naked before the men, shame filled her, and she clutched her clothing close with her free hand.

"P–please," she said, her lips trembling from cold and fear. "M–may I dress?"

"Shut up, slut." Henry raised his hand and brought it

hard across her face. The force of the attack sent her crashing to the ground.

Thomas knelt beside her, trying to cover her with her clothing. He glared up at Henry. "What kind of man are you, sir? I've half a mind to call you out."

"Tread lightly, Son," his father cautioned. "You don't know the whole truth here."

Attempting to keep her nudity covered from the other two men, Thomas helped her to her feet, then stood in front of her as a shield. "I know that a young lady has just been accosted by this. . .this. . ."

The blood left Cat's face at the filthy word Thomas used to describe Henry. She recognized the warning glint in Henry's eyes; but undaunted, Thomas continued, "This lady is unclad and freezing, and you gentlemen haven't the decency to avert your gaze and allow her to dress."

"Put on your clothes," Henry commanded, jerking his head toward an empty stall. Cat knew from the darkness in his eyes that everything he was holding back from Thomas he would unleash on her as soon as he had her alone.

"The least you can do is allow her some privacy," Thomas said, his words a command. The older men looked away, but not before Cat saw Henry's face redden with fury.

Cat dressed quickly. She watched the unsteady rise and fall of Thomas's shoulders, and she longed to go to him once more before he learned the truth.

As if sensing her need for his strength, Thomas moved to her, gathering her to him quickly before Henry could grab her again. "Pa, I know we're young, but I love Cat. I'm sure you'll agree that she's been compromised and we have no choice but to marry immediately."

Mr. Hanson regarded Cat for a moment. The absence of anger in his blue eyes caused more pain than a thousand lashes. His countenance told her Thomas would never be hers. All she could do was prevent Thomas from fighting his pa and breaking his ma's heart. The outcome of tonight's disaster lay securely in Cat's hands. She nodded to Mr. Hanson, then moved from the protection of Thomas's arms.

Lifting her chin, she turned to face her beloved, relishing the love in his eyes one last time.

She squared her shoulders and gathered a deep breath. "Thomas, it's not possible for us to marry. You haven't compromised me." She stepped toward Henry.

His expression changed to confusion. "What do you mean? Don't you see? We have to get married now. They won't stop us."

"Yes, they will," she whispered, unable to meet his gaze.

Henry took her by the arm and led her roughly to the door. "I don't mind young Thomas using my girl," he said with a leering grin at Mr. Hanson. "But if he got her with child, I'm not paying a stud fee."

"Must you be so coarse?" Thomas's father scowled. "The boy made an unfortunate mistake."

A short laugh escaped Henry's throat. "No hard feelings. Young Thomas couldn't help himself. These black wenches have a way about them white men can't resist. Especially this one. Believe me, I know from experience."

Bile rose to Cat's throat as he turned his dark gaze on her, eyes flashing with the threat of what she knew was to come.

"What do you mean, calling Cat a black wench?" Indignation edged Thomas's tone. "You dare compare her to a common. . ."

"The girl is a slave." Mr. Hanson released a resolute sigh and clapped his hand down on Thomas's shoulder. "She belongs to Mr. Penbrook, Son. You know Mrs. Penbrook's family is outspokenly abolitionist. She insisted they raise this girl as a white. Against his better judgment, Henry graciously allowed his wife her fancy. But when he realized the girl was coming to meet you, he did what any respectable gentleman would do and informed me immediately. And it's a good thing he did before you made quite an embarrassing error. Taking your pleasure is one thing. . .and understandable for a young man of your age. But imagine if you had followed through with a marriage. Though it would not have been binding, obviously, it most certainly would have humiliated your uncle and abused the hospitality of his home. Not to mention the embarrassment your mother would have been forced to endure."

Cat stared at the tops of her boots during Mr. Hanson's inflectionless discourse, but as silence filled the barn, she could no more have kept her head down than she could drain the Negro blood from her veins. She lifted her gaze to find Thomas staring at her in horrified disbelief. Her stomach sank. Somehow she had hoped. . .of course, it had been a foolish hope, but a dream nonetheless. She had hoped Thomas loved her enough to overlook her one-eighth Negro blood.

A shiver coursed through her. She rubbed her arms. Looking down at her own pale skin, she felt tears prick her eyes. Wasn't she as white as any one of the men standing in the barn? Yet they stood, as though better than she, accusing her, condemning her for being in love with a man of the wrong color. Did they expect her to fall in love with and marry a black man? An ignorant slave? God forbid. There was no place for her. She was too black to be white and too white to be black.

I'm too white to be black and too black to be white. I'm nothing.
Andy almost dropped the journal as he read the words he had spoken of himself countless times. From his bed, he glanced out the window into the darkness illuminated by intermittent flashes of lightning. Rain beat insistently against the glass, demanding attention. Striding to the window, Andy glanced out and frowned at the water standing in the streets. If the rain didn't let up soon, he'd be stuck in the room another day. Not that he minded reading the diaries, but he had hoped to visit with Miss Penbrook as soon as possible to fill in a few details. So far, he had read Madeline's and Cat's accounts of the years living in Missouri—fascinating reading, but not much he could use in writing Miss Penbrook's memoirs.

Readers were interested in her travels and in her rise to fame as a poet and author of novels. They wouldn't care about the slave girl's love for a white boy. Henry's abuses might be of interest to some, especially Negroes who screamed for civil rights for their Southern-born brothers and sisters, and the Northern whites out to prove they weren't like their Southern counterparts. But those weren't things he could put into print if he expected to keep his job. He was not interested in civil rights as a movement, nor the NAACP. All he cared about was making a respected name for himself so he could hold his head high.

Shaking himself from his least favorite subject, Andy

gathered a long breath, rubbed his gritty eyes, and started to return to the diaries, when his stomach rumbled. Remembering the promised slice of lemon pie Mrs. Purdue had wrapped up after supper, he decided to sneak downstairs and grab the snack before resuming his reading.

Quiet darkness met him when he stepped into the hallway. He pulled off his shoes and set them inside his room, then tiptoed down the stairs, grimacing when the next-to-last step groaned beneath his feet. A glance at the grandfather clock at the bottom of the stairs revealed a few minutes past midnight. He blinked in surprise at the late hour. Perhaps he'd better turn in when he got back to his room.

When he reached the telephone, he paused, debating whether to try to reach Lexie or wait until morning. She'd been pretty clear the marriage was over after the last time he'd failed to come home all night. He'd truly been working. Oh, he didn't blame her for refusing to believe him. He hadn't exactly been a choirboy during their marriage. But it had been a full year since his resolve to remain faithful to his wife. He loved Lexie. He had to find a way to get her back when he got home.

The urge to speak to her was too strong to resist, so he grabbed the receiver and put in a call to Chicago.

A relieved sigh escaped him when she picked up after a series of rings.

"Hi, honey," he said, keeping his voice low so as not to disturb the Purdues. "It's me."

"What time is it?" she asked, sleep thick in her voice.

"Midnight here, so I guess it's eleven there."

"It's a little late to be calling, don't you think?"

Andy frowned at her cool tone. His stomach dropped at

the thought that he might just have lost her this time. "So, how are you, Lex?"

"Listen, Andy, I know you didn't call me all the way from Georgia just to see how I am."

"I don't know why I called. I guess I just needed to hear your voice. I love you, honey."

A short laugh escaped through the line, burning Andy's ear. "Mama isn't sure you even have the capacity to love me."

"I thought your mother wanted you to take me back. When did she go over to your side?"

"Oh, Andy. Maybe that's the problem. There shouldn't be your side and my side. Shouldn't we be in this life together? Working to make a living? A family?"

A knot formed in Andy's stomach. Why bring up a family when she knew that was never going to be? "I guess so."

"We have some things to discuss. Do you know when you'll be home?"

"In a few days. Miss Penbrook is a little addled. I'm trying to piece my story together through old diaries and bits of conversation with her, but so far I don't have much." A sharp, insistent knocking interrupted his thought. "Listen, honey, I have to go. Someone's at the door."

"This late?"

"I'll try to call again in a few days."

"All right." The phone clicked before he could say good-bye.

Andy replaced the receiver and hurried across the foyer.

He jerked open the door to find a waterlogged young woman shivering on the porch, her arms wrapped tightly about her body. "It's about time," she snapped. "My hair is ruined."

Andy gaped as she pushed past him into the foyer and stepped in front of the mirror that hung beside the coat rack. She scowled at her reflection and squeezed water from her hair.

"Sorry," Andy finally managed. "I got to the door as quick as I could. Hang on. Let me get you a towel."

"Sure," she said with a lift of slender shoulders.

Andy tore his eyes away long enough to run up to the bathroom and grab a fluffy towel from the shelf above the sink. "Here you go. I apologize for being the cause of your soaked condition," he said, then cleared his throat in embarrassment, thinking the words sounded foolish.

"That's some fancy talk," she said, raising an eyebrow and observing him through the mirror. "Where're you from?"

"Chicago."

She turned and faced him, her eyes searching his. He felt his ears warm as her gaze slid boldly over his body, then back to his eyes. Andy felt a stirring as a slow smile touched her full lips. He breathed in sharply, unable to keep himself from returning her appraisal. The wet, yellow dress clung to full curves, igniting senses in Andy better left ignored if he had any chance of winning his wife back.

Laughter bubbled from her lips. "I look a sight."

Andy thought she was about the most beautiful woman he'd ever seen. Perfectly shaped mahogany arms supported slender hands. She grabbed a hanky from her purse and dabbed at the raindrops on her face.

"Can you believe that water is standing a foot deep on some streets?" she chattered. "My date's car stalled six blocks from here, so I just decided to walk." She laughed again, a throaty sound that quickened Andy's pulse. "God didn't bless that man with one lick of mechanical sense"—she sent him a saucy grin that Andy couldn't help but return—"but he sure can dance."

At the mention of another man, Andy's senses returned. "Did you need a room or something?"

"Huh? Oh." She raised her head in understanding and gave a dismissive wave. "I live here. I'm the Purdues' maid. I figure, shoot, if I'm going to have to clean for a living, I might as well clean for my own kind and be treated a whole lot better. Know what I mean?"

"Sounds like a good idea to me."

"So, what do you do, Yankee boy?" Her teasing smile sent warmth up his neck, and he fought to swallow around a sudden lump in his throat. Lexie hadn't given him a look like that in longer than he could remember. As a matter of fact, he couldn't recall the last time they'd shared more than a cursory kiss as he hurried out the door for work.

"Call me Andy," he said, his voice cracking like a twelve-year-old boy's.

A giggle bubbled musically to her lips, and she stepped forward, reaching toward him. Her long, bloodred finger-nails tickled his palm as he took her proffered hand.

Lexie's soft voice and sweet face played across his mind. He wanted his wife back more than he wanted to be with a woman he didn't love. The voluptuous wet figure lost some of its allure. He smiled, the fire suddenly gone from him. "I'm a writer," he said, "and I have a ton of work to finish, so if you'll excuse me. . ."

She brightened. "I ain't never met a writer." Keeping his hand firmly gripped in hers, she smiled up at him. "How about having a cup of tea with me and you can tell me all about it?"

Gently, he slid his hand from her grasp, winning him a quick scowl from the beauty. Even with a frown on her face and bedraggled from the rain, she was lovely.

He tossed out a self-deprecating smile to let her know he was tempted but resisting her seduction. " 'Fraid not."

She shrugged and flashed her white teeth at him again. "If you change your mind, come find me. I'm up the stairs and four doors down on the right. You didn't ask my name. But I'll tell you anyway. It's Ella."

He stepped back. "Nice to meet you, Ella. Good night."

"I'll be seeing you," she said softly.

He climbed the steps, knowing she was watching him. When he returned to his room, he quickly undressed, removed the diaries from the bed, and crawled under the covers. But sleep eluded him as his thoughts warred inside. He thought of Lexie, her coldness, her constant accusations—only a few of which had been warranted. The last one—the proverbial straw that broke the camel's back and caused Lexie to leave him and move back into her mother's house—had been completely unwarranted. For once, he was as innocent as a newborn babe. He'd been faithful for a year. But no amount of explaining had sufficed. He frowned into the dark room. Lexie could have been with him right now, keeping herself occupied during the day while he worked, and keeping him occupied at night. Instead, she'd chosen to leave. Had chosen not to believe him.

Against his will, his mind conjured up the wet form of Ella—warm, and willing to share more than tea.

With a frustrated growl, Andy flung back the covers, switched on the lamp beside his bed, and grabbed the next diary. As he skimmed through the pages of Cat's anguished words, anger rose in him at the account of Henry's brutal beating after he caught her in the barn with Thomas. And he had resumed his rapes of the poor girl. As a cloudy dawn slowly pushed back the night, all thoughts of the temptation down the hall were swallowed by Madeline's words.

GEORGIA, SEPTEMBER 1861

Cat's child has been born.

"She's paid back what she took," Henry said when he laid his son in my arms this morning. Henry's breath smelled of brandy, and his eyes were clouded from drunkenness. I have never understood the depth of his agony over losing our baby so long ago, but in that simple sentence, I finally understood what I have been too blind to see all these years. Henry doesn't blame me. He blames Cat. A little girl who only wanted to play with a doll. That is the reason he has poured his hatred into making her life miserable. Her misery is complete, for he's taken the child she bore him and has given him to me to raise as my flesh and blood.

Camilla is fit to be tied and understandably so, for Henry Jr. will inherit Penbrook House and the lands. Camilla will be given a dowry and the money I have for her from my own inheritance. This infuriates her.

Mrs. Penbrook has vowed she will never acknowledge the child as her grandson, but I know she would rather pretend the boy is mine than to bear the humiliation of her ladies' society becoming aware that her son is raising his illegitimate Negro son. With Mr. Penbrook lying in his grave, no one will protest for long, and

Henry's plans for his son will prevail.

I will never forgive myself for being unable to stop Henry from sinning with Cat. Nor, I fear, will I ever be able to forgive Henry. I despise him with every breath in my body for his betrayal. I bear the poor girl no ill will. A slave has no power over her master.

I have insisted Cat at least be allowed to be her son's nurse. I will obey my husband's wishes and raise young Henry as my own, but I will not deny Cat access to him. And praise be to God, Henry has agreed to this.

CHAPTER FOUR
~GEORGIA, DECEMBER 1861

"Oh, Mother, don't they look just marvelous?" Camilla's face glowed as Toby pulled the carriage to the edge of the road and allowed a company of home-guard soldiers to march past. They stepped together without one break in formation, each Confederate soldier as skilled in marching as the most highly trained West Point cadet.

Madeline had to admit they were a magnificent-looking bunch, though she prayed diligently that they would soon cast off their uniforms and return to the duties of husbands, fathers, sons, and brothers.

Though the war had yet to claim the lives of any of the boys in the Penbrooks' circle of friends, Madeline knew it was only a matter of time if the fighting did not end soon. And her heart broke for the mothers whose sons were spoiling for the chance to thrust their swords into the battle-grounds of Virginia.

"Camilla, dear, do not crane your neck, please."

Madeline observed her daughter as the carriage lurched forward once again. Tendrils of her chestnut curls sprang loose and fanned her flushed cheeks. At barely fifteen, the child was enamored of the men in uniform, and they were equally taken with her.

"Did I see Randall Jones marching with those men?" Madeline asked. "I understand he spoke to your father about coming to call on you."

Camilla let out a contemptuous sniff. "As though I'd want him for my beau." She cut a glance to the driver's seat where Cat sat next to Toby. "Besides, the Hansons arrive tomorrow, and I much prefer Thomas to any of the young men in Floyd County." Her voice rose to slightly louder than necessary, and Madeline shifted uncomfortably. Why must Camilla be so cruel?

Madeline frowned and shook her head at her daughter, but Camilla ignored her and continued without so much as a pause. "That may be the one good thing about this war. Thomas and his parents can't go north for the holidays like they always do, so Father invited them to spend Christmas with us. I believe Thomas will ask me to marry him during the visit. After all, I imagine he will want to have things settled between us before he heads to Virginia."

A smirk twisted Camilla's lips as Cat's back stiffened. "Won't that be just wonderful, Mother? I know this may not be the most opportune time to plan a wedding, but ever so many girls are getting engaged nowadays. Why, Amber Calhoun says it's our duty to send our men off to war with the assurance that we'll be waiting for them upon their return. She says it gives them something to fight for."

Cat twisted around in her seat and looked at Madeline. A frown etched her brow. "Is Thomas going to go fight, Miss Maddy?"

"I believe you mean Mister Thomas." Camilla's blue eyes flashed like sapphires.

"I said what I meant," Cat retorted, never taking her gaze from Madeline's.

"Why, you insolent girl. I'll whip the hide right off you when we get back to Penbrook House."

"Camilla, please. What do you expect when you provoke her?"

"It isn't possible to provoke a proper slave," Camilla replied, obviously uncaring of her disrespectful tone. "I will speak to Father about this girl's conduct." She cast her glance to Cat. "What do you think of that?"

A shrug lifted Cat's much-too-thin shoulders. "Do as you please, Camilla."

"You will address me as Miss Camilla."

Maddy released a sigh and raised her gloved hand to her temple in an attempt to ease the ache. "I wish you wouldn't speak of this to your father, Camilla. It will only upset the household. Cat meant no disrespect, I am sure, but only showed concern for an old friend. Isn't that right, Cat?"

Cat stared back at her, anger slowly receding from her fawnlike brown eyes. "Yes, ma'am. I apologize, Miss Camilla. I—I forgot my place for a moment."

"See that you don't forget it again!" Camilla straightened in her seat and plucked at her skirt as though the matter was suddenly beneath her. Cat slowly turned and stared straight ahead.

Relieved that the incident appeared to be over, Madeline leaned back and closed her eyes as the swaying carriage sent waves of nausea through her. More and more lately, her stomach ached and her head pounded until she took to her bed for days at a time. Henry despised her for her weakness, as though her frequent bouts of illness were a personal assault against him.

But she wasn't the only one he railed against. Henry seemed to be angry most of the time. Maddy knew the Penbrook plantation was suffering, mainly, she surmised, from Henry's mismanagement since his father's death. But of course Henry insisted it was because of the Yankees blockading all ports in and out of the South.

Money was dwindling away, but for Maddy this was no concern. She knew her inheritance was secure under her father's capable control, and if need be, she and Henry could borrow the money to get back on their feet once the war ended. When she said as much to Henry just the other day, she saw his fists clench and feared he might strike her. Instead, he only shouted, "I'll not have my wife trying to manage my affairs!" He stormed out of the house and didn't return until well into the night. Madeline suspected he was frequenting one of the gaming houses on the seedier side of town, but since she would rather die than admit she knew of such places, she had never confronted him about his return to gambling.

The following morning he was in good spirits, so Madeline could only conclude he had not lost in his gambling. For that she was grateful.

"Mother?"

Madeline opened her eyes, then quickly shut them again as the sun's blinding rays stabbed like knives into her sockets.

"We're home, Mother."

Madeline groaned in response.

"Is she all right, Camilla?" Even with her head spinning, Madeline couldn't help but warm to the care in Cat's tone.

"Miss Camilla. And I don't know." For once Camilla's acid tone smoothed to concern.

"I'll be fine, girls. But it hurts too much to open my eyes

in the sunlight. Will you help me to my room?"

"What should we do, Cat?"

"Take that arm, and I'll take the other. We'll support her as she steps down. You don't have to carry her, just guide her."

Madeline winced as her daughter's fingers sank into the fleshy part of her upper arm.

"Gently!" Cat scolded.

"I am being gentle."

"No, you are not."

"Girls, please do not argue."

"I'm sorry, Mother, but she. . ."

"Yes, Miss Maddy," Cat murmured. "We're sorry. Step down now. We won't let you fall."

Maddy allowed herself to be led inside and felt the girls guide her toward the stairs.

"What is this?"

Cringing at the sound of Henry's clipped voice, Madeline opened her eyes slightly and nearly cried out as the light stabbed at her once again. She tried to focus on her husband.

"Mother is ill," Camilla explained, "and we are helping her to her bed."

"Another headache, dearest?" Sarcasm laced his words.

"I do apologize, Henry. But I am afraid so."

He seemed to soften at her gentle response. "Move away," he instructed Cat, who still clung protectively to Maddy's arm. "I'll carry her up." He gave Cat a shove toward the stairs. "Go feed my son. Cook used up all the sugar in the pies for the Christmas dinner, so there was none left to make sugar water. Naomi has been trying to get him to suck on a soaked rag, but he won't take it. He's been squalling for an hour."

"Yes, Mister Henry," Cat murmured and headed up the

stairs, taking two at a time.

Feeling herself being swung into strong arms, Madeline closed her eyes once more and leaned against Henry's shoulder. For a moment, she could almost pretend he was the same man with whom she had lived happily for the first six years of their marriage. But after he tenderly laid her on the bed, the memories were shattered by a stark reality as he climbed in next to her and buried his face in the curve of her neck. She moaned as his passion grew, and her stomach rebelled against his brandy-laced breath.

"I'm sorry, Henry." She rolled from his touch and grabbed the chamber pot in time to keep from vomiting all over the bed.

"Is this what we've come to?" Henry exploded. "My attentions cause you to be ill?"

In misery, Madeline retched, unable to answer until she was weak and spent and lying back on her bed, pressing a handkerchief to her lips.

"My illness has nothing to do with you," she said with a weary sigh. "I don't know why these episodes come. Had I that knowledge, I would do everything possible to prevent them from interfering with our intimacy."

He gave a short, mocking laugh. "Don't give it another thought. I believe Cat has missed me since my son's birth. I'm almost sure I see the desire in her eyes when she looks at me."

"More likely it's the same contempt I feel for you at this instant, Henry. Leave the child alone. Haven't you hurt her enough?"

"Hurt her?" Henry came close until he lay inches from her. "I give her pleasure, as I once gave you. What better position could Cat have than to be nurse to my only son? And if she bears me another, so much the better for her."

Opening her eyes, Madeline couldn't keep the tears from escaping and trickling down her face and onto her neck. "Why must you humiliate me so?" she asked, her voice a hoarse whisper. "Could you not have picked another woman and remained discreet?"

"Things are as they are, dearest." He rose from the bed and stalked to the door. "Do not expect my return to your room this evening. I'll send Tessa in to attend you."

Madeline barely noticed when Tessa quietly entered the room and placed a wet cloth on her head. The coolness brought some measure of relief, enough so that the pain slowly faded into a merciful sleep.

Baby Henry's lusty cries from the nursery across the hall awoke her sometime later. She opened her eyes, relieved that the pain in her head had dulled to a minor ache. The moon was low in the sky, so she knew it was nearing dawn.

With a sigh, she pushed aside the covers and went to the nursery. A quick look in the corner revealed Cat's cot was empty. Cringing, Madeline couldn't help the vivid image that sprang to her mind. She knew Cat had been sent for and could be found in Henry's bedroom.

"It's all right, sweetums," she cooed. "We'll get you out of those wet clothes. and you'll be more comfortable."

Baby Henry stopped wailing at the sound of a sympathetic voice, but as soon as the cool air hit his wet bottom, he screwed up his face and let out a howl loud enough to raise the roof.

"Well, now. Aren't you the angry little fellow?" Madeline smiled at the baby's indignant hollering. But she didn't know what she would do if Cat didn't arrive soon to feed her son.

When the baby was properly dry and comfortable, Madeline scooped him up and snuggled him close. She stroked his silken head and breathed deeply of his fresh baby scent, accepting comfort from the warmth of his little body. He sighed softly, his head resting against her shoulder. Then, as though realizing this wasn't the comfort he sought, he bobbed around her neck. Not finding the source of his much-needed meal, he let out a bloodcurdling scream.

She bounced him and walked him back and forth across the nursery floor until Cat finally hurried in, disheveled, her dress torn at the collar. "I'm sorry, Miss Maddy."

Madeline observed the slightly swollen lip and the purple bruise on her right cheek, and her heart nearly stopped. Henry had become a monster. She handed over the baby and slipped her arm about Cat's shoulders. "It's all right. He's hungry but not starving to death."

With a nod, Cat moved to her cot.

The baby's cries stopped the instant he was put to his mother's breast. Madeline smiled as he suckled and cooed, euphoric in Cat's arms. "He's a dear, isn't he?"

A light glimmered in Cat's eyes. "He's perfect. I never thought I'd. . ." She broke off her sentence but kept her loving gaze on baby Henry's face.

"Oh, Cat. I'm so sorry you've had to give him up to me, though I love him dearly."

"It's all right. He's better off being raised as a white boy."

"I'll make sure he knows who his real mother is."

A frown creased Cat's brow. "He mustn't know. Not until after he's received his proper inheritance." She took Madeline's hand. "Please, Miss Maddy. Promise me we will

never speak of this again. Henry is your son. Yours and the
master's. He's a white boy and will grow to be a white man."

"It's so unfair, Cat."

"But Henry Jr. will be luckier than most boys. He'll be
loved by two mothers. Please. It's how I want it to be."

As Madeline returned her steady gaze, a bond formed between them. A bond that went beyond mother and daughter,
mistress and slave. They were two women united in mother-
hood of one small boy and the commitment to make him
greater than either could have accomplished alone.

1 9 4 8

Andy closed the journal and gave a short laugh. So Miss
Penbrook had a partly colored little brother. Did she know
what her mother's diaries revealed? He stood and stretched
his back. What would it do to the pride of Oak Junction to
learn that their most prominent citizen had a Negro brother
raised as a white man? He could just imagine the outcry. But
that wasn't his affair. He was more than ready to get his story
and get out of Georgia.

The Purdues had invited him to eat dinner with them
again. And since water still stood in the streets from the
two-day onslaught of rain, he accepted rather than getting
himself soaked.

He glanced at the clock and noted it was too early for
dinner. Only four o'clock. Mrs. Purdue had instructed
him to be downstairs and ready to eat at 6:30 sharp. He
groaned as his stomach rumbled. After staying up all night,
he'd skipped breakfast in lieu of sleep and hadn't awakened
until after lunch. That meant he hadn't eaten in almost
twenty-four hours, and he was famished.

Just as he was trying to decide whether or not to brave the ankle-deep water outside and grab a licorice stick from the grocery store across the street, he heard a tap on the door.

Standing, he opened the door.

He gulped when he found Ella smiling back at him, a pile of linens in her arms. "Hey, Yankee boy. Miz Purdue says I should see if you want your room straightened and your sheets changed."

"Uh, I'm not sure." He glanced at the journals and notebooks spread out on the bed.

"Come on now. How about letting me do my job?"

"I guess so." He opened the door wider and drew a sharp breath as she brushed by him, filling his senses with the sweet fragrance of her perfume. Ella glided to the bed, hips swaying. "You really are a writer, aren't you?" She grinned up at him. "To tell you the truth, I thought you were just trying to impress me. Now I'm not sure whether to be disappointed or not."

Gathering his wits about him, Andy couldn't help returning the infectious, toothy grin. "Here," he said, stepping toward the bed. "Let me get those things off of there so you can work."

Ella grabbed one of the open notebooks he'd been using to take notes from the journals. She whistled as she glanced at the writings. "Penbrook? Don't tell me you're writing an article about rich, white Miz Penbrook?"

"More than an article, but yes, Miss Penbrook is the subject."

"Whoo-ee. How'd you manage that?"

Taking the notebook, he shook his head. "To tell you the truth, I haven't the faintest idea."

"Well, if you ask me, you've been working too much. Don't you know you have to take some time off every now and then?"

"Now you sound like my wife," he mumbled, carrying an armload of books to a small table next to the window. He sat in the single chair as though guarding the journals.

A short, throaty laugh escaped Ella's lips. "Well now, no one has ever compared me to a wife before. But in this case, your woman is right." She pulled the covers off the bed and tossed them to the floor. Andy averted his gaze as she crawled across the bare mattress and pulled the sheets free. "Tell me, Andy," she said, "when was the last time you went out on the town and had yourself a good time?"

Andy glanced up, and to his relief, she stood facing him, brows raised as she awaited his answer.

Expelling a breath, Andy allowed himself to be drawn into what he knew to be a trap. "Too long."

A light glimmered in Ella's eyes, and a slow smile stretched her mouth. "How about letting me take you to the best swing club this side of Atlanta?"

Andy hesitated. It could be innocent enough. It wasn't like she was suggesting a date or a night in a motel. Still. . .

He sat, a refusal poised on his lips. Then he saw her press her lips together as she watched him, and suddenly he didn't want to disappoint her. "I'll consider it."

She smiled and gathered up the dirty linens. "That's better than a no. You can decide and let me know at supper. Unless. . ." She turned at the doorway. "Unless you'd like to grab a bite to eat before we go to Georgie's club?"

His empty stomach urged him to say yes. But that sounded a little too much like a date for comfort. Andy swallowed hard. "I already told Mrs. Purdue I'd be here for supper."

Disappointment clouded her features, but she rallied quickly and flashed him a smile. "Another time, maybe?"

"Maybe." Hopefully he'd be able to finish his research and get home within a couple of days. "I'll let you know."

Ella gave him a knowing glance that said she realized he was trying to find a way to escape her charms. With a satisfied smile, she stepped out and closed the door behind her.

Andy shook his head and decided to grab an early bath. Twenty minutes later, he emerged feeling more relaxed, more refreshed, and slightly more human. As he walked down the hall back to his room, he pulled his watch from his pocket. 5:30. Lexie should be home from her cleaning job at the Bells'. Deciding to go ahead and call brought a smile to his lips.

"Too bad that smile's not for me, Yankee boy." Ella came out of one of the rooms carrying an armful of dirty linens, stopping Andy dead in his tracks.

He stiffened, guilt washing over him at the very thought of calling Lexie when he was contemplating having a night on the town with this woman. He had to settle that right now.

"Ella, I'm going to have to pass on the club. I think I'd better finish what I came to do and get back home to my wife."

She opened her mouth, but before she could protest, Andy smiled. "I hope you understand."

"Shoot, of course I do. But that don't mean I'm not disappointed." She shrugged. "Well, you still have a couple of hours. If you change your mind, just let me know. I won't call Leroy until I'm sure you won't decide to come along after all." Giving him no opportunity to reply, she slid past him and moved down the hall.

Andy had to smile at her efforts as he sauntered back to his room to drop off his dirty clothes. Still, Ella would have to accept his refusal. She was too much of a temptation, and he couldn't risk taking her up on what she had to offer.

The house seemed unusually quiet when he stepped down the stairs. Mouthwatering smells drifted from the kitchen, making his stomach growl loud enough for him to hear.

Pushing aside thoughts of his hunger, he dialed the operator, mentally calculating how much it was going to cost him to call long distance every day. Joy rushed through him when the connection went through and Lexie's voice came through the line.

"Hi, it's me."

"Andy?" she sounded breathless and surprised.

"Did I catch you at a bad time? You fixing supper or something?"

"I just walked in the door a few minutes ago. June and Petey and the girls are here for dinner."

Andy frowned at the hesitation in her tone. What about her sister and brother-in-law could cause her to be nervous?

"Hey, Robert." Andy heard a child's voice on the other end of the line. "It's my turn for a piggyback ride!"

"Robert?" Anger seized him, and his stomach clenched, squeezing the breath from him. "Robert Kline?"

"Andy, don't overreact."

Her calm voice heated his blood. "You think I'm overreacting?"

"Robert just came over to—"

"I know exactly what that guy came over to do. I don't know what he said he came over for. But I think you and I both know what he wants."

"Oh, Andy, really. . ." But her tone said it all. She knew she was playing with fire by not telling that guy to shove off.

"Are you keeping him sniffing around for insurance, just in case I don't come through for you?"

"You're acting like a child." She lowered her voice. "I can't discuss this right now. Mama's kitchen is in chaos, and she needs my help with supper."

"Is Robert eating with you?"

"Yes. The least I could do was invite him after he carried my groceries home for me."

The image of Robert sitting at his place at his mother-in-law's supper table while Lexie poured him coffee and brought him dessert nearly overwhelmed Andy, forming a knot in his gut the size of a baseball.

"If you can't respect my wishes about that idiot, we have nothing more to discuss," he said, the tension in his throat reducing his words to barely more than a whisper.

"What did you say? I couldn't hear you?"

"I said good-bye, Lexie."

He hung up the phone, stunned that Lexie would blatantly disregard his wishes about Robert. Any man who would weasel his way into another man's life when he was off trying to provide a decent living wasn't worth his salt as far as Andy was concerned. The fact that Lexie couldn't see through him escaped Andy's realm of understanding. For crying out loud, the guy was giving his nieces piggyback rides. How transparent did he need to be for her to see him for what he truly was?

Without heading back upstairs, Andy made his way to the kitchen. Mrs. Purdue scurried about, giving orders to her two oldest daughters, whom Andy remembered from supper the night before. Ella turned toward him, a serving dish in her hands. She remained silent but smiled her slow smile. Andy's blood warmed.

"Oh, Mr. Carmichael," said a breathless Mrs. Purdue. "Supper isn't quite ready yet."

"Anything I can do to help?"

"How sweet. But no, thank you. We have it under control. Go ahead and sit and have some coffee while we finish up. Ella, pour Mr. Carmichael a cup, will you?"

"My pleasure, Miz Purdue."

Andy sat, trying not to watch the sway of Ella's hips as she sashayed to the cabinet, took down a cup, and filled it with steaming coffee.

She kept her eyes fixed on his as she walked the short distance from the counter to the table. He knew he should feel guilty, and he wanted to turn away and pretend she didn't exist, but the image of Robert and Lexie flashed through his mind like a motion picture. He allowed Ella's hand to brush his as she set down the cup, then he looked up at her and smiled.

A sense of foreboding washed over Lexie as she hung up the phone. *A foolish woman tears her house apart with her own hands.*

Her temper flared at the recalled words. Mama always took Andy's side. In eleven years of marriage, he had been away chasing assignments more than he had been home—practically. What about a man neglecting his wife, huh?

What about a husband tearing down his house with his own hands? Besides, no one had the kind of fairy-tale romance Mama and Pop had.

"Everything okay, Lexie-girl?" The deep voice came so close behind her, Lexie could feel Robert's hot breath against her neck.

She cleared her throat and stepped away quickly. "Everything's fine. Andy misses me real bad." With forced cheerfulness, she moved to the counter to unload her groceries. "I swear, he'll be so glad when he makes editor and doesn't have to travel anymore."

He gave her a lazy smile. "Can't say that I'll be too happy when that day comes."

Alone in the hallway, Lexie felt the forbidden pleasure of attraction for a man who was not her husband. His closeness sent fingers of excitement blazing a trail up her spine. She shook off the feeling and stepped back. "Listen, Robert, I don't mean to be rude, but I think I'm going to have to ask you to leave without supper. Andy wasn't too happy about your being here."

"Sure thing, Lexie-girl."

Lexie stepped around the counter and preceded him down the hall. When they reached the door, he donned his hat. "Call me if you need me for anything while your husband is off doing what he loves most."

Lexie stiffened and reached for the door. He caught her wrist and pulled her toward him. "If you were my woman, there's no way I'd leave your bed for even one night."

Warmth radiated from him, and Lexie trembled at his nearness. "Robert, please. . .don't."

He towered above her slight frame, and when he leaned

closer, Lexie felt as though she were being engulfed in a wave of warmth. The feeling both excited her and terrified her. She tried to summon the image of Andy's face, but everything was a blur except Robert, who stood close enough that if he moved an inch, his lips would be on hers.

"Lexie?" Mama's voice preceded her presence in the front hallway. Robert stepped back.

With a relieved sigh, Lexie shrugged and grinned up at Robert. His amused expression warmed her. . .and worried her. If he had been upset by the interruption, she could have despised him, but his good-humored acceptance made him all the more appealing.

"Good-bye, Robert." She opened the door, then moved aside while he stepped across the threshold.

"Good-bye, Lexie-girl." He tossed her that award-winning smile. "Your husband has every reason to be worried, because I mean to have you for myself."

Lexie gasped, but before she could respond, he tipped his hat, shoved his hands inside the pockets of his pleated slacks, and exited the house whistling to himself.

CHRISTMAS EVE, 1861

Thomas is here at last. My joy in seeing him is marred by my present circumstances, but I cannot help but glory in his presence. Of course I will have no opportunity to be alone with Thomas during his family's weeklong stay, but I hope to catch a glimpse of him from time to time.

Camilla is determined to have Thomas for herself, but I believe it is only to spite me. I pretend I don't care—but I do. She will never love him the way I do. There isn't enough love in her heart to warm a flea, let alone a man like Thomas. I hope and, yes, even pray that Thomas will not be fooled by her ruse. I wish for him to fall in love with a woman who truly loves him the way I do. But I cannot say these things to my beloved. When he sees me again, he will be ashamed at what I've become. But he is not alone, for I nearly die of shame daily.

CHAPTER FIVE

A haze of smoke hovered over the table in Georgie's club,
providing just the right atmosphere for Andy's foul mood.
He swallowed down his third shot of whiskey. This time the
amber liquid didn't burn quite so much. Either that or he
was becoming numb. He preferred the latter. He wanted to
become so numb he couldn't hear the sound of Lexie's voice
screaming in his mind.

*It's your fault, Andy. You left me alone when I needed you.
You drove me into the arms of another man.*

Robert's image gave him a taunting smile just before
he buried his face in the tender curve of Lexie's neck. Andy
growled and drained another shot.

"Honey, you're going to have to stop thinking so much."

He blinked at the sound of Ella's voice. He'd forgotten she was even there. With a lazy smile, she kept her eyes
focused on his and leaned forward to light her cigarette from
the candle on the table. His gaze flickered to her revealing
neckline and then settled on her lips. They puckered slightly
as a trail of smoke escaped and curled seductively into the
air. She put the cigarette in the ashtray and smiled.

"Come on," she said softly, her smoldering eyes inviting.
"Let's dance." She stood as though taking no for an answer

was completely out of the question.

Andy allowed her to pull him up. Blood rushed to his head, and he made a quick grab for the table to steady himself.

"Easy there, Yankee boy."

She took his hand and led him toward the dance floor. The band played while the singer crooned "Embraceable You" in a poor imitation of Nat King Cole. Andy stumbled on the slight step-up to the dance floor and collided with a hard body.

"Hey, watch where you're walking, boy."

Andy turned and focused on the deep Southern drawl. He glanced up into a reddish-blond beard. "I don't like being called 'boy.' " Angered to see a young black beauty in the white man's arms, Andy sneered, "What's the matter, can't you find one of your own kind to dance with?"

"Boy, you better shut your mouth before I forget my manners."

Heedless of the warning in the young giant's voice, Andy continued to vent, all the while seeing Henry's rotten face. "All you white boys are the same, aren't you, Bubba? Our girls are good enough for fun, but don't let anyone see you coming back from the slave quarters."

"Leave it alone, Rafe, please," begged the young black girl in his arms. "He's just drunk."

"That's right," Ella said, grabbing Andy by the arm and tugging. "Come on, Andy. You promised me a dance."

Andy jerked away. "I don't like you, Bubba," he said. "I don't like your kind." He turned to the girl, whose eyes flashed in anger. "And you should be ashamed, turning your back on your own kind and dancing with this. . ." He pointed at the white man. ". . .this massuh."

Rafe glared down at Andy. "Let's take this outside."

"Fine by me."

"Please don't, Rafe. What do we care if he doesn't like us dancing? He's just an ignorant drunk. Let's go, please. Don't ruin our time together."

Rafe looked into her pleading eyes, and for an instant, Andy recognized a look of tenderness. But when he fixed his steely baby blues on Andy, all traces of tenderness were gone. "Sure, baby," he said, never taking his iron gaze from Andy's. "We'll go."

Ella breathed a sigh of relief as they walked away. She turned to Andy with reproachful eyes. "Honey, you're going to have to ease up. Rafe and Ruthie have been seeing each other for two years. They'd get married if her family would allow it. And I'd bet my last dime it won't be long before they run off and do it anyway. Rafe is good to her. Always has been. And I've never seen a man more in love. You're lucky his sweet Ruthie can't stand violence, or Rafe would have flattened you and hung you on Georgie's wall for decoration."

"I'd like to see him try it," Andy sneered.

Ella grinned up at him as she wrapped her arms around his neck. "I wouldn't. I like you just the way you are. Besides, I thought we were going to dance."

Her soft curves distracted Andy, clouding his senses. He could see her mouth moving but had no idea what she said. "Huh?"

"Never mind, honey. We don't have to talk." She laid her head on his shoulder and began to sway with the music. "My sweet embraceable you," she sang, her breath tickling his neck.

Andy's blood warmed despite his confusion. He placed his hands on her hips and pulled her closer, drinking in her sweet scent. She stroked his head, his shoulders, his back until, unable to take any more, he pulled away, enough so that he could look into her dark eyes. Her message was clear.

Suddenly he couldn't remember why he was resisting her in the first place. It had been months since he'd held a pliable woman in his arms. And he liked it.

Unbidden, Lexie's face came to his mind. He hesitated, guilt sifting the desire from him. Then, as quickly, came the memory of Robert. With his family. Just how far had Lexie allowed Robert to replace him anyway?

"Are you okay?" Ella's soft voice broke through. He watched her lips as they formed his name. "Andy?"

In an instant, he covered her mouth with his, then became lost as she softened against him, kissing him back with a fervor that fed his passion.

The music ended, and Ella pulled away, bringing Andy slowly to his senses.

"I'm sorry," he said. "I don't know what came over me." But he did know. She was a willing body, and he was a warm-blooded man trying to forget that the woman he loved wanted someone else. And he had no one to blame but himself. "Let's go, okay? I need to walk off this booze." He stumbled as if to punctuate his words.

Ella chuckled and took his arm. "Not much of a drinker, are you?"

Andy tried to focus on his feet, wishing the floor would be still before he fell on his face.

"Oh boy. You're sloshed. Wait here," she commanded. "I'll get your hat and jacket, and we'll be just in time to catch the last bus home."

Andy leaned heavily against the wall for support. He watched the people walking by. They swayed, and Andy swayed with them.

"Whoa there, Yankee boy." Ella caught his arm.

"Careful. You just about hit the ground."

The humid warmth of the evening did nothing to alleviate Andy's spinning head. If possible, he felt worse. Time seemed to stand still and run together at once, and Andy regretted taking that first drink. Without Ella he would be helpless. Men and women on the sidewalks hooted and called to them as they walked past.

"Ella, sweetie," one man sneered, "what are you doing wasting your time with that fool? You know you could be taking me home and tucking me into bed. All he's going to do is pass out."

"You can dream if it makes you happy, Leroy," Ella shot back. "You know that's all of me you're going to get."

Indignant, Andy tried to locate the offensive man, but Ella held him firmly by the arm. "Lemme teach him how to speak to a lady."

She laughed. "Honey, you're having trouble speaking to a lady yourself. Besides, if I let you go, you'll fall on your face, and how'll I look then? I have my pride, you know."

Andy stopped and grabbed her, suddenly filled with an onrush of gratitude. "You're so nice, Ella. I like you. And I like kissing you." He leaned forward. Ella's eyes grew enormous, and she gasped, looking past him.

"Rafe, no!"

The earth spun, and Andy came face-to-face with Rafe's hard eyes and fist.

Something bit into Andy's lip as he slowly came to consciousness. He tried to sit up, but pain slammed into his head and sent him back down with a moan.

"Don't try to get up, son. Ol' Rafe sure did a number on you."

Andy struggled to open his eyes. Panic rose inside him. "What's wrong with my eyes?"

"Your right eye is completely swollen shut, and the other one probably will be by morning."

It all came back to him. *Rafe.* "Who are you?"

"Dr. Mayfield. A friend of Buck and Lottie's."

"I'm back in my room?"

"Yep."

"So what's the damage?" he asked. "How long before my eyes work again?"

"A few days maybe. You probably have a concussion, and your ribs are definitely bruised, if not cracked. I have them taped, and I advise limited to no movement for the next several days. Do you want to know how Ella is?"

"Ella?" Alarm shot through Andy. "Did he hurt her?"

"No. She's fine. Lucky for you, she stepped between you and Rafe, or you probably wouldn't be with us."

"There were at least twenty black men on the street. How come they just stood by and let a white man beat one of their kind senseless?"

"Let me tell you something. Everyone around here knows Rafe. He's helped more families than I can count in more ways than I can count, and he does it because he wants to. He's in love with one of ours, but of course he can't marry her. You, on the other hand, are a married man, kissing and groping one of our girls in public while so drunk you can hardly stand without help."

Shame cut a line in Andy's heart, and he swore to himself never to touch another drop of booze as long as he lived. His head pounded, and he wished the doc would just give him some aspirin and let him sleep. But the doctor didn't seem inclined to put him out of his misery just yet.

"Loyalty runs deep around here. And those men on the street, whom you feel should have come to your rescue. . . Rafe has their loyalty because he's earned it. You insulted little Ruthie. Ten men would have been happy to do the same thing Rafe did to you. So be glad he didn't give them each a turn at your face."

"As bad as I feel, I don't think a few more blows would make much difference anyway."

The doctor chuckled, and Andy heard his bag snap shut. "You might be right. Take it easy, and I'll be back to see you in the morning. I left some pills by your bed in case the pain gets too bad. But I wouldn't get too used to them if I were you."

"Thanks, Doc."

The door closed, and Andy settled back. What on earth was he going to do? If he couldn't see to read, he'd never get his research finished. He groaned and slammed his fist against the bed.

His body felt like he had been hit with a wrecking ball, and he longed for Lexie's soothing touch. She always seemed to know just what kind of care he needed when he was sick.

Lexie. . .

He drifted to sleep, dreaming of her sweet voice and gentle hands.

After hours of fitful sleep, Lexie awoke, unable to shake the feeling of dread that had been her companion since Robert's visit two nights before. She shook her head in the predawn darkness. How could she have come so close to allowing another man to kiss her? Not only had she almost allowed it, but she had been disappointed when they were interrupted. Had she completely lost her sense of morality? She cringed to think what Mama and Pop would say if they knew. Mama had said plenty at the mere suspicion after Robert had left.

"God, what am I going to do?" she whispered into the still air. She thumbed the gold band Andy had lovingly slipped onto her finger eleven years ago. A smiled touched her lips at the thought of him so long ago. Fresh out of college, he had worked in her parents' cafe while he pounded the pavement trying to find a writing job. Filled with ambition, he had been rejected by every white-owned-and-operated newspaper in Chicago until Mr. Daniel Riley of the *Chicago Observer* had called him, offering him a job writing obituaries and selling advertisements to local businesses. For some reason, Andy had resisted, but finally, at Lexie's insistence, he agreed to go to work for the man.

He'd moved up quickly, despite the resentment he was forced to contend with every day from his coworkers. White men who felt Andy should work for the *Defender* or another exclusively black newspaper. But Andy wanted real exposure in the mainstream. He wanted to report on black issues. But also white issues. American issues.

Andy firmly believed in fighting ignorance with intelligence. If coloreds were ever to gain equal footing with the whites, he believed it would come as a natural progression of integration into white society. Not by fighting or demanding rights. Lexie had told him he was a dreamer. No white paper was going to hire him. But he refused to give up, and he had been right.

Lexie still didn't understand how it had happened. Mama said, "Some things you just have to leave in the hands of almighty God and thank Him for the miracles when they happen." But even she had to admit, this one was a mighty big miracle, and it wasn't as though Andy was a praying man.

With Andy's first paycheck and the money they'd saved during two years of marriage, they had moved out of Mama and Pop's basement and into their own little flat. They were so happy back then. Lexie did domestic work, and Andy had his hands covered with ink each night. He was ecstatic. Filled with dreams for the future, of the day when they would have a home of their own, a car—and children. Lots and lots of strapping boys to carry on his name. Tears pricked Lexie's eyes. She'd failed him in that department. Twice.

Andy said it didn't matter. But to Lexie it mattered a great deal. She wanted him to have his dreams. And she had ruined this one for him. No wonder he never came home to face the reminder. No wonder he wanted to be with other women. Why would he want half a woman?

❧

Andy leaned against the four propped pillows on his bed and tried to organize his thoughts into anything that might make sense for a first chapter. An award-winning book that would launch him right into the *New York Times* or the *Washington Post*. He would love to move Lexie to New York City.

A light tap on the door distracted Andy from his Fifth Avenue fantasy. He glanced up, then scowled. Even after three days, he couldn't see a blasted thing through his swollen eyes.

"It's me, Andy. Can I come in?"

Irritation rolled through him at the honey-toned Southern drawl. This was all Ella's fault. If she hadn't been trying to seduce him with her luscious curves and perfume and soft lips. . .

"Andy? Are you sleeping?"

"Come in," he said grudgingly.

She did.

"What do you want?"

"Well, shoot, Andy. You don't have to be so snarly. I just came to change your bedding."

"I don't need it changed."

"Yes, you do. And I'm opening a window. It stinks in here. Now, what do you want to wear today?"

"Are you going to change me, too?"

"Not unless you want me to, sweetie." She kept her voice low and suggestive.

"What I'm wearing is fine. It's not like I can go anywhere."

Ella clucked her tongue and released a loud sigh.

"What?"

"Oh, nothing," she said with another sigh.

"Fine."

"I just never took you for the type to bull up and feel sorry for yourself."

"Who says I am?"

"Ha! Don't freshen my bed." Her mimicking tone sent heat to Andy's ears. "Let me stay in dirty, stinky clothes. I want to pout because I got my face bashed in."

"Pout?"

"Yes. And let me tell you, Yankee boy, you deserved that roughing up you got from Rafe."

"So I've been told," Andy said wryly.

"Anyway"—her tone softened—"there's a bath running for you, and Buck's coming up in a few minutes to help you get up and down the hall. By the time you get back here, I'll have your bed all nice and fresh for you. Now, what clothes should I get out?"

❧

Andy returned to his room an hour later to the scent of freshly starched linens on his bed, the sounds of traffic and laughter on the street from the open window, and the clean scent of a dusted and swept room. He had to hand it to Elia. She'd made things more comfortable.

He settled onto his bed just as Ella returned with a tray. "I brought your lunch."

Andy wasn't particularly hungry, but mealtime broke up the monotony of sitting in the darkness.

"Thanks."

She set the tray on his lap, the soft fragrance of her rose-scented perfume quickening his pulse. The bed moved as she sat next to him. "Andy?"

"Yeah?" He felt around on the tray, self-conscious to know she was watching his feeble attempts at trying to do a task that he had always taken for granted. *Eating.* One of those things a person should be able to do without thinking. But trying to find his fork, cut his meat, separate his food. . . He preferred to eat alone, where he wouldn't humiliate himself.

"Aren't you going to eat?"

"I think I'll just wait awhile."

"Shoot, Andy. Just eat. Here, take your sandwich."

Andy felt the bread in his hands and sent her a sheepish grin. "Thanks."

"Now, listen. I talked it over with Mr. Purdue, and he says I can stay up here and read to you for a while." She released a throaty laugh. "As long as I keep the door open."

"That's not really—" He was going to say "necessary," but she gave him no chance.

"Don't mention it. You can't just sit up here every day all by yourself with nothing to do. You'll go crazy. The least we can do is read to you."

"We?"

"Yep. Buck liked my idea so much he said we can take turns."

Andy shifted uncomfortably. "Why should any of you put yourself out like this?"

He felt Ella lean closer. "To tell you the truth, I like being around you. But Buck and Lottie are good people, and they just want to help."

Andy's blood warmed at her nearness. It was probably a good thing that door had to stay open. "Okay then. How about grabbing the diary on the nightstand, and you can start reading where I have the place marked. And would you mind sitting in the chair instead of on the bed? When you move it makes my ribs hurt." A small but necessary lie.

She gave a low chuckle, obviously aware of her effect on him, and moved away. "Okay, handsome, here goes."

CHRISTMAS, 1861

Cat stood in baby Henry's nursery staring out at the carriage block below. Her heart raced, and she snuggled her son closer. "He's here," she whispered against his downy head.

Mr. Hanson stepped out of the carriage, tall and handsome like Thomas. Cat shuddered, remembering the kindness in his eyes when he'd silently beseeched her to let Thomas go. She had been grateful for his gentleness at the time, but as she watched him bend gracefully over Camilla's hand, then offer her his arm, hatred surged through Cat.

Camilla would not have Thomas. Even if Cat couldn't have him, she'd die before allowing Camilla Penbrook anywhere near him.

Pushing away the dark thoughts, she caught her breath as Thomas emerged. Even from the window, she could feel the warmth of his presence. Cat noted with a sense of satisfaction that he hesitated before accepting Henry's proffered hand, then shook it stiffly. He had not forgotten either.

"Look up, Thomas," she whispered.

As though he had heard, Thomas raised his chin. For a moment, his gaze captured hers and his eyes widened. Then a sneer twisted his lips, and he looked away.

Tears pricked Cat's eyes. She turned in defeat from the window. She laid the sleeping baby in his crib, then sat on her cot, tears sliding down her cheeks. Hugging her legs to her chest, she rested her forehead on her knees and allowed the tears to flow.

Henry had ordered her to stay away from their guests. "If you go anywhere near the Hanson boy," he'd said the night before, his fingers biting into the soft flesh of Cat's upper arm, "I'll kill you."

Cat shuddered at the memory of his cold blue eyes. She would have willingly risked death to see Thomas, but it was obvious he no longer cared for her.

The door creaked slowly open, and Cat glanced up. She stiffened at the sight of her mother.

"Miss Maddy want you to get the baby washed and dressed. Master Henry want to show off his son at dinner tonight."

"Am I to take the baby down there?" Cat asked, horrified at the thought of Thomas figuring out that she had borne Henry a son.

"No," Naomi said softly. "I's gonna take him down when Master Henry call for him."

Cat nodded. "I'll have him fed and ready." She waited for Naomi to leave, but her mother stood there, scrutinizing her.

Finally she spoke. "Why you was crying."

"I wasn't." Cat jerked her chin up and glanced away from her mother.

Naomi placed her hand under Cat's chin and pressed, forcing Cat to look at her. "Yes, you was."

Cat scowled. "I wasn't." She jutted her chin.

Naomi settled next to her on the cot and placed her work-hardened hands over Cat's. "Sometime de tears jus' come and dere ain't nothin' you can do about it, baby. Jesus takes dem tears and puts 'em in a bottle."

"I'm sick of crying. And don't tell me about Jesus. He's a white man's God, not mine."

Naomi gasped. "Cat! Don' talk dat way."

"I will talk that way. Do you hear me, God?" Her voice rose, and she glared at the ceiling. "I think You're just like the rest of the white men in the world."

Naomi shot to her feet, casting fearful wide eyes around

the room as though afraid Cat's blasphemy might bring the walls crashing down around them.

Shaking with self-induced fury, Cat rose and paced the floor. "What kind of God allows people to be work animals for other people? We're nothing more than dogs or mules at the whim and mercy of cruel taskmasters. What kind of life is this?" Tears streamed down her face.

Naomi placed her hands upon Cat's shoulders. "You thinks you got it worse dan other slaves? At least you don' have to work in de fields from sunup to sundown. Sweating in the sun, freezing in the cold. Den go back to the quarters and lay down with de master or any of de men on the plantation. You might have to put up with Master Henry, but he won't let any other men near ya."

Cat laughed. Loudly, hysterically. "Do you really think Henry has me hidden away because he cares about me? Lord Almighty, Naomi. I love Thomas Hanson. And he loved me until he found out I have Negro blood. Henry's just afraid Thomas might want to run off with me."

"Oh, baby. My baby." Naomi gathered Cat close. Cat resisted, but her mother tightened her hold until Cat relaxed against her.

"Oh, Mama, why? Why does life have to be this way? Don't I have skin as white as Camilla's? Why should she have Thomas?"

"Dat's jus' de way things be, baby."

"What if the Yankees win and we go free?"

Naomi held her at arm's length and looked sadly into her eyes. "Will dat change who you be? Will it change de African blood in your body? You find a strong man of your own kind. A man who know what it is to belong to another man.

A man like dat will treat you good because he know where you's been. He know what you's come through."

Cat snorted. "I'd rather be alone forever."

Naomi narrowed her eyes but said nothing. Cat met her gaze, unwavering. She had not been raised in Miss Maddy's parlor to throw away her refinement on a man who would never understand her. How could a slave, or even a former slave, ever know how to sit properly at a dinner table? Would he read Lord Byron to her in bed at night? It was out of the question.

Little Henry stirred in his crib, mewling softly. Cat glanced lovingly at her son, feeling her milk let down as he opened his eyes and whimpered. Right now he was the only bright thing in her life. At least as Henry's son, no one would ever know he had any Negro blood. He would be a white man in every sense of the word and would inherit Penbrook. The family Bible listed young Henry next to Camilla as Miss Maddy and Henry's child. Cat nodded in satisfaction. She would endure what she must as long as her son was cared for.

❧

Two days later, Cat sat in the garden behind Penbrook House nursing her baby. While Henry took the Hansons on a tour of Penbrook's extensive fields, Cat had taken advantage of the unseasonably warm December day to allow baby Henry and herself a respite from confinement within the four walls.

Thomas and his family would leave Penbrook tomorrow. Cat had hoped for a moment to speak with Thomas alone, but there had been no opportunity. Other than his arrival, she hadn't even seen him. A sigh escaped her lips. There would be no opportunity to thwart any marriage plans Camilla might snag him into.

"What are we going to do, my sweet baby?" She looked down at her son nursing euphorically, eyes wide open. He grinned in response to her voice. Cat laughed as milk ran from his mouth.

"That's quite a boy you have there."

Cat gasped. She stood quickly as Mr. Hanson stepped into the garden.

Baby Henry let up a squeal of protest as her nipple bobbed from his mouth. Cat pulled her dress closed and adjusted Henry to her shoulder. "I—I didn't know anyone was home."

"Ah yes. I thought I'd stay and prepare for our departure tomorrow." His eyes reflected the same kindness she'd observed that night in the barn. Still, Cat watched him warily. If he took one step toward her, she'd run screaming for the house.

"Don't worry, my dear. I have no intention of molesting you. Please sit. I can imagine Henry's had you locked away to keep you out of Thomas's sight. And it appears with good reason."

"I don't understand what you mean." She wanted to bolt. To return to the safety of the nursery before anyone found out she had disobeyed Henry's orders and left the room in the first place. After three days without his abuse, she didn't relish the thought of what he would do to her.

"I take it the child is yours and not Mrs. Penbrook's?"

Heat suffused Cat's cheeks, and she glanced away. "He belongs to Miss Maddy. I'm his wet nurse."

"I'm not a fool," he said without a trace of gruffness. "Give me the baby."

Fear gripped Cat, and she tightened her hold.

"It's all right. Let me see him."

Reluctantly Cat released Henry, who had drifted off to sleep. He didn't stir as Mr. Hanson held him in his arms.

"How old is he?"

"A few months."

"How many months?" he pressed. "And don't lie to me."

Cat cleared her throat. "Three." Dear God, was he going to expose them all? "Please, Mr. Hanson. . ."

"Surely you've noticed the resemblance. I noticed it the moment I saw this child our first night at Penbrook."

"I don't understand."

His gaze flicked across hers, and then his expression changed. He handed her the baby and rose, straightening his vest. "It doesn't matter. Forgive my intrusion."

Cat frowned as she watched him turn to head back to the house. Then realization dawned. She glanced at baby Henry and gasped, "Oh."

Mr. Hanson spun on his heel and walked quickly back to where Cat sat. He cupped her chin and forced her gaze upward. "I assumed you knew my son fathered this child. The resemblance is unmistakable."

Joy shot through Cat's heart like a ray of sunshine slicing through a black cloud. "Thomas?" A smile curved her lips. She glanced down at her son, and a new surge of love shot through her. Why had she never seen it before?

"He must never know."

Confused, Cat sought understanding in the depth of Mr. Hanson's gaze. There was no anger, no condemnation, only concern. She remained silent, knowing if she tried to speak, she would burst into tears.

With a heavy sigh, Mr. Hanson sat next to her on the bench. "If my son knew he had fathered this child, he would take you both away from here, someplace where you could pass as a white woman."

"No, he wouldn't. You didn't see the way he looked at me."

"He's seen you since our arrival?" He grabbed her arms. "What did he do?"

"N—nothing. I only saw him through the window. He—he didn't look happy to see me."

He released her and raked fingers through his graying hair. "I apologize for scaring you."

"Y—you didn't."

"Thomas is my only son. My only heir. His sister and her husband live out west, so there is no one else to run the plantation when I am gone."

Tears pricked Cat's eyes. If she thought Thomas loved her, nothing would keep her from telling him about his son. No one. "I won't tell him," she said softly. "You have my word."

Mr. Hanson's eyes softened, and he reached forward to cup her cheek. "It's no wonder my son fancied himself in love with you. If only. . ."

He stood once more, patted baby Henry on the head, and strode to the house without another word.

Trembling, Cat gathered the baby in her arms and returned to the nursery. How could she allow a monster like Henry to raise Thomas's son? If only. . . Mr. Hanson's words hung in her mind. If only she had no Negro blood coursing through her veins.

She allowed herself a brief moment to dream of what life might be like should Thomas whisk her away like a prince in a fairy tale. She sighed. Thomas was a prince, but she was far from a princess. And he would never leave his kingdom for the likes of her.

1948

Ella closed the diary and set it on the nightstand as Buck entered the room.

"I'll take over the reading now, Ella. Lottie needs you in the kitchen."

"Duty calls, Yankee boy. I'll see you later." She ducked out the door.

"You really don't have to read to me, Buck. To tell you the truth, I was having trouble keeping from dozing off while Ella read."

"Your wife telephoned."

"She did?" Andy's heart leaped, and he started to get up.

"Lie down, boy. I told her you was hurt and shouldn't get out of bed."

Andy scowled. "You shouldn't have done that. I would have talked to her."

"I figured you might, but she didn't want you hurtin' yourself more. Just told me to tell ya she hoped you'd get to feelin' better soon."

Disappointment swept through Andy. She hoped he felt better soon? No words of love and devotion?

"Thanks for the message, Buck."

"Weren't no trouble, son." He hesitated a moment, then Andy heard the squeak of his shoes as he headed toward the door. "I suppose if you don't want me to read, I'll leave you to your nap. Just holler if you need anything."

"Thanks."

Andy scooted more deeply under the covers and tossed aside a couple of his pillows until he was comfortable in the bed. His head throbbed, and he reached for the bottle of painkillers on the nightstand. He felt around until he found them, took two, and swallowed them down without water.

Loneliness drifted over him. He lay awake for what seemed like hours thinking of Lexie and wishing desperately he had never gone with Ella to Georgie's.

APRIL 1863

There are only women in the house now. Henry rode off to fight in the war right after the holidays. If there truly is a God, he will not return alive. Most of the slaves have run away, as there are very few men left to patrol and keep them in hand. The militia is too busy conducting mock drills to bother with the runaways.

Many of the women are afraid to step out onto their porches at night for fear the runaway slaves will accost them. I find this amusing. Camilla is beside herself with worry and taxes my patience unendingly. I wear myself out doing her bidding while I try to care for her poor mother.

I'm afraid Miss Maddy will not be with us much longer. Her strange illness has taken all of her strength, and she has lost vision in her right eye. I remain at Penbrook only because she needs me. Camilla is useless, and old Mrs. Penbrook has left us and returned to her childhood home in Louisiana to live with a spinster sister.

She took Naomi with her. My mother hugged me and cried as though she will never see me again. I try to find it in my heart to miss her. But I spent so many years away from her that I hardly think of her as my mother at all. Maddy has always been more so to me.

That is why I can hardly bear to see Miss Maddy so ill. If not for her illness, I would take my son and travel north, even if I had to walk every step of the way. But I cannot leave her now. Not while she lives.

Chapter Six
~Summer 1864

From sunup until sundown, the work was endless. The day had barely begun, and already exhaustion weakened Cat's legs, making the walk up the long staircase tortuously slow. She entered Miss Maddy's room carrying a basin of water and a fresh cloth.

"Cat? Is that you?" Miss Maddy's feeble voice barely carried across the length of the room.

Cat made her way quickly to the bedside. "I'm here, ma'am." Setting the bowl of water on the nightstand, she dipped the cloth and squeezed out the excess liquid. "How are you feeling?"

Maddy seemed to relax as Cat wiped the cloth across her forehead. "Not quite as bad today. The cool cloth helps. Thank you."

A sense of helplessness crept through Cat. A familiar enemy. If only there were some way she could help relieve the pain. Cat would give almost anything to see Miss Maddy well again. But there was no doctor for miles. Perhaps in Atlanta. But Cat knew even if she walked the entire thirty miles, the chances of convincing a doctor to leave the wounded soldiers to attend one woman were pretty slim.

A moan brought her back to the present. "What is it? Can I do something?"

Miss Maddy shook her head. "It won't be long now. I can feel it."

Fear shot through Cat at the very sound of the words. "Don't say it. I won't believe it."

"Oh, Cat. You must know it's true. My eyesight is gone. The shape of my head has changed. I can feel the deformity, so I know you must be able to see it."

She was right. Miss Maddy's forehead was almost grotesque in appearance. But Cat refused to acknowledge the statement. She couldn't bear the thought of telling the once-beautiful woman that she was beautiful no more.

"Henry Jr. recognized some letters today," she said brightly.

A pleased smile lifted Miss Maddy's pale, chapped lips. "Already? I've never heard of a two-year-old with such intelligence. He must take after you, Cat. You always were so bright."

Pain twisted Cat's heart. She dipped the cloth into the basin again and squeezed out the excess water. "Please. We agreed never to speak of little Henry as my child." She folded the cloth and laid it across Miss Maddy's forehead.

Maddy reached up weakly and pressed at the cloth as though trying to enhance its soothing affects. "Oh, what does it matter anymore? Really. The money from Penbrook Estate is all gone. Henry Jr. won't inherit much anyway. Even if his father does make it back from the war."

Cat pushed back the thought. She prayed every night that Henry would die in battle or from any one of the horrific diseases of which they'd heard rumors. "Don't you see,

Miss Maddy?" Cat sat next to her, folding her hands in her lap. "It's not about money. It's about this land. I'll make sure he has something worth inheriting."

"What do you mean, you'll make sure?" Camilla's haughty voice raked through the room as she entered, grating on Cat's already taut nerves. "What have you to do with any of it?"

"Camilla, please," Miss Maddy pleaded. "Don't start an argument."

"I'm sorry, Mama. But really, who does she think she is?"

"Come here and sit with me." She held her hand in the direction of the doorway where Camilla still stood.

Cat rose to leave. "I'll be back in a little while with some breakfast for you, ma'am."

"No, Cat. Stay. I wish to speak with you both." She patted the bed on either side of her.

Camilla walked around and sat carefully. "I didn't hurt you, did I, Mama?"

Miss Maddy attempted a smile, but weakness caused it to falter, reducing the effort to little more than a quiver. "No, sweetheart. You didn't hurt me."

Camilla took her mother's hand and pressed it against her own cheek. During times such as this, when Camilla's eyes clouded with pain and fear, Cat almost allowed herself a moment of compassion. But her dislike for the girl was too strong for any other emotion to last for long.

"Cat?" Miss Maddy reached for her. Cat sat on her other side and took the outstretched hand between hers.

"What do you want to tell us?"

Miss Maddy grimaced.

"I can see you're in pain, Mama." Camilla pressed a kiss to her mother's palm. "We should let you rest for now. Can't this little talk come later?"

"Every minute draws me closer to the end."

Camilla gasped. "You mustn't speak that way, Mama. It's tempting the fates."

"We don't believe in the fates. You know that, dear. We believe in divine destiny. If it is appointed for me to die at this time, there is nothing I can say or not say to stop it."

Cat squeezed her hand gently. "What did you want to tell us, Miss Maddy?"

She gave Cat's hand a weak squeeze in response. "When I'm gone, there will only be little Henry and the two of you left at Penbrook."

Camilla turned and stared wide-eyed at Cat as though the thought hadn't occurred to her. Cat had thought of little else. How on earth could she live in the house with Camilla as mistress?

"We'll get along fine, Mama. Don't you worry about anything. Just concentrate on getting better."

"My dear girl, I am not going to get better. We must speak of this. There will be dark days ahead, whether the war ends soon or not. The two of you must work together to survive and take care of Henry Jr." She turned unseeing eyes to Cat. "I know you've tried to keep from me how scarce provisions are. But I can tell we have very little. I also know we have no money to replenish."

"Don't worry about anything, Miss Maddy. We still have some canned goods and seed potatoes. We'll be planting soon. And I'm getting pretty good with a rifle. I noticed some deer tracks out by the well yesterday. I'm thinking of going hunting in the morning. And with the money we've been able to bring in from washing the Yankee soldiers' laundry, we're going to be able to buy some cotton seed and plant just as soon as there are men enough to hire on."

Cat felt Camilla's dark gaze on her at the mention of doing the Yankee laundry. It had been a stroke of luck that Cat had caught the eye of Captain Stuart Riley, the Yankee soldier who had saved Penbrook from burning to the ground when the occupiers had come through a few months earlier. But Camilla hated the sight of the blue uniform with such passion that she didn't even try to be civil when the captain came to call on Cat. Which he did often.

Oblivious to the silent exchange, Miss Maddy squeezed Cat's hand. "You're such a good girl. I know you'll take good care of Camilla and Henry Jr."

Cat felt Camilla stiffen. She gave her a sharp look and shook her head. A scowl marred the other girl's features, but to her credit, she didn't voice her opinion of her mother's statement.

Miss Maddy grimaced and closed her eyes.

Cat motioned to Camilla with her head and slipped her hands from Miss Maddy's. "We'll leave you to get some rest."

Madeline straightened and clung to Cat. "Wait. Promise me that you'll stick together and behave like the sisters I raised you to be."

Camilla's face grew red with anger. Her lips pressed together tightly.

Cat spoke up quickly. "We promise." She bent forward and pressed a kiss to Miss Maddy's cheek. Camilla followed her example. They tiptoed away. The dying woman was asleep before they reached the door.

In the hallway, Camilla turned on her heel, fire blazing in her blue eyes. "I will never think of you as a sister."

A heavy sigh escaped Cat, and she stood unflinching before the girl's anger. "Nor will I think of you that way. But it was good of you to let Miss Maddy have the peace of thinking we will stick together once she's gone."

"I'm not entirely heartless, you know."

"No, I didn't. But I'm glad to hear it." Weary of Camilla's presence, Cat turned to go. "I'll be in the kitchen preparing breakfast."

"I'll have mine in my bedroom."

"Then you'll have to come down and get it, because the only tray I'm carrying up is your mother's."

Camilla gave a huff and flounced away.

Cat leaned against the wall and closed her eyes. Food was scarce. The constant ache in the pit of her stomach was becoming more than she could bear.

Her mind flitted to the line of Yankee soldiers who had marched into town a few months earlier. Madeline's status as a Northerner had allowed Captain Riley to justify not burning the house. Cat knew none of these diehard Southerners would have anything to do with the soldiers. But Yankees had money. She needed a way to care for Miss Maddy, Camilla, and little Henry. And whether her neighbors or Camilla liked it or not, she would do laundry for the soldiers. She had no choice.

1948

Andy leaned against his propped-up pillows and frowned. He'd come to the end of this journal. At the worst moment.

He moved carefully from the bed, clutching his side as he made his way to the boxes of tablets and journals. Thankfully, they were organized into some semblance of order, or he'd have wasted hours, maybe days, trying to sequence the writings. After a few minutes of moving boxes here and there, he found the next journal. He settled down and read through eyes that, after a week of being swollen shut, had only the day before gone down enough to allow for reading, difficult though it was. It was slow, unfocused at times, but certainly preferable to sitting idly, listening to the sounds of the house while everyone was too busy to visit him or read to him from the journals.

"Andy?" A tap sounded at his door.

"Come in."

"Is everything all right up here?" Miss Lottie's soft-spoken Southern accent brought about the nostalgic longing he often experienced in her presence. He couldn't quite put his finger on it. Wasn't sure he wanted to. No, he knew he didn't want to. Most likely it was only a residual effect of spending the latter half of his childhood without his mother, who in his memory spoke very much like Lottie.

"Yes, ma'am. Everything's fine."

A frown marred the otherwise smooth brow. She planted her hands on her hips. "Then what was all that banging around?"

Andy smiled. "I was just finding the next of Miss Penbrook's journals."

"Oh, I see your eyes are beginning to open. That's good. You'll be back to normal in no time."

A grin tipped Andy's lips. "I've been a real bother, haven't I?"

"Of course not." Sincerity rang in her tone, leaving no doubt that she spoke her true feelings. "Buck says Miss Penbrook's diaries are real interesting."

"They are."

"Should you be reading much?"

With a sigh, Andy set the book aside. "I guess my head is aching from trying to focus."

Miss Lottie walked closer to the bed. "My work is finished until time to start supper. I wouldn't mind reading to you for a while."

"I'd hate to impose."

"Nonsense. It'd be my pleasure." A hint of starch lingered as she leaned over him to retrieve the book. In truth, she was a young woman, probably several years his junior, but her demeanor made him long for his mother.

She settled into the chair next to his bed. "From the beginning?"

"Yes. I was just about to start reading when you knocked."

AUGUST 1864

Even the sky wept the spring day Miss Maddy was laid to rest. As the last shovelful of dirt was thrown, Cat looped her arm with Camilla's. Had she not, the young woman would have fallen under the weight of grief. Years of animosity were set aside as they shared an umbrella and watched the makeshift casket, crafted by the blue-coated soldiers occupying town, being lowered into the earth.

Not many mourners joined them. After all, Maddy wasn't one of their kind. And neither were the girls. The few neighbors who did attend made their displeasure known as soon as it was apparent that Yankee Captain Stuart Riley and his men were tending to the burial.

Their closest neighbor, Mrs. George, an old dowager who lived five miles away, made a beeline for the girls as soon as the minister said the final prayer. "You two should

be ashamed of yourselves letting Yankee soldiers bury anyone on Georgia soil." She zeroed in on them both as though
not quite sure which was which. "I always liked your ma,
even if she was a Yank. But I can't abide the presence of
those infidels. You should be ashamed."

Camilla's forlorn expression tugged at even Cat's heart,
but she remained silent. No one seemed to question her
presence at the graveside. There had been so little inter-
action between the Penbrook plantation and the other
families in the county that Cat doubted anyone knew
of her roots. This emboldened her. She returned the old
dowager's glare.

Camilla pressed a handkerchief to her red nose. "Th–
there was no one else to build a casket or dig a grave."

Mrs. George harrumphed. "I would rather blister my
hands and dig the grave myself than allow the enemy to step
a foot on my place."

"But Captain Riley has been so kind," Camilla tried to
explain. "Why, if not for the men allowing us to take in
their washing and ironing, we would have starved."

A gasp left the older woman. "You're washing the filth
from Yankee uniforms? The very Yankees who have stripped
us of our land? Our very existence? I'd rather starve!" Without another word, she swept her skirt aside and scurried
away as though one more moment in their presence might
sully her very status as a Confederate woman.

"Good! Go!" Camilla shouted after Mrs. George and the
others who were slowly trudging away through the mud.
"My mother wouldn't have wanted you here anyway!" She
dipped and snatched a rock from the rain-soaked ground.
Cat grabbed her wrist before she could chuck it at the old

woman's back. Secretly, she admired Camilla's spunk, but reason prevailed.

"Camilla," Cat murmured next to her ear. "Don't give her the satisfaction. Your mother would expect you to behave properly. Besides, think about little Henry. He might need friends among these people some day."

Camilla's face crumpled before Cat's mild rebuke. She dissolved into tears, clutching at Cat's slim shoulders. Cat's knees nearly buckled as Camilla went limp in her arms. Struggling beneath the weight of an unconscious body, Cat pulled at the young woman's gown. "Wake up before I'm forced to let you drop to the ground." Nothing would have given her greater pleasure than to see the haughty girl, who had made her life a living hell, lying flat on her back in the mud. But she'd promised Miss Maddy that she'd be good to Camilla—as though they were sisters. Still, she was only physically capable of holding so much weight. Rain trickled down her neck as she struggled to stay on her feet.

"Let me take her for you, Miss Cat."

Cat looked up into the handsome face of Captain Stuart Riley. Relief flooded her as he relieved her of her burden. He swept Camilla into his arms and whisked her away from the family grave site. Once inside, he turned to Cat. "Where do you want me to lay her down?"

"In the parlor." Cat led the way and slid open the door. "Put her on the sofa. She hasn't slept or had anything to eat for two days. I'm surprised she held up as long as she did."

Gently he deposited his burden on the sofa.

In the foyer, Cat smiled up at the young officer. Dark sideburns adorned his face, and a fashionable mustache hung over his lip. He smiled down at her, his brown eyes filled with tenderness. "Thank you, Stuart. I don't know how to express my gratitude to you and your men for all you've done." Tears filled her eyes. "Miss Maddy would have liked you, I think."

Stuart's soft gaze caressed her face. He lifted her hand and pressed a warm kiss to her knuckles. "You and your sister have made life bearable during the past two months. Do you know how much we admire your determination to survive?"

Early in their acquaintance, Stuart had made the erroneous assumption that she and Camilla were sisters. Cat had not bothered to correct him. "There's really no choice but to survive or die, is there?"

"That's the spirit I'm talking about." His grip tightened on her fingers. "I admire you more than any woman I've ever met."

Cat's heart lifted with the praise. "Thank you, Stuart."

He reached out and trailed his finger along her jawline. "So brave."

Warmth filled her belly at the expression of tenderness in his eyes. Closing her eyes, she leaned into his palm, grateful for the comfort. Before she quite knew what was happening, she felt him shift, and warm lips covered hers. Her eyes flew open. She stepped back, staring at the captain.

"What's wrong?" he asked.

"D-don't do that."

"I'm sorry, Cat." He took a step forward.

Cat retreated. She held up a restraining palm.

He placed his hat on his head and slapped his gloves into his palm. "If I've misread your feelings for me, I apologize. But I thought—"

"Please, just go."

Bowing at the waist, Stuart turned. Cat held her breath

as his boots thudded against the hardwood floor. She released it only when the door shut behind him. Her hands began to tremble and then the rest of her.

Captain Riley was certainly nice enough, and Cat was grateful for all he and his men had done for them, but that didn't mean she'd allow pawing and kissing and God knew what else he had in mind. She was finished with men. Henry's interest in her had resulted in physical pain and demoralization. Even her love for Thomas had brought nothing but heartache. She wasn't sure what Stuart wanted from her, but whatever it was. . .

Outside, she heard Captain Riley order the men to mount. Unease pricked her as she replayed her response to his advances. What if he stopped bringing his laundry? Sudden fear clutched at her belly. What if he ordered his men to go to one of the army wives from town who had joined their Yankee husbands? Panic licked her insides, and she fairly flew to the door. The men were already beginning to enter the canopy of oaks flanking the lane to and from Penbrook House.

"Stuart, wait!"

Looking over his shoulder, he reined in his horse and motioned his men to continue on ahead. Then he nudged his horse and galloped back to the house.

He remained in the saddle and stared down at her as a soaking rain continued to fall. "What's wrong?"

Swallowing hard, Cat clenched her fists. "I. . .just wanted to apologize for my reaction."

He remained silent, his questioning gaze demanding an answer as she descended the steps. She pressed her hand flat against her stomach, trying to ward off a knot of nerves. Rain trickled down her neck. She forced a smile. Too much was at stake. "I can't let you ride away if you're angry."

Captain Riley dismounted. "Cat, honey, you're getting soaked. Let's go back on the porch." He wrapped his arm around her shoulders and headed her back up the steps. She reached for the door, but his hand restrained her. He turned her to face him. "Now, what's this about?"

"I—I just. . ." She tore her gaze from his and stared at the brass buttons on his blue coat. "I hope you aren't angry with me. I—You just took me by surprise, that's all."

"Look at me." He placed a finger beneath her chin and pressed upward until her eyes met his. "Do you mean to tell me you welcomed my kiss? That you return my feelings?"

Confusion clouded her mind. What were her feelings for Stuart? Gratitude for his kindness, to be sure. But romance? She swallowed hard and nodded, forcing the lie through her trembling lips. "I do. Truly."

His lips curved upward into a smile, showing white straight teeth. He pulled her to him.

Cat knew what she had to do. How many times had she been forced to pretend she cared? She allowed instinct to take over. She'd been well trained. Rising to her toes, she slipped her arms around his neck and met his kiss. She melted against him, feigning a passion she didn't, couldn't feel. When his lips left hers, he kept her close, his breathing heavy. He pressed his forehead against hers. "Cat. . .I need to tell you something."

The door shot open. Camilla stood, shaking with fury, her eyes wide, face white as a ghost. "What do you think you're doing?"

"Camilla, go back inside and mind your own business."

"You are standing on my steps, behaving like a

common. . ." She glared at Cat, fury burning red in every line of her face. "You pretend to love Mother and yet less than an hour after her burial, I find you like this." Tears pooled in her large blue eyes.

Stuart released Cat. He bowed to Camilla. "I apologize for giving in to my feelings on a most inopportune day."

"Indeed." She drew herself up to her full height, pulling her shawl closer about her.

Cat knew she had to appease Camilla quickly before the girl began another rant. "I'm sorry, Camilla. You are right. It was not the right time. H–how are you feeling?" Weariness suddenly overcame her strength, and it was all she could do to remain standing.

"A lot you care. You left me alone."

Irritation and embarrassment nipped at Cat. "What would you have me do? Sit and watch you sleep?"

Brows narrowing, Camilla fixed her with a dangerous glare. "I think you're forgetting yourself."

Stuart looked from Cat to Camilla. Cat's face burned.

Ever the hero, Stuart inclined his head. "I'm sorry, Miss Camilla. I'm afraid it's my fault your sister wasn't there when you awoke."

A short laugh shot from Camilla's lips. "Sister? Is that what she told you?"

"Camilla, please." Cat would have gladly scratched out the other girl's eyes. Or cut out her tongue to prevent her from speaking the inevitable.

Ignoring her, Camilla fixed Stuart with a rigid glare. "No Negro girl is my sister, Captain Riley. And yes, that is what this girl is. She is a slave in the Penbrook household. Nothing more."

Bile rose to Cat's throat. Anger blinded her. Camilla

continued her spiel to the speechless captain. "Or perhaps she was a little more than a slave. She was also my pa's mistress."

Humiliated beyond words, Cat stared at Camilla, then looked into the blanched face of the Yankee captain. She backed away a few steps, turned, and fled into the rain.

1 9 4 8

Lottie's choked voice read the last few lines of Cat's diary entry for the day of Madeline Penbrook's funeral. "Poor girl."

"Yeah."

She heaved a sigh and set the book on the table beside Andy's bed. "I'm so grateful to God that my girls are free and will never have to go through what our grandmothers did."

"I wouldn't exactly call our state being 'free,' " Andy retorted. "Especially in the South."

Lottie gave a short laugh. "At least it's a higher degree of freedom than the slavery our ancestors had to endure." Her voice faltered. "My girls can go to school. Even college if they want."

"Colored schools. Colored colleges. Substandard educations, Miss Lottie. That's not freedom. If your daughter drinks from a whites-only fountain, you think she can tell the policeman arresting her that she's free to drink wherever she wants?"

"Those things will change in time."

"Yes, but will it be in our lifetime?"

Her features softened, and her eyes seemed to look past him, as though she were attempting to look into the future. "I don't know. But for now, I'm satisfied that neither I nor my daughters have to fear being raped by our masters. We make our own living. My husband will never be beaten for not picking enough cotton to suit a white trash overseer."

Remembering the young men who had stopped him on the road to Penbrook House on the day he arrived in Oak Junction, Andy shrugged. "There are other things he can be beaten for."

Lottie laughed without humor. "Perhaps, for example, insulting a colored girl in front of the white man who loves her so deeply he can't see straight?"

Heat shot to his ears at her pointed comment. "A valid observation. Forgive my cynicism."

"Tell me about your family, Mr. Carmichael. I know your wife must miss you terribly. I'd die if Buck took off for even a few days."

Andy closed his aching eyes. Lexie's beautiful face floated across his mind. Robert's oily chuckle followed the image, souring it. "No one is dying of loneliness over me."

She cleared her throat. "What about your parents?"

"I don't have parents." His tone was harsh. He knew it, but he couldn't find the strength to apologize.

"I'm sorry to be so nosy." She shuffled to her feet. "I'll let you rest for now."

Andy listened to her soft steps as she made her way across the room and quietly closed the door behind her.

From Camilla's diary
September 1864

Mother has been buried for two weeks. To my great joy, I have discovered her diaries. She wrote in them every day before her illness forced her to stop. There are many, many tablets and books upon which she wrote, from the time she married my pa until only a few months before her demise.

Reading her thoughts brings me closer to her. To know the depth of her love for me. It disconcerts me to read that she loved Cat as a daughter. She has said it enough times, but somehow the reading of these—her deepest and most honest thoughts—makes it more painful.

Cat. I admit I can't abide her uppity ways. But then I suppose now that she perceives herself as free and seems to have taken it upon herself to provide for us, she must feel as though she is justified in disobeying God's laws. "Slaves, obey your masters." For that is what the scriptures command.

She scoffed when I reminded her of this. I have no choice but to allow the insolent girl to continue as she has. I am ashamed to say that I cannot care for myself. But then, I have not been raised to care for myself, have I? I am only waiting for the war to be over so that Thomas will return and marry me. Then he will take care of me, and all the drudgery and difficulty will be over.

I regretted my hasty outburst of truthfulness with Captain Riley, as I feared it would cause him to turn away and leave us to our own devices. Oddly enough, however, the news does not seem to have cooled his affection for Cat. This relieves me greatly. I only hope he will marry her soon.

Before Thomas returns from the war.

CHAPTER SEVEN
~ DECEMBER 1864

Cold wind bit through Camilla's threadbare shawl and whipped at her thin dress as she gripped her rifle and crept stealthily toward the moving bushes. Her stomach growled, and hope rose in her throat. Only last week, Mrs. George's last remaining slave had knocked on the door, asking Camilla if she'd seen a loose pig. Apparently the animal had broken its rope on the way to the slaughterhouse and had gone missing.

She had not seen the pig. And if she were to find such a treasure, she certainly wouldn't be returning it to Mrs. George. How could she forget the woman's insulting words to her on the day Mother was buried? Besides, the thought of roasted ham made her mouth water and her stomach ache.

The bushes moved again. Camilla cocked the rifle, ready to plug a hole into the pig as soon as it stuck its little pink snout out of that brush.

"Lawd Almighty, don' shoot, miss."

Fear shook Camilla from her head to her toes, and she nearly dropped the rifle. "Wh–who is it?"

"Now, I be coming out wif my hands in the air. You gonna shoot me?"

"I'm making no promises. Show yourself immediately."

Slowly a young man appeared, as black as night. Obviously a runaway.

"What are you doing on my land?" Forcing a bravado she was far from feeling, Camilla pointed the gun barrel at the slave. "I insist you tell me where you've come from. Who is your master?"

"I don' got no master no mo'."

"Fiddlesticks. You must tell me so that I may send you home immediately." Perhaps there was a reward for such a strapping young buck as this.

He smiled, the flash of his white teeth making a startling contrast to the darkness of his skin. "I guess you ain't heard. Pres-ee-dent Lincoln done freed all us slaves. You cain't send me nowheres."

Alarm shot through Camilla at his audacity. "Yes, well. That fool Lincoln doesn't make the rules for the Confederacy."

"Miss, I–I'd be beholden to ya if ya'd point dat dere gun somewheres else than at my gut."

"You're in no position to be asking for favors, boy."

"Yes'm, I knows dat. But seein' as how dere's a mean-lookin' hawg over by dat tree lookin' like he might charge, I'd like da chance to mebbe hep ya."

"Wh–what?" Camilla turned and came face-to-face with an angry hog.

"Now, miss, don' run."

Ignoring the soft words, Camilla screamed, dropped the rifle, and took off toward the house.

Behind her, she heard the squeals and grunts of an angry hog, mixed with a scream of pain. She stopped short, tears flowing, and turned. Horrified, she observed a wrestling match between man and beast. And the beast seemed to be winning.

Fighting the urge to plug her ears against the sounds, Camilla knew what had to be done. Strength from deep inside flooded her, and she flew into action. She raced back to where she'd flung the rifle. Her movement drew the hog's attention.

The man lay still. Even from her distant vantage point, Camilla saw his bloody arm.

Stuffing the rising fear, she grabbed up the gun, which miraculously had failed to discharge when she dropped it, despite the fact that it was cocked. Her heart beat furiously in her ears.

The beast barreled toward her. As though time slowed, she worked methodically. She raised the rifle, aimed carefully, remembering Cat's instructions, and squeezed the trigger. The hog let out a bloodcurdling squeal and dropped dead at her feet, a bullet lodged between its open eyes. Camilla dared not move. She held her breath and stared unblinking at the hog until her lungs screamed for air. Only when she was sure the thing was really dead could she find the courage to look past the beast.

"Boy, are you alive?"

A weak moan came in reply.

Shaking violently, she took an unsteady step toward the slave. She kept a tight grip on the rifle, eyeing the hog as though it might come back to life and attack.

"Camilla?" Cat's voice called from the edge of the woods. "Where are you?"

"O–over here, Cat. I need help."

Seconds later, Cat crashed through the brush. She

stopped short and stared. Camilla relished the priceless look of surprise on her face.

The need to remain in control bolstered her courage. She resisted the urge to run crying into Cat's arms and turn everything over to her. If only Mother could see her now. She, Camilla, had killed a hog and possibly saved a man's life. Even if he were just a slave.

"What on earth happened here? Who is that?"

"I don't know, but he needs our help."

"He's fainted." Cat knelt beside the Negro man. "His arm is bleeding badly. Give me your shawl."

"I'll freeze!"

Cat scowled deeply, turning flashing brown eyes on her. "I need something to tie up his wound before he bleeds to death. Give it to me before I take it away from you by force."

Indignation rose in Camilla. She removed the shawl from her shoulders and stomped toward Cat. "Move aside. I will bind the wound myself. You ride for the Yankee doctor in town. The Northerners came all the way down here and fought this war to free slaves like him; surely they'll travel five miles to offer medical help."

Cat made no move to do as she was told. Rather, she stared up at Camilla. "How will you get him inside?"

She hadn't thought of that. "Bring me some blankets to keep him warm. Then hurry to town and bring back your Captain Riley to help."

"All right." Cat nodded and stood. "But bind the wound tightly. As badly as he's bleeding, he'll be dead before I return if you don't slow it down."

Camilla's stomach weakened at the sight of the bloody arm. She gathered a deep breath and fought against the swimming in her head. This was no time to faint. But suddenly her bravado fled.

Cat shook her arm. "Can you do this? Or should I stay here while you go for the supplies and Captain Riley?"

"I–I'll do it. Just show me—"

"For mercy's sake, Camilla." Cat snatched the shawl and knelt beside the wounded man.

The man's eyes shot open. He snatched at Cat's hands.

"Shh." Cat took his hands and laid them on his chest. "I must bind your wound, or you're going to lose too much blood before I can return with help. Do you understand?"

"My eyes thought dey be starin' straight at a angel of de Lawd."

Cat smiled. "Your eyes are going to feel mighty foolish when you get well. I'm no angel."

" 'Bout as close as dey come."

Over Cat's shoulder, Camilla observed the wounded man slide his massive hand over Cat's. A bold move for a slave to do to a white woman. Or one who looked white anyway. Somehow he held Cat's gaze, and the young woman ceased her ministrations.

"For heaven's sake, Cat. Are you going to finish binding the wound, or sit and stare at him all day? You're the one who said we had to hurry or he's as good as dead. I'm feeling better. I'll finish up here. You go."

The sharp words had their intended effect, snapping Cat from her trance. She stood. With a lingering look at the stranger, she took off through the woods.

The man's eyelids shuttered down, and Camilla knew he teetered between consciousness and unconsciousness. She knelt and resumed where Cat had left off.

Blood immediately began to seep through the white shawl. Frantically Camilla yanked tighter, eliciting a groan from the patient.

"I'm sorry," she whispered.

"God bless ya, miss." His eyes rolled back in his head, and consciousness lost the battle.

By the time Cat appeared with blankets, Camilla had bound the wound. Cat looked it over and patted Camilla's shoulder. "You did a good job. More than likely saved his life. Your ma would be proud of you. Here, take some snow and wash your hands."

Camilla looked down at the blood on her hands and burst into tears.

1 9 4 8

A surge of pride shot through Andy. For the past week and a half, he'd come to know the young Miss Penbrook only through Madeline Penbrook's disappointment and Cat's animosity. He felt a bit more sympathetic toward the old lady now that he saw she wasn't completely useless, selfish, and downright mean. Perhaps there was something of interest in her early years after all. The fact that she'd saved a black man's life increased his opinion of her tremendously.

He set the diary aside and carefully sat up, his legs hanging over the side of the bed. Other than bruises and a few painful spots in his ribs, he was feeling almost well. No one needed to read to him anymore. At first he was relieved by that fact. But after three days of seeing Lottie or Ella only when they brought his food trays, he had to admit he missed the long hours of company with various members of the family. Even ten-year-old Titus had been allowed to take a turn reading, though the others were too young to read parts of the disturbing history in such detail.

The delicious aromas wafting through the floor vents tempted his stomach and caused his mouth to water. He stood, snatched a white shirt from the chair next to his bed, and made himself presentable enough to join the family for supper. He knew it was a bit early, but he relished the thought of joining Lottie for a chat while she finished up dinner preparations.

Her smile brightened the day as he stepped into the kitchen. "Andy! What a nice surprise. I was just about to fix your tray."

"I thought I might join your family tonight if you don't mind."

"Mind? We'd be thrilled."

Andy found himself the center of attention once the meal began. How was he feeling? Did his eye feel as bad as it looked? Bet he wouldn't smart-mouth ol' Rafe again any time soon.

The last comment, spoken by Titus, received a stern rebuke from Buck. "What do you know about Rafe Cooper?"

Titus shrugged. "I hear stuff."

"Well, don't you go believing everything you hear." Lottie sent Andy a silent look of apology.

He smiled. He'd lived in a private world for so long, the thought of having anyone care about his life felt like being on foreign soil.

"Any word from Miss Penbrook this week?" Lottie asked.

Andy shook his head. "I suppose I should telephone Penbrook House and make sure they haven't forgotten about me."

"My aunt Delta ain't forgot," Buck said. "She asked about you yesterday during services."

Andy nodded. He'd forgotten that Buck was Miss Penbrook's maid's nephew. "Did she say if I should come back to the house?"

Buck speared a slice of ham from the platter in the middle of the table. "Nope. Just asked how you was gettin' along after Rafe's beatin'."

"Does the whole town know about that?"

"This end does." Buck shook his head. "It takes a lot to rile ol' Rafe. You must have really lit into Ruthie for him to tear up your face like that."

"It was the booze talking."

"The devil's drink." Miss Lottie scowled. "Maybe you'll think twice before you give in to that temptation again." She gave him a pointed look. "Or any others for that matter."

Silence thickened the air as the children, obviously recognizing their mother's stern tone, waited to see if Andy would respond. He glanced around from one wide-eyed brown face to the next. Finally he gave a broad wink that encompassed all six children.

"Miss Lottie, you make me want to be a better man. I will certainly think twice before succumbing to any devilish wiles from now on."

Buck snickered. Lottie raised her eyebrow and shoveled a spoonful of brown beans into little Lester's baby mouth. "Good. Children, stop gawking and eat your supper before it gets cold."

Andy's heart lifted. A week ago, he might have suggested she mind her own business. But he was growing fond of Lottie, Buck, and their large, rowdy, fun-loving family.

Even Ella's playful seduction had become part of his everyday life.

Lexie's face came to mind less and less, and when it did, anger always followed, so he tried to push her memory away. If she hadn't already given in to Robert, he imagined it wouldn't be long. Robert wasn't the sort of man to wait forever. Neither was he the sort to give up easily. He'd be laying it on thick. Flowers, compliments, love letters. It wouldn't take much for Lexie to be seduced.

Andy shifted uncomfortably at the thought. Was he ready to give up the only woman he'd ever loved? Was he willing to toss her to another man? If Lexie surrendered to Robert, it would be Andy's fault. Only he could stop it from happening.

Chicago

"A boy delivered these." Lexie's mother slung a bouquet of daisies on the table as though it were a sack of baking flour. "When's that fool man gonna get it through his head that you is a married woman?"

"I don't know, Mama." Lexie tried not to show her excitement as she nonchalantly slid her hand to the attached card.

Meet me at Sheila's. 9 p.m. Don't stand me up, girl.

"Well? What's it say this time?"

"Oh, the usual." Lexie waved her hand as the lie rolled from her tongue. "He wants me to know he's here for me if I ever want to talk."

A snort left Mama. Lexie looked up slowly, dreading eye contact. Mama's eyes were narrowed, and her lower lip pushed out with disapproval. "Talkin' is the last thing on that man's mind, and you been a married woman long enough to know I'm tellin' the truth."

Lexie's cheeks warmed beneath the scrutiny and frank words. "Maybe so, but that doesn't mean he's getting more than talk from me."

"Be not ignorant of Satan's devices, baby. He knows your weaknesses."

"Weaknesses? Oh, Mama. What are you talking about?"

"You sittin' home night after night, missin' your man. Angry 'cause he ain't telephoned you again. Don't cast your pearls before swine, girl. You hold out. Wait for your husband to come home, then be the godly wife he needs."

"The wife he needs? What about the kind of husband I need? Andy's been running around on me since I had my first miscarriage. I guess I'm just damaged goods to him. I can't give him a child, so he'll go make bastard children with whoever will crawl into bed with him."

A loud crack split the air as pain exploded onto Lexie's cheeks. Her eyes widened as she stared at her mother.

"Girl, I hated to smack you, but I won't have that kind of language used in my house. I don't care how old you is. You is goin' to respect the rules."

Tears burned Lexie's eyes. Tears of anger, hurt, humiliation, remorse. Oh, how she had ruined her life by marrying Andy Carmichael. What was she now? A woman past her prime childbearing years, separated from her husband, and living with her parents. Why shouldn't she enjoy a night of music and dancing with a man who actually thought she was worth investing some time in?

Her cheek still smarted as she rose, took her daisies, and walked out of the kitchen without a word.

PENBROOK HOUSE

The old woman curled into a ball on her bed, clutching her chest. The pain was unbearable.

"Not yet, Lord," she gasped. "Not until he knows. Not until I can make it right. Please. Just a few more days."

~ *Part Two: Bitterness* ~

The heart knoweth his own bitterness.

PROVERBS 14:10

Chapter Eight

Andy leaned against the porch railing, hands stuffed in his trouser pockets. He watched the neighborhood children playing baseball in the street. Buck rocked back and forth in the wooden rocker. "Yessiree, ain't nothin' like havin' a quiver full of little arrows."

"Excuse me?" Andy turned.

" 'Children are an heritage of the Lord. Happy is the man that hath his quiver full of them.' That's from the Bible."

"Oh." Religion. He'd had enough of it growing up. Had no need for it now.

"No children of your own, huh?"

Andy shook his head.

"Well, don't lose heart. Sometimes it just takes awhile."

Andy turned back to watching the children in the street. "My wife left me. We didn't have children."

"Your wife left you? What are you doin' about gettin' her back?"

Andy shrugged. "Not a thing. She's through with me. Can't say that I blame her all that much."

"A woman just wants to be treated with a gentle hand. Wants to know she's the most important thing in the whole world to ya. I bet it wouldn't take much soft talk from you to get her back."

A short laugh spurted from Andy's throat. "At the moment, another man is giving her enough soft talk for the both of us."

"Another man, eh?" Buck fell silent for a few minutes. Then he stopped rocking and sat forward in the chair. "What brings you to Georgia, Andy?"

Expelling his breath, Andy faced his newfound friend. "You already know. The chance to write old Miss Penbrook's memoirs."

"Ain't got much writin' done yet, though, have ya? What with the beatin' and all."

Andy's neck warmed. "Are you ready for me to leave?"

Buck chuckled. "Nope. You're more than welcome here for as long as you pay your rent. But if you don't mind my sayin' so, it sounds like you have things to take care of at home."

Ah, so the man hadn't dropped the subject after all. "If Lexie's still my wife when I get home, I'll try to do right by her. If not, there's nothing I can do about it."

Buck resumed his rocking but didn't speak. The silence made Andy as uncomfortable as if Buck had come up with another sermon.

They remained silent until the door opened and Lottie appeared on the steps. "Delta just called."

Andy perked up. "Did she leave a message for me?"

Lottie nodded. "Miss Penbrook would like to see you in the morning."

Excitement, combined with a sense of dread, knotted into a ball in Andy's stomach. He wasn't sure why he felt such anxiety. But he did.

The diaries, the women, the history. They tore at him. He felt he knew these people. Wanted to know them better.

After a few more minutes of polite conversation, he retreated to his bedroom.

He slept fitfully and rose before dawn. The town of Oak Junction didn't stir as he quietly left the Purdues' rooming house and began the five-mile trek. He was sitting on the steps of Penbrook House as the sun made a grand entrance on the eastern horizon.

"Nothin' as pretty as a Georgia sunrise," his mama used to say. "Unless it's a Georgia sunset."

He leaned back against a thick white pillar and stretched out his legs as he watched the orange and pink fingerprints slide across the sky.

He could hear his mama's voice, but no matter how hard he tried, he wasn't able to connect a face to the soft tones. He leaned his head back against the pillar and closed his eyes. Sketchy memories invaded his mind.

"What are we going to do about him?"
Desperate whispers in the night.
"Elijah's gonna kill 'im if I don' get my boy outta here. I knows dat's what he's plannin'."
"Calm yourself, Rae. We won't allow Elijah to harm the child. You'll both stay here until I work out a solution."
"He'll find me."
"He won't try anything here. You know he hasn't the gumption."
Mama's wet tears on his neck. Shadows and whispers.

That was the extent of his memories. Nothing he could

put his finger on to make any sense of.

Andy opened his eyes and looked out across the green field beyond the house. The dew lifted as he stared. His heart raced for no reason.

Finally, when he thought the hour acceptable, he rang the bell.

"Took you long enough." Delta's amused scolding greeted him when she opened the door.

"You mean to tell me you knew I was out there?"

"Naturally. Nothin' happens around here that I don't know about." She looked him over. "I'm guessing you ain't had a bite of breakfast. Follow me."

"What about Miss Penbrook?"

"She ain't had no breakfast neither. Her mind works better when her stomach's full."

Then by all means feed her. Please.

He followed Delta to the back of the house and into a large kitchen.

"How are you getting along at Buck's?" Delta asked, waving him into a seat at the long wooden table.

"Fine. They're exceptional people."

"What's exceptional mean?"

Andy heaved a sigh. "It means extraspecial."

Delta beamed. "They sure are that. Every single one of 'em." She eyed him. " 'Specially that Lottie. Now, she's one exceptional gal. Don't you think?"

"Mrs. Purdue is a woman any man would be lucky to have as a wife. Buck's got himself a priceless gem."

"Yep." She placed slices of bacon into a skillet and lifted the coffeepot from the stove. "Want some? Miz Penbrook only drinks tea. But I can't abide it. I prefer me some strong coffee."

"Yes, ma'am. Me, too. Thanks."

She set a couple of cups on the table and poured the steaming black brew. After returning the pot to the stove, she sank into the chair across from him.

"How long have you worked for Miss Penbrook?"

Her face clouded as she tried to recall. "Let's see. Your mama hadn't yet married that no-good Elijah. . . ."

Andy stared. "What do you mean? You knew my parents?"

Her eyes grew round and she stood quickly. "I best check on that bacon. If it's too crisp, Miz Penbrook tosses it on the floor. And the good Lord knows my back aches when I got to bend over too much."

"It's too late to pretend you didn't just say something about my mother, Delta. Turn around here and finish your thought."

"It ain't none of my business, boy. And don't think you can bully me into telling things I ain't got no business tellin'."

Andy took a deep breath. "I've been having memories, Delta. . .flashes in my mind about my past. My mama's voice, all afraid and whispering. Somehow I know I'm linked to Miss Penbrook. Maybe I can figure out why I keep having these memories if you at least tell me what you know."

"You ain't here to figure out nothin' about you. You's here to write down Miz Penbrook's life so she can be re-membered rightly."

"True." Still, he couldn't resist the memories trying to surface in his mind. Whether he wanted them to surface or not, his mind seemed to be ready to share hidden parts of his life.

If only Delta were as ready to share what she knew. But she became a rock wall. Impenetrable. After a couple of attempts at conversation, Andy gave up. He sipped his coffee, his mind mulling over Delta's slipup. He would definitely get more information out of her another time. When she wasn't on the defensive.

Delta set his breakfast before him, then made up a tray. "I'll be back when Miz Penbrook is ready to see you. Help yourself to more of that coffee if you run out."

"Thank you, ma'am."

Andy finished his breakfast and washed his dishes. He went to the kitchen door and stepped outside. From the back porch, he could observe the smokehouse, stables, and a path that he instinctively knew led to slave quarters. The woods beyond called to him.

Remember.

Somehow he knew that the Penbrook property stretched across vast acres and acres.

The door groaned open behind him. "Miz Penbrook is asking for you now."

Andy nodded and returned to the house. He followed Delta through the kitchen and toward the long staircase. "Are the Penbrook lands sharecropped?"

"Some of 'em. Miz Penbrook sold some of the land to faithful tenants."

"Were my parents sharecroppers?" He knew his heritage was tied to this place. His vague memories were growing more prominent as he allowed them admittance. "I have brothers and sisters. Are they still living? Do you know where they are?"

Rather than giving him the angry reply he expected, Delta stopped short, causing him to halt his steps. She placed her hand on his face, much as a mother might.

"I know you be wantin' answers. You're gonna get them. Slowly. But you best get on in to see Miz Penbrook while her mind's all there. Don't forget to talk loud so she can hear ya."

Delta pushed open the door at the end of the hallway. "He's here, ma'am."

Andy stepped into the dark room and across the floor until he stood over the old woman. "Good morning, Miss Penbrook. I hope you're doing well today."

"As well as can be expected at my age." She gave a tired wave. "Sit down. Are you finding the diaries helpful?"

Andy took the chair she indicated. "I am enjoying them very much. I'm only just to the entries you made, though."

"Oh?"

"Yes, ma'am. Until yesterday, everything I'd read was written by Madeline Penbrook and Cat, the slave girl."

"And what do you think of Cat?"

Andy shrugged. "I admire her spirit. She was a survivor."

Miss Penbrook emitted a broken sigh. "Yes. And much of what she did went beyond morality and good judgment."

Andy chuckled. "Even now, you can't see your way clear to be kind to Cat?"

"You feel sorry for her?"

"Any decent person would. She had it rough."

"How far into the diaries have you gotten?"

Andy told her about the hog in the woods and the runaway slave.

"Shaw was a godsend."

"Shaw?"

"The slave who was almost killed by the hog. He never left us. Just like he promised. At least not until thirty-eight years ago." Her voice seemed to come from far away. "He died."

"Did he sharecrop?"

"Sharecrop? For a time, I suppose."

"When did you start to sharecrop the land, Miss Penbrook?"

"I suppose that's a good story to tell."

Andy settled into his chair as Miss Penbrook retreated eighty years, to a time when she was a young, beautiful, strong woman.

1 8 6 6

Sunlight streamed through the long windows, illuminating Camilla's fair skin as she stood, arms folded stubbornly across her chest, looking out at the weeping willow in the yard.

"Camilla," Cat bellowed at the young woman, "use the brain God gave you!" She was beyond her wit's end with the stubborn ignoramus.

Camilla whipped around, anger flashing in her wide blue eyes. "How dare you speak to me that way?"

"How dare I? I dare, my dear, because you are hoarding the money your grandmother sent you for nothing! It must be invested back into the land, or it will soon run out again, and then where will you be?"

"Grandmother Wilson said she sent only a portion of my inheritance early, so there is plenty more where that came from."

Cat gathered a breath and looked to Shaw for help.

He clutched his hat tightly between massive, scarred hands. "Miss Camilla."

Camilla turned to him and her face softened. It was beyond Cat what sort of relationship these two had. And frankly, she couldn't care less. But it did come in handy on occasions such as this one, where she needed someone who could talk sense into Camilla's thick head.

"Do you agree with Cat?" Her blue eyes pleaded for him to be on her side. "Should we use all my money to plant cotton?"

"Well, miss," he said, carefully choosing his words, "the facts be dat dis here money ya gots. . .well, if ya was to spend it on purty clothes and furniture and sech, ya'd just be sprucin' things up around here and makin' yo'self look even purtier than ya already are."

Camilla preened like a peacock at his praise of her looks.

"But, if ya use jes' a little bit and buy material to make a nice dress for yo'self and one for Miss Cat, then ya might have enough left to buy the plow and a couple o' mules, like Miss Cat suggests."

"And seed." Unable to keep quiet any longer, Cat reentered the negotiations. "Listen, Camilla, we have to get the land going again. That's the most important thing. Shaw has been talking to some of the other free darkies. Lots of them are talking about going back to the plantations where they were slaves."

"If they had any gratitude, they would never have left to begin with. I think they should go back and beg forgiveness." She looked at Shaw. "Not you, of course. You belong with us."

His face softened to what Cat could only describe as pure affection. She pushed the odd relationship away once more. "The point is, Camilla, that if we can get extra plows and mules, we can sharecrop the land."

"Sharecrop? Whatever is that?"

Camilla's frown irritated Cat. Was the girl completely ignorant? Or only playing dumb?

"We give the slaves a certain amount of land to work. In exchange, they owe us a percentage of the profits from their crops."

Camilla gasped. She glared at Cat, her eyes blazing. "I might have expected you'd want to give all my land to your darkie friends. No. I will not do it."

Cat had to fight to keep from slapping the foolish girl across the cheek. "Shaw, try to explain it to her, will you? Though I sincerely doubt she has enough brains to understand." She turned on the worn heels of her boots, leaving Camilla sputtering in anger.

The low tones of Shaw's deep voice followed her from the room.

The war had been over barely a year. Soon after Lee's surrender at Appomattox, Captain Riley and his company had been called to Atlanta to help keep the peace there. He came to see her often. Cat had grown fond of him. He didn't concern himself with her heritage. He told her she looked every bit as white as his own mother, who was of French descent.

She learned to enjoy his kisses and caresses. Thankfully he hadn't pursued a more intimate relationship, though Cat suspected he frequented the fancy women in town.

Rather than anger her, the thought relieved her. As long as he was satisfied elsewhere, he would leave her be. Once she'd thought he might propose marriage, and she would have accepted in order to have help caring for Penbrook. But one day it had dawned on Cat that Camilla's Missouri grandmother was wealthy, and they had investments in the North. It had taken time for mail to start making it to Oak

Junction, but once the letters started flowing again, she'd coerced Camilla into writing; and her grandmother had straightaway sent a bank draft.

Now that ignorant girl wanted to buy gowns and furniture and carpets for the floors. At least she also wanted to buy a cow or two and some chickens and pigs.

The library door opened, and Camilla flounced into the foyer, followed by Shaw. She slapped a stack of money into Cat's hand. "There. Take it. Buy your plows and seeds and mules. But I'd also like you to buy enough material for three dresses for me and one for you. No, two. One nice one and one to work in, as I'm sure you won't allow anyone to oversee the fields but you."

Cat fought to squelch the excitement rising at the thought of fields white with cotton. Little Henry's fields. Penbrook would be more profitable than it had ever been. "Anything else?"

"Yes. Shaw needs a new shirt and some trousers. And little Henry has all but worn through what he hasn't outgrown. Mind you pick out material for those, as well. And everyone must have new shoes."

Cat began mentally calculating how much she thought those items might cost. "All right. Shaw and I will go to Atlanta in the morning. We'll need to go into Oak Junction first and buy another wagon and a couple of mules." She turned to Shaw. "We'll need some of your men to help load and unload supplies. Can you speak with them tonight? Bring at least three. Ask them to be ready first thing in the morning, all right?"

"Yes'm." He nodded to each woman, then strode across the foyer and out the heavy door.

"Cat, surely you don't intend to travel thirty miles with four darkies? How on earth will it look? I mean, we know what you are, but you do look white."

Bitter laughter bubbled to Cat's lips. "I don't care how it looks. All I know is that I need supplies. And I'm taking no chances that a shopkeeper might not give Shaw a fair deal."

"Shaw is smarter than most," Camilla defended her friend. "He won't let himself be hornswoggled."

"He won't intentionally, but he doesn't know how to figure his numbers, nor can he read. He can't negotiate until he learns those things."

"Then I shall teach him." The determination on Camilla's face left no room for doubt.

"I think that would be very nice of you."

Surprise shot to Camilla's eyes. "Well, then, perhaps you'd best buy a couple of books and a slate and pencil while you're in Atlanta."

Cat scowled. If she'd known it would cost more money, she'd have let Shaw stay illiterate. She sighed. "Fine. But that's all. The rest of the money goes straight for supplies."

"You're doing all this for little Henry, aren't you?" Camilla asked. "If not for him, you would have left long ago, despite the promise to Mother that we stick together. Wouldn't you?"

Cat regarded her evenly. "Yes. Your pa promised Henry would inherit this land."

"What about me?"

"You have your mother's inheritance. You don't need Penbrook. My son shall inherit the land. I know where the will is, and I know your pa made good on his word." That was the one decent thing he had done.

"Oh, who cares anyway? I don't intend to live here any longer than absolutely necessary."

"Missus, we gots company," Shaw's voice carried from the porch.

Cat frowned and looked at Camilla. "Who on earth?"

Camilla shrugged and headed toward the door, leaving Cat to follow.

"Oh my!" Cat heard Camilla shriek.

"What?" Camilla blocked her view. Impatiently Cat pushed around her. She gasped at the sight of the man standing next to Shaw. "Thomas," she whispered.

"This be Mister Thomas?" Shaw directed his question to Camilla. Irritation shot through Cat. What exactly had Shaw been told?

There wasn't time to wonder. Thomas's face lit up at the sight of Cat and Camilla. "You two are a refreshing sight."

Cat couldn't speak past the lump in her throat. Quick tears sprang to her eyes.

Camilla squealed as though she were still the adolescent girl she'd been the last time Thomas had stood on this porch. She flew into his arms. Thomas's laughter rang into the air as he swung her around. He set her down, cupped her face in his hands, and kissed her soundly on the lips. "You're still as beautiful as I remembered."

Jealousy burned in Cat's stomach. Pain clutched her chest, squeezing breath from her lungs. Her head began to swim, and before she knew it, darkness engulfed her.

FROM CAMILLA'S DIARY
Thomas is home. Thomas is home. Thomas is home.
And I think he loves me. He certainly seemed happy

to see me. He brings with him the news of my father's death. I feel little grief. Cat is, of course, jubilant.

I've watched Cat and Thomas carefully. There seems to be nothing left of the childhood love they shared. She is content with Stuart Riley, I believe.

Thomas returned home to Atlanta to find his home burned to the ground. He discovered from a friend that his mother has traveled to Texas to join his sister's family. With his father dead by the second year of the war, Thomas is alone. We have invited him to live at Penbrook. He has gratefully accepted and vows to help in any way he can. I suspect it will only be a matter of time before he proposes marriage.

CHAPTER NINE
~ CHICAGO

Lexie stared at Dr. Harmon as a slow smile played beneath his mustache. "First time I ever saw you shocked to silence," he said with a chuckle.

"I. . . Are you sure, Doctor?" Another disappointment would be more than she could bear. She had to be absolutely positive before she could stand to get her hopes up.

"Little girl, I've been delivering babies for nearly thirty years. I think I know by now when there's a bun in the oven."

Lexie's cheeks warmed.

A bubble of excitement shot through her, and she hopped up from the chair, throwing herself into the old doctor's arms. "A baby!"

She practically floated along the busy sidewalks toward home, her secret securely tucked away, safe, protected from harm. A smile refused to be stifled, her joy spilling over to everyone who passed by. A baby! Her baby! After all these years.

Why now?

No, she wouldn't even think about the whys of it. Rather, she would revel in unspeakable joy and imagine the warmth of holding her baby in her arms.

Her monthly cycles had been sporadic at best her entire

adult life, so cessation had come as no real surprise. When she'd stopped bleeding a few months back, she'd assumed her days for bearing children had ended. She'd almost been relieved. No more hoping, month after month. No more crying every time her hopes were dashed.

The thought that she might be pregnant this time hadn't even entered her mind. Conception must have occurred right before Andy's last fling. Right before she moved out of their apartment and into Mama's house.

Andy.

She would stop seeing Robert immediately, of course. Thank God she hadn't given in to his tempting offer to share his bed. Andy would have no cause to wonder whether this was his baby or not. Given that she was at least four months along, he should know better anyway. But thankfully she could honestly tell him she'd remained faithful.

They were going to have plenty of hurdles to jump if their marriage was to survive. Andy's infidelities alone were going to be difficult enough. Her heart clenched at the thought. Funny how only yesterday she'd been sure her love for Andy was a thing of the past. Now, as she looked down at the small bulge in her stomach—a bulge she'd thought was a result of Mama's home cooking—love stronger than reason swelled her heart. Love for her child and for her child's father.

Oh, Andy. I'm finally giving you a baby.

GEORGIA, 1948

The old lady was more coherent this time. She rattled on for two hours. Thomas this, Henry Jr. that. Shaw, Camilla, Cat. The sharecroppers. She never spoke in first person. Every time she told a story, it was as though she hadn't been part of the fascinating stories, but only a spectator. He wasn't sure how much she was remembering and how much she'd simply learned or remembered from reading the diaries herself.

The biggest question plaguing his mind since reading the last diary still hadn't been answered, though. He waited for her to pause, then he broached the topic. "I have a question, Miss Penbrook."

She glared at him, her toothless bottom gums pressing out beyond her top lip. "I don't like being interrupted, boy."

Annoyance shot through him. "Then we're even," he said without taking even a second to consider his words. "I don't like being called boy."

Her eyebrows shot up. She chuckled. "I suppose I don't blame you. What's your question?"

"You haven't mentioned Thomas in a while. You've talked about buying supplies, gathering sharecroppers from among Shaw's friends. Talked about plowing and planting and the first profitable harvest. But nothing about Thomas from a personal level. As a writer, I'm aware that you might have kept Penbrook as a pen name. So, which of you did he choose? You or Cat?"

Miss Penbrook heaved a sigh. "I thought you might ask that. It wasn't so much as who he chose as who we decided should have him."

"I'm not sure I understand."

She leveled her gaze at him. "You will."

FROM CAMILLA'S DIARY
1867

Camilla stood on the wide porch and listened for the sound of the wagons returning from the fields. Long, lonely days with only Henry Jr. as company left her desperate for conversation. Why Cat felt the need to work in the fields alongside the Negroes and the men was beyond Camilla's understanding.

Thomas, too, spent his days in the fields. At first Camilla fought against this. But Thomas had been adamant. "I have to do my fair share of the work."

Finally she'd stopped protesting and life became routine. Planting, waiting, harvesting. Back to planting. The waiting was finally over, and now they were harvesting for the second year. The first year had yielded a minor profit for the plantation, and Cat had allowed Camilla to begin fixing up the house after the years they had been forced to neglect its upkeep.

Allowed.

Somehow Cat had become the unofficial head of the house. Everyone looked to her for guidance, even Thomas. The one time Camilla complained to Thomas about a Negress giving orders, he'd turned on her, fury in his eyes. "Cat is no more a Negress than you are, Camilla Penbrook. She's the reason you and I have food on the table, so mind how you speak about her!"

Stunned to silence and hurt beyond words, Camilla had refrained from mentioning that it was, after all, her money that had funded Cat's venture; and without Shaw and the other free darkies, Cat wouldn't have known how to plant or care for the cotton, let alone how to bring in the harvest.

Was Camilla the only one who saw the truth?

Despite the fact that Cat was a woman, and therefore had no business managing a plantation, she was also nothing more than a former slave in the Penbrook household. It wasn't fitting or proper for her to be in charge. But Thomas's defense of Cat made it impossible for Camilla to restore the correct order of things.

If Thomas had no objection to taking orders from a woman, then by all rights, Camilla should be in charge. She'd be happy to turn over control to Thomas if he'd propose marriage. He could take his place as the master of Penbrook. But he didn't seem to be in a hurry to ask for her hand.

In fact, he barely even noticed her. Was there something between Cat and Thomas that had escaped her notice?

Surely not. After all, Cat still made time to see Captain Riley when he came to visit. The tension between the two men was thick as dumplings. But Camilla wanted him to keep coming. As long as he distracted Cat, she wasn't focusing her attention on Thomas.

When she heard the sound of a horse's hooves in the distance, Camilla hurried inside to set the table for supper. She pumped water into the coffeepot, carefully measured grounds into it, and set it on the stove to boil. Thomas enjoyed a cup each day when he came in from the fields.

She returned to the porch just as the rider dismounted. Disappointment gnawed her stomach. Stuart Riley. Not Thomas.

He removed his hat. "Good evening, Miss Camilla."

"Good evening. What brings you out so late in the day?"

"I've just received news, and I need to speak with Cat. Is she here?"

Camilla shook her head. "I'm afraid not. She hasn't returned from the fields. Would you care to come in and wait? I've just put on a pot of coffee, and supper will be ready soon. You're more than welcome to join us."

He shook his head, already putting his boot in the stirrup to remount his horse. "I'm afraid there isn't time. I'll just ride out and find her."

Camilla watched him ride across the fields into the red horizon, where the sun displayed its glorious departure from this day. Her curiosity mingled with a sense of excitement. Had Riley finally decided the time had come to ask for Cat's hand? A smile tipped the corners of her lips. What would tomorrow bring?

From Cat's diary
1867

Cat gripped the reins tighter as the sound of a horse's hooves gave the mules an excuse to nervously pull in different directions. She looked up, trying to figure out who was coming down the dusty road.

"Riley." The disgust in Thomas's voice at Stuart's presence always gave Cat a bit of a thrill. Thomas maintained his distance from her. But that didn't keep her from catching him, in unguarded moments, staring at her with longing in his eyes. He'd been home for nearly a year and a half but had never sought to be alone with her. At first the disappointment had been nearly more than she could bear. But as time went on, she grew accustomed to the pleasure of simple things. Seeing him playing with his son, working in the fields alongside Shaw and the others, and listening lazily while Camilla read poetry or the occasional novel aloud in the sitting room during the evening. The routine had become pleasant and familiar.

Though she'd been tempted to reveal Henry Jr.'s true

paternity, she'd decided against it. Thomas had nothing to give her son. As Henry Penbrook Jr., he would inherit everything she was working so hard to build for him.

A sense of dread formed a ball in her stomach as Stuart's eyes met hers in grim greeting.

"What's wrong?"

"I need to speak with you alone."

Thomas reined in his horse alongside the wagon and glared at Stuart. "Cat needs to go home and eat something. She didn't even stop for lunch today."

"This is important."

The urgency in his voice sent alarm through her. "It's all right." She looked from Shaw to Thomas. "You go on back to the house. I'll be along soon."

Thomas glowered, his jealousy apparent. Cat couldn't understand why he didn't speak for himself if he still cared for her.

Riley dismounted and held out his hand to help her down. "Let's walk by the river."

Cat nodded, slipping her hand into his. He curled his fingers around hers and silently walked the few yards to the water's edge. "What's this all about, Stuart?"

He looked across the water, where the setting sun shimmered off the ripples brought on by a south wind. He took a sharp breath and tightened his fingers. "I'm going home."

Cat knew the home he was talking about was not Atlanta, where he'd been stationed since the end of the war. After three years away, he was going back to Chicago. Her mind flashed with the image of life without the occasional diversion of Stuart to brighten her days.

She sighed. "When?"

"My train leaves in the morning."

Alarm seized her. "So soon?"

"I just received word that my father died two weeks ago. I must return home immediately. My mother needs me to keep the newspapers rolling."

Disappointment swept through Cat. "I'll miss you." Her stomach jumped as she realized her words were true. She would miss Stuart. When had he become more than a diversion? Although she knew she didn't love him the way she loved Thomas, her feelings had grown beyond mere fondness.

He cleared his throat. "I need to tell you something. I tried once before, but. . ." He scowled and shrugged. "I chose the coward's way out."

"What is it?"

He swallowed hard and turned to face her, taking her other hand. "Cat, I–I'm married."

He said it so quickly that for an instant Cat wasn't sure she'd heard him correctly. Then understanding shot through her, igniting her ire. She jerked her hands free and stomped away toward the bank of the river.

Stuart remained rooted to his spot. "I'm sorry. I wanted to tell you so many times. But I couldn't take the chance you'd refuse to see me."

"Which I most certainly would have done," Cat retorted over her shoulder. This betrayal brought a tremble to her lips.

"I know." A twig snapped as Stuart closed the distance between them. He stood behind her, circling her waist with his arms.

Cat wanted to fight him, wanted to hit him, wanted to make him hurt like she was hurting. Lash out at him for

making a fool of her. Instead, the fight sifted from her, and
she leaned back against him. "Why tell me now, when it's
too late for us anyway?"

He turned her to face him, then tipped her chin to look
into her eyes. "Do you care about me, Cat? Even a little?"

"How can you even ask? Of course I do."

"You never said."

"I've kissed you, haven't I? Many times."

His gaze moved to her mouth and back to her eyes. "Yes.
You have. But a man like me needs to hear the words." He
pulled her against him. "How many times have I said 'I love
you' over the last three years?"

Too many to count.

"Do you love me?"

"Don't ask me to say the words, Stuart. It isn't fair. Not
with you leaving. Not when you're going home to your
wife."

He scowled. "Fine. Don't say the words then. It will
make what I'm about to say easier for me."

"Go on," she encouraged.

"If I could, I would ask you to marry me and take you
away from all this backbreaking work and sweat and dirt."

Cat frowned. She loved working the land. The dirt didn't
bother her. She was working for Henry Jr.'s future. But Stuart
didn't know that. He didn't know that the little boy he often
carried on his shoulder or held in his lap while sitting on the
porch in the lazy twilight was flesh of her flesh.

"I understand, Stuart."

"My wife is not an affectionate woman. She is barren,
and I believe that has made her indifferent toward me. I am
not proud of the fact that I have not been faithful to her."

"I'm sure you tried to be."

His mustache twitched. "Thank you for your confidence in me. Unfortunately I haven't tried very hard."

Cat saw no humor in his flippant reply. Riley was the one thing she'd come to count on. She'd expected him to ask her to marry him someday. That's why she'd allowed his continued presence in her life. If he loved her enough to marry her, she could finally have a life of her own. Security. Respectability. But that dream was now impossible.

"Cat, I—I want to ask you something. I—I want you to come to Chicago with me."

Cat's jaw went slack. "What do you mean? You just said you're married."

His gaze never faltered. "I know. I can't make you my wife. But I'm offering you a life away from this drudgery. I'll buy you a home of your own and take care of you as though you were my wife. Any children born of the union would be given my name."

Any children born of the union? "What about your wife?" Cat released a short laugh. "Do you honestly believe she's going to stand for her husband keeping another woman right under her nose?"

"Chicago is a big city."

"No city is so big that a wife will put up with people laughing behind her back. Or worse yet, pitying her."

"Believe me," Stuart drawled, "she won't be pitied. Sarah is quite wealthy and has many admirers of her own." His arms tightened, and he pulled her closer. "I don't care about your bloodline, or if you were another man's slave. All I know is that I love you and this is the only way I can have you in my life."

Cat observed him with frank appraisal. "If you didn't know what I was to Camilla's father, would you still ask this of me?"

His averted gaze told her all she needed to know. Anger snapped through her. How would this relationship be any different from the one she had endured at the hands of Henry Sr.?

She pushed at his arms and backed away. "You may say I am no different to you than a white woman, but your actions say differently. You would never insult someone like Camilla by asking her to be your mistress, yet you don't hesitate to do so with me. I'd be nothing more to you than I was to Henry."

Anger flashed in Stuart's eyes, and Cat's stomach tightened, ancient fears igniting within her. She wanted to cower, to run, to fight. But she stood her ground and watched in wary readiness as he stepped toward her.

"Maybe, if you were a virgin, I wouldn't ask you to be my mistress," he conceded. "I don't know. But it doesn't lessen my love for you. I would marry you if I could."

"So you say."

A frustrated growl rumbled deep in his throat. He pulled her to him and covered her mouth with his in one swift movement. Cat didn't fight him.

"I know you love me," Stuart whispered, his voice filled with passion.

"Oh, Stuart." She laid her head against his chest, her heart swelling with affection for this man. Though she couldn't condone his deception or his infidelity, she had no doubt that he loved her. The thought of leaving her was obviously breaking his heart. It pained her, too, to think of what her life would be like without him. "I do care for you. But I can't leave Penbrook. It's my home."

Stuart gripped her arms and looked her in the eye. "A home where you are a virtual prisoner, a slave, nothing more than a possession. You don't owe Camilla anything. You've made a success of this plantation when practically every other planter around here was either burned out during the war or became so poor they can barely scratch out a living. Penbrook is thriving. Camilla will be the queen of the county if she keeps up the sharecropping. She and Thomas can marry and raise Hank as their own."

Cat bristled. "Thomas doesn't love Camilla." And there was no way she'd allow Camilla to raise her son.

"There are other reasons to marry a woman."

"Oh? And what were the reasons you married your wife, Stuart? Is she rich? Beautiful?" She didn't even try to hide her contempt. Let him rescind his offer. She didn't need to be another man's whore.

He offered her a sheepish grin. "I married Sarah at my father's suggestion. He was in the newspaper business, and Sarah's dad was in publishing. It seemed a good match. At the time." He slipped his arm around her waist and pulled her close again. Inches from her face, he looked deeply into her eyes. "Please say yes."

"I don't know, Stuart. I just can't leave on a whim." How could she tell him what was really keeping her at Penbrook? That little Henry was her child. That she could never take him away from his inheritance.

For the first time, a hint of doubt niggled at her. What if Thomas and Camilla were to marry? Staying at Penbrook would be intolerable. Perhaps she could take Henry with her after all. Penbrook would still be his. He could come back when he was grown.

Stuart's voice broke through her thoughts. "Look, I'm not asking you to come with me tomorrow. It'll take a few weeks for me to settle in, take care of business, and find you a place to live. But if you say yes, I will send for you when the time is right."

Cat clenched her fists so tightly her broken nails dug into her palms. "I—I have to think about it."

And think about it she did. All the way back to the house. To leave the South and move north. . .to Chicago. To finally get away from the land of her oppression. And from Camilla.

Her growing enthusiasm at the possibilities was dulled by only one thought. If she left, Thomas would certainly marry Camilla. Then again, Cat could never have him anyway. He knew the truth about her and had already made his contempt clear.

When they neared the house, the sun had completely descended, leaving the earth covered in darkness. Stuart declined a dinner invitation. "I have to return tonight. My train leaves early in the morning." Without waiting for permission, he pulled her close and kissed her long and passionately.

Cat wrapped her arms around his neck, snuggled closer, and allowed his embrace.

"I'll send for you in a few weeks."

"I haven't agreed to go."

He gave her another long look. "You will. You hate the memories in that house. This may not be the kind of future you envisioned for us. But be honest for once. You've been waiting for me to take you away from this place, haven't you?"

Cat fought for the energy to order him away from Penbrook once and for all. "You seem very sure of yourself."

"I'm sure of you." With that, he mounted his horse and cantered off.

Cat watched him ride away, then turned to walk into the house. She stopped short at the sight of Shaw standing in the shadows of the porch.

"Mercy, Shaw. You nearly scared me to death." How much had he heard? "What do you mean lurking around, listening to people's private conversations?"

"What are peoples doin' havin' private talks wifout first makin' sure ain't nobody on de porch?"

Cat scowled. For all of his ignorant grammar and lack of education, Shaw had a pretty quick wit and a morality about him that always made her feel a little unclean.

"Well, you should have stepped out. That would have been the polite thing to do."

He shrugged. "Seems like I'd a been interruptin' somethin' special."

Cat plopped down on the bench Shaw had crafted soon after his recovery from the hog attack. They had spent many evenings together on that bench, enjoying the cool of the night.

"It wasn't really anything special, Shaw." She turned her gaze toward the man whose presence filled her with such confusion. Her defenses rose. "I guess you think I have no business kissing a man I don't love."

"Ain't none of my business, Miss Cat."

"Stop calling me that. You know I was just as much a slave as you were. Technically, we're no different."

He made no move to contradict her. Irritation bit her hard, and her defenses rose. Why didn't he state the obvious differences? She was almost white, while he was black as pitch. She was educated. To be sure, her station in life was higher than his. But only because she lived as a white woman. Shaw was one of the few people who knew her secret.

"You think we're no different?"

Her snappy tone must have taken him by surprise. "What you mean, miss?"

"I said we're no different, and you never said one word."

He expelled a heavy breath. "One thing I's learned, Miss Cat, is de Bible say dey ain't no difference 'twixt any of us."

"What do you mean? That God agrees with the slave-holders? That one drop of Negro blood makes us equal?"

By the light of the moon, Shaw leaned in close, the whites of his eyes startling against skin made even darker by the night. He took her hand and pressed it against his chest. Cat's pulse picked up at his closeness. She tried to pull away, but he held her palm there. "Feel dat?"

Confused, Cat couldn't look away from the dark brown eyes. Warmth flooded her stomach. "F—feel what?"

"My heart beating fastlike." His whisper sent a shiver up her spine. "I's a man. You is a woman. Dere ain't no denyin' it. It ain't about color, Miss Cat. Dere ain't no mans nor womans, no black nor white. In Jesus, we's de same. We's equal in God's eyes."

"Religion again, huh?" Swift disappointment shot through her. Why did he always have to speak of the good Lawd this and Jesus that?

"Not religion, Miss Cat." He turned her loose. "Jus' de truth."

"It's only truth in your mind. If you honestly believe there is no difference between black and white, men and women, then you're nothing but a fool."

"De world don' think de way de Lawd do." He smiled a bit sadly. "I'd rather be a fool for believin' what de Bible say dan agreein' wif folks who don' know no better."

Cat sniffed and jerked her head. She stared up at the moon. "Maybe you're the one who doesn't know any better."

He smiled and stood, holding out his hand to help her up. Surprise raised her brow. He'd never shown such familiarity. But as she took his rough, calloused hand, she suddenly didn't care. "Do you have a family, Shaw?"

"A fambly?"

Heat rushed to her face, and she was glad for the cover of darkness to hide her blush. "A wife, children?"

"Oh no. De only woman I ever loved was my ma, and dey sold me away when I was jus' a boy."

"How old are you?"

He shrugged. "Somewheres 'bout thirty, near as I can figger."

"And you've never been in love?"

"Not 'til now." He tightened his grip on her hand, and Cat felt the sheer force of his admission.

For a second, her breath refused to come. They had never spoken of their feelings. Shaw was her friend, the one who understood her. The one she could always count on. But she could never. . .

She looked into his dear face, and tears misted her eyes. "Oh, Shaw."

"Don' feel bad for ol' Shaw. I knows you be too good for de likes of me. I jus' couldn' be tellin' no lies."

"Too good for you, Shaw? I thought we were all equal." Cat nudged him with her elbow, trying to lighten the tension.

A deep chuckle rumbled as he stared up into the star-filled sky. "See, Lawd? She be listenin' after all." He turned to her and dropped her hand. "G'night, Miss Cat. Oh, and about dat cap'n. . ."

"Yes?"

"Love ain't selfish."

"What are you saying?"

Shaw shrugged. "If de cap'n truly loved ya, he wouldn't ask ya to accept a life o' sin. He be wantin' to use ya for his own pleasure. Is he thinkin' what's best fer you?" He shook his head.

Anger flashed through Cat. Mostly because she knew he was right. "Well, maybe I'm the one using him. Maybe I want to leave this godforsaken place. Maybe I just want to live like a queen. Stuart is rich, you know. I'd have my own house and basically be able to come and go as I please."

Shaw shook his head again.

"What?"

"You'd be more a slave dan ya ever been if ya do dis thing."

"That's my business." Without awaiting an answer, Cat slammed into the house and stomped upstairs to her room.

FROM CAMILLA'S DIARY

My fear has been realized. Captain Riley has been gone for several weeks, and Cat has turned her attention to Thomas. What is it about her that men seem to find so hard to resist? My pa, Thomas, Stuart Riley, even Shaw is in love with her, though he tries hard not to show it. Sometimes I think she cares for him, as well, but I suppose that is a silly thought. Though it would be a fitting union.

Each day I watch as Thomas falls more and more under her spell. I am powerless, as he has eyes only for Cat.

What shall I do if they marry? My life will be unbearable, living in this house, though I know they will not ask me to leave my home. Common decency prevents such a thing. But I know they will only suffer my presence. I must somehow prevent their union. I accomplished that very thing once. I can do it again. I must.

CHAPTER TEN

Andy hooked the collar of his jacket with his index finger and slung it over his shoulder as he walked the dusty road back to town. The midday sun beat down, scorching the red dirt beneath his feet. Sweat trickled along his spine and soaked his white shirt. His mind replayed Miss Penbrook's latest story. He would have to confer with the diaries as soon as he arrived back at Buck's place. The old lady had trailed off in her mind once again before revealing which of the girls ended up with Thomas.

Andy shook his head and smiled. Romance had never interested him before. But he had a real curiosity about Thomas and which woman he'd chosen. Why take so long to declare himself one way or the other? According to Miss Penbrook, he'd been home more than a year before Stuart Riley's little proposition to Cat.

Riley. . . Riley. . . The name bothered him. Was it too much to be a coincidence?

His mind drifted back twenty-six years.

"Hello, Andy."

Ten-year-old Andy stared way up. The man standing before him was so tall he could probably knock a bird right out of the sky with his head. With a smile, he bent so that he came eye to eye with Andy. His eyes creased with humor. Andy relaxed and took the massive proffered hand.

"My name's Daniel Riley. You're going to be living with my family. Do you know why?"

Andy shook his head.

Mama had never told him why. All he remembered were wild whispers from Mama. Her wet tears on his neck. Being shoved onto the train as it slowly inched forward. Mama walked, then ran alongside, her hand stretched toward him. "You be a good boy for them white folks. Don't ya make no trouble, ya hear?"

He'd promised, fear and confusion playing a discordant tune inside him.

The shrill of the train whistle had drowned out his pleas to stay with his mama.

Hours later, he stood on the wooden platform, being greeted by the tall, white Mr. Riley, who had kind eyes and a deep, rumbly voice.

"Where's your bag, son?"

"Ain't got no bag, suh."

"What about your clothes?"

Andy felt the embarrassment clear to his worn-out boots. "All I gots is on me."

"Well, no worry. We'll fix that lickety-split."

"You mean I's gettin' me some new britches?"

"Of course. I'll have my wife take you shopping tomorrow."

"Ain't never had me no new britches befo'."

Mr. Riley chuckled and rubbed Andy's head. "Well, I can see the first thing we're going to have to work on is your speech. I'm told you're about the brightest boy who ever lived. So I'm sure you'll catch on fast."

Andy felt a stab of pride at the praise. Someone thought he was a bright boy? "Yes, suh."

Maybe living in Chicago wouldn't be so bad after all. But geez, he was gonna miss his mama.

❧

A honk, a roaring motor, and the crash of pain on the side of his head all yanked Andy from long-buried memories. He hit the dirt amid shouts of laughter. His case flew from his grasp and popped open. On hands and knees, he scurried to retrieve the papers that were scattering in the breeze.

A truck skidded to a halt, and five white boys, three of whom he recognized, hopped out. A telltale beer bottle in the dirt near his face solved the mystery as to what had knocked him in the head.

"What are you doing back on our road, boy?" said fat, freckled, redheaded Gabe. Still up to no good.

"Nothin', suh," Andy said, rising to his feet. "I's jus' walkin'."

Gabe snatched Andy's jacket. "Why you all dressed up? You going prowling? Caught the scent of a fresh young nigga gal?"

"No, suh."

"Maybe you think you're too good for a colored? You after a white girl?"

Oh, God. Help.

"Oh no, suh."

"What's that you're carrying there?"

He clutched his case containing all of his notes from the diaries and his conversations with Miss Penbrook. "What, this?" He hoped his eyes conveyed ignorance. "This ain't nothin' but a bunch o' papers Ol' Miz Penbrook axed me to carry to town for her."

"Miss Penbrook?" A slightly built, handsome man came forward, his brown eyes snapping, not in anger but something else. Something akin to curiosity. He snatched the case from Andy's hand. "What's she doing sending papers to town with a colored?"

"I don' know, suh."

The man scrutinized him, and Andy knew he saw more than the rest. His gaze drifted over Andy's clothing. "You're not from around here."

"No, suh."

"From the North?"

Andy nodded.

The redhead laughed without humor. "Looks like we got us a real live, uppity, Yankee colored. What do you say we teach him his place?"

"Wait." The other man raised his hand. "What are you doing down here with Miss Penbrook? And stop the ignorant act."

Andy gathered a breath. "She has enlisted my services to help write her memoirs."

The man's eyes narrowed. "You're a writer?"

"Yes."

"See what I mean? Uppity."

The man glared at the redhead. "Shut up, Gabe." He

turned back to Andy. "Why would Miss Penbrook hire on a colored from the North to write her memoirs?"

Andy shrugged. "I've been trying to figure that one out myself."

"Aw, Sam, he's too ignorant to figure anything out. Let's just string him up."

"Shut up, Gabe!"

The redhead seemed stunned to silence.

The man stared Andy hard in the eye. "Where'd you say you were born?"

"I come from Chicago."

The man called Sam narrowed his gaze once more. "That's not what I asked."

"I was born around here. I don't remember much about living here, though. I moved north when I was ten."

Anger fired in Sam's eyes. His face reddened. "What's your whore mama's name?"

Andy squeezed his hands into fists to keep from lashing out. "My mother was no whore, mister."

Sam stepped forward, nose to nose with Andy. The stink of alcohol on his breath, combined with the stale stench of tobacco, churned Andy's gut. Sam bared stained teeth and practically growled. "Her name?"

"Rae Carmichael."

His eyes took on a wild fury, and he sprang before Andy could brace himself or step aside. They crashed heavily to the ground, rolling. The case flew from Sam's hands.

Andy knew better than to fight back. He covered his head and took the blows.

"Fight me, you worthless nigger!" Sam shoved Andy's face in the dirt.

Andy clamped his lips shut against the rocks and dirt and shook his head vehemently.

"Fight me!"

"No! I'm not giving you an excuse to hang me."

A stream of violent expletives shot from Sam's lips. "I don't need an excuse." Sam shoved up from the ground and turned to his friends. "Get a rope."

Disbelief shot through Andy as two of the thugs hauled him to his feet. How could this be happening?

C H I C A G O

"I'm going, Mama." Lexie snapped her suitcase shut and grabbed the handle, sliding the burden off the bed. "Nothing you say is going to change my mind."

"Honey, you ain't never been down south. You don't know what I knows. That husband o' yours'll be back soon enough. Ain't no need fo' you to put yourself in danger."

"It's important. Too important to leave anything to chance. Andy may not even be planning to come back to me. I have to get to him before he does something stupid."

"Nothin' more stupid than traipsin' off to somewhere you ain't got no business traipsin'."

Lexie stopped at the fear-filled brown eyes. She set her bag on the floor. "Mama, listen. Andy was furious about Robert being here the other night. He thinks I'm doing more than I was with Robert, and that alone might cause him to turn to someone else. Or. . .I don't know. I just have a bad feeling. He needs me."

Tears flooded the soft, dark eyes. "Call the roomin' house where he's stayin' and at least let him know to expect you. That way he'll be at the station waitin' when you gets there."

Lexie hesitated. As much as she preferred to surprise Andy, it might not be a bad idea to have him waiting when she arrived. "All right, Mama. Dry your eyes. I'll put in a call to Oak Junction and talk to Andy before I leave."

GEORGIA

Andy scrambled to keep his footing as the white boys led him like a dog on a leash to the back of the truck. Oh, God, they were going to drag him? Better to be hung. Every ounce of dignity within him fought against a swelling tide of tears. He fought against the urge to plead for his life. A futile plea, he knew.

The rope burned his wrists. Fear tore the breath from his lungs as he faced the inevitability of the next few minutes. The only possible outcome could be death.

Lexie's precious face flashed before him. If he had another chance, he'd tell her that she was the only woman he'd ever loved. The only woman he ever could love. He would beg her forgiveness and pledge his undying fidelity. But now she'd never know how much he cared.

The rope tightened as Sam looped it around the chrome bumper and began to tie it.

"Hey, Sam." Gabe's voice shook. "You ain't really doing this, right?"

Sam looked up and sneered. "You a nigger lover like your brother?"

"It's the middle of the day! My pa or one of his deputies could catch us."

A blond-haired young man wearing a red and blue shirt stepped up, his brow furrowed. "Come on, Sam. Havin' a little fun is one thing. But there's no need to take it too

181~

far. And it ain't about lovin' this colored." For emphasis, he doubled Andy with a fast gut punch. "You know Gabe's pa runs a clean county."

"Then maybe it's time for a new sheriff." Sam's lips curled again as he spoke the words like a challenge.

"You sayin' there's something wrong with my pa?"

"Yeah. He's too soft on coloreds. That's why your brother ain't been run outta town by now."

"Now look, Sam," the blond-headed man interjected. "Ain't no call to be insultin' Gabe just because his brother can't stay away from the colored gals. It's a sickness in some men."

"Yeah," Gabe said. "You think I like it that my own flesh and blood is taken in by some black witch's voodoo? Besides, Sam, you should know that, after your own—"

"You want me to put a bullet through your skull?" The fury in Sam's face seemed to take the others by surprise.

In the distance, Andy heard the sound of a motor. A cloud of dust swirled up from the road. A truck slammed to a halt, and the driver got out in what seemed like one motion. He whipped a shotgun from behind the seat and slammed the door shut. "Hey! What do you think you're doing?"

"Well, looky there," Sam sneered. "Just the fella we were discussing. Maybe we ought to drag him after the nigger and rid the town of two filthy vermin."

Andy blinked in surprise at the sight of the man he'd met in Georgie's club. How ironic that the person who had beaten him senseless was now coming to his defense.

"Watch it, Sam," Gabe said. "I know that's the liquor talking, but I'm gonna knock the tar out of you if you don't quit insultin' my family." He shot a glance at the road. "Get outta here and mind your own business, Rafe."

"Not until you turn him loose. I can't stand by and watch you murder a man in cold blood."

"We're just having a little fun, that's all. We're just scarin' him."

Rafe kept coming. "Let him go. Now."

"What are you gonna do, raise your shotgun against your own flesh and blood?"

"If I have to. I'd rather see you shot in the leg or the arm than be hung for killing this man without cause."

Sam stepped in front of Gabe. "Then shoot me."

"This ain't like you, Sam. What's botherin' you?" Rafe's enormous body towered over Sam's slight form. Andy knew he could take him easily. Instead, he placed his hand on the younger man's shoulder and looked down with compassion.

Sam shook off his hand. He turned a venomous gaze on Andy. "This ain't over." A quick glance to his cohorts conveyed a clear message, and they piled into the truck. He shifted his eyes back to Rafe. "You have until I get back behind the wheel to save him." He headed for the driver's door of the truck.

Andy's knees weakened.

Rafe pulled a knife from his pocket and sawed through the ropes binding his wrists. Just as the engine fired up, sending black fumes into the air, the rope released. Sam spun rocks and dirt as he gunned the motor and sped down the road.

"Thanks," Andy said, rubbing his raw skin. "The would-be assassin becomes the hero."

Rafe jammed a meaty finger into Andy's chest. "Listen to me. You'd best stay off this road from here on out."

Andy shook his head. "Can't. I have a story to finish

researching before I can go home." He gave a wry grin. "But I'll travel by night and follow the river so the patrollers and bloodhounds won't find me."

Rafe scowled. "Spare me the runaway slave references. Get in the truck. I'll drive you back to Buck's place."

Andy's brow rose. "You want me to ride in back?"

"Don't be stupid. You think I make my Ruthie ride in back? We're both targets as it is, so no one will be surprised to see us together."

"Suit yourself." Andy climbed into the truck, refusing to acknowledge that his gut was clenched with nervous tension.

When they arrived at Buck's rooming house, Rafe pulled along the edge of the street.

Andy reached for the door handle, then turned back. "Look. Under the circumstances—"

"You don't need to apologize for your opinion about me and Ruthie. We don't care what you think."

"I wasn't." Andy stared with frank perusal at the giant of a man. "Personally I think relationships between races are a mistake. There are too many repercussions. But that doesn't excuse the way I spoke to you or Ruthie."

Rafe nodded. "Well, we already settled that, didn't we? And don't expect me to apologize for thrashing you. You're just lucky they pulled me off of you when they did."

Andy's lips tilted. "Yeah, I suppose so. Anyway, I'm obliged for the intervention today and for the ride."

"You take care. And next time you need to go out to Miss Penbrook's, have Buck send word and I'll drive you out there. No sense tempting Gabe and his boys."

"Why do you care?"

"I care about my brother. I don't want to see him messed up in something he can't get out of. My family has enough trouble to deal with."

"If you're so worried about your family, why don't you give up Ruthie?"

Rafe gave him a sad smile. "Might as well ask me to rip out my heart. Believe me, I've tried. I can't. She can't. We need each other."

"Then why not leave town? Go north to Canada?"

He gave a shrug. "I don't know. We might if things get worse."

The house was quiet when Andy entered. He headed straight to his room and slipped off his shoes. Prayer seemed the only appropriate course of action as he stretched out on the bed and closed his eyes. "I don't know why You'd spare my life after I walked out on You so many years ago," he spoke into the darkness. "But thank You."

He touched the spot on his wrists where the rope had rubbed him raw. Tears formed quickly, and before he could wipe one away, another made a trek down his cheek. Today he'd almost been killed. For what? The look of utter hatred in Sam's eyes haunted him. Curling into a ball, he sobbed until no tears remained.

1924

Twelve-year-old Andy sat on the step and watched Jonas Riley playing baseball in the street with his friends. White friends. Usually Andy didn't care about being excluded. He'd rather be reading a book or writing a short story anyway. But today Aunt Lois had sent him outside with the other boys, insisting he was going to be sickly if he didn't get some fresh air once in a while.

"Andy, come be our fourth man," Jonas called. "We need another player."

"Hey, he ain't playing." Karl Starnes held the ball tightly in his hand and stood his ground.

Jonas stepped forward and faced him nose to nose. "Who says?"

"I do."

Standing to his full height, Jonas looked down on Karl. "Well, I say he's playing. And I'm a lot bigger than you."

Jonas was a true friend. Andy's best friend. Mrs. Riley always said they could have been brothers. Like two peas in a pod. Jonas and Andy laughed when she said that. Andy's happiest times were when he stayed inside the Riley home and read or played cowboys and Indians with Jonas.

The times he hated were when Jonas got into fights because of him. Like he was about to do now. Anger popped out Jonas's freckles, and Andy almost felt sorry for Karl. He was about to get a thrashing.

Karl obviously saw the same thing. With a scowl, he backed down. "All right. He can play. But I don't want him on my team."

"You couldn't have him if you did want him. He's too good for your team."

It was a lie that all too soon became obvious. But even losing the game for Jonas couldn't diminish Andy's sense of pride. Jonas was a good buddy. Easily the most popular boy in school and well liked. And he was Andy's champion.

Wrapped in a cocoon of love and acceptance, it was only in the dark of night that Andy longed for home.

Andy's eyes opened at the sound of a knock on his door. He called a welcome.

Ella stepped inside. "There's a phone call for you."

Frowning, Andy sat up. "Miss Penbrook?"

She shook her head. "It's a woman who says she's your wife. This is the third time today she's called."

Andy shot from his bed and sprinted past Ella. In the hallway downstairs, he snatched up the phone. "Lexie?"

"Hi, Andy." Something was different. That hard-edged tone he'd become accustomed to over the past year was noticeably absent.

His pulse picked up. "Is everything all right?"

"Yes. I—I just have to tell you something."

Dread formed a knot in his gut. "Go ahead."

"Not on the phone."

He gave a short laugh. "Then why did you call?"

"Don't be nasty." Hurt deepened her voice.

"I'm sorry, honey. But I don't understand why you called only to tell me you can't tell me something over the phone."

"Well, if you'll listen, I'll explain."

Andy released a sigh. "I'm sorry."

"I'm taking a bus down there tomorrow."

The thought of seeing Lexie sent a shock of joy spreading through his chest.

"I wanted to surprise you, but Mama is worried I might run into trouble."

Like a jolt, Andy recalled the haunting hatred in Sam's eyes. The rope. The blows. "Your mama's right. I don't think it's a good idea, Lexie."

"What do you mean? You don't want to see me?"

"It's not that." He didn't want to explain. Admit that he had become some sort of target. And that Lexie might become a target, too.

"Andy, I do have to speak with you. But I can't do it over the phone."

He could well imagine. Most likely she wanted a divorce. Better to wait until he was back in Chicago to let her rip his heart to shreds. At least he could make an effort to win her back on safe ground. "I'm sorry, Lex. You'll just have to wait until I get home."

"But why? I won't be in any danger with you there."

Torn between the pride that she believed in him and the knowledge that he couldn't allow himself to weaken, Andy spoke more bluntly than he desired. "Listen, I don't want you here distracting me from my work. All right? I'll be home as soon as I can, and then we can talk about whatever you want. It won't be much longer."

"That's what you said when you left. You've already been gone a lot longer than you thought."

"I know. Things happened."

"I can just imagine what things." The hard-edged tone was back.

"I doubt you can. If you come down here, you could be in danger, like your mama said."

"Sure, Andy. How convenient. You just make sure you come by and see me when you get home. I won't bother you anymore."

"Lexie. . ."

But it was too late. The phone clicked.

With a frustrated growl, Andy slammed down the receiver.

"Troubles at home?" Ella's husky voice pierced the silence.

"That's none of your concern."

"Shoot, Andy. No need to be mean." She stood between him and the steps. He'd have to brush past her to return to his room. But he'd definitely made a new commitment today while standing with a rope around his neck.

"Excuse me."

"Sure, Andy." Her sultry voice had its intended effect. Andy felt himself responding to the way she swayed to the side to let him pass.

He let his eyes linger too long. A smile slid across her lips, and she pressed close as he walked by. She wrapped long, slender fingers around his arm. "We're alone in the house," she said, her lips close to his ear. "The family went to a church meeting two counties away. They won't be back until the wee hours of the morning."

Fire shot through his belly as temptation wound a chain around his heart.

Ella laid her head against his shoulder, her soft breath tickling his neck, her fragrance wafting to his nostrils, clouding his senses.

He truly did want to make a new start with Lexie. But Ella. . .

Swallowing hard, he tried something new. *Help, God.*

In a beat, he had the answer. "No." The word seemed to come from outside of him, though he knew he had spoken it.

"What did you say?" Ella lifted her head and stared

into his eyes. She wrapped her arms around his neck, pressing her curves against him.

Help, God. Andy shook her off. "I said no."

She stepped back, pressing her hand to her cheek as though she'd received a hard slap. "Do you mean that?"

"I love my wife. I want to make things right between us. The only way I can do that is to stay away from you."

"Aw, Andy. She'd never know."

"I would. And that's enough."

"Don't expect me to offer again."

"I'd appreciate it if you didn't." A wry grin twisted his lips. "You're not easy to resist."

She let out a huff, and her face twisted in anger. In that instant, Andy felt no attraction for her at all.

As she walked away, a feeling of exultation rose inside him. He felt as though he'd passed a test, grown some as a man.

A smile remained on his lips as he retreated to his room, stretched out on the bed, and opened the diary on his nightstand.

Chapter Eleven
~December 1867

After two months passed with no word from Chicago, Cat had begun to believe Stuart Riley had forgotten all about her. But as she stared at the telegram in her trembling hands, the truth came back with startling reality.

Will arrive in Oak Junction three days before Christmas
STOP
Will purchase two tickets for return trip dated December 26
STOP
Looking forward to seeing you again
STOP

She couldn't stall much longer. Soon she would have to make a decision one way or another. Would she accept Stuart's proposition or stay at Penbrook?

"What's that?"

Cat jumped at the sound of Camilla's voice. "Mercy, Camilla. Don't sneak up on people like that."

"I didn't sneak." She eyed the telegram. "Who's it from?"

"Stuart."

Camilla smiled. "That's lovely. How is he?"

"You can ask him yourself." Cat shrugged. "He's coming for Christmas."

"Wonderful."

"Yes. Isn't it?" Cat said absently.

Camilla gave an exasperated huff and planted her hands on her hips, which had become quite round since the lean days of the war. "For heaven's sake, Cat. He was your beau for three years. Aren't you the least bit excited that he's coming?"

Cat faced Camilla with a forced smile. "Of course I am. I'll bake a sweet potato pie, and we can fix that chestnut stuffing your ma used to make. We haven't had that since the Christmas—"

A high-pitched scream pierced the air, cutting off the rest of her comment.

Henry!

Cat's heart lurched at the sound of her boy's cry. She and Camilla both sprang into action. "Where is he?" Cat asked, more to herself than Camilla, as they ran out of the study and into the foyer.

The door flew open and Shaw rushed inside, cradling the screeching child in his arms. Cat nearly fainted at the sight of blood covering his mouth. "What happened?"

"He done took a fall."

"A fall off of what?" Cat demanded. "You've been told over and over not to—"

"For heaven's sake, Cat. Let's take care of his injuries before you fuss at the child."

The two women followed on Shaw's heels as he hurried to the kitchen. He laid Henry on the table.

"I don' think he be hurt too awful bad, Miss Cat."

He held the thrashing child down. "Get somethin' to clean up the blood," he instructed.

Cat could no more have crossed the room for water than she could have carried the cast-iron stove on her back. She grabbed Henry's trembling hand as the room began to spin. Shaw snatched up a wooden chair and pressed it into the back of her knees. "Here, Miss Cat. Sit befo' you falls down."

Giving a grateful nod, she sat heavily, staying firmly at Henry's side.

Camilla pumped water into a bowl. She wet a towel and gently began to cleanse away the blood. "There now," she soothed. "You lost your front tooth. But guess what? You were going to lose it anyway in another year or so."

"I wath?" The loss of his tooth caused an adorable lisp.

Camilla caught him close, mindless of the sticky blood from his shirt staining her yellow bodice. "I'm so happy you're all right." She set him back on the table and held him at arm's length. "Now, young man. Tell me how you lost that tooth."

Henry hesitated, averting his gaze.

"Come on now," Camilla prodded. "Let's have it. The truth."

"I fell off Claud."

A gasp escaped Cat's lips. "What were you doing on Claud in the first place? How many times have you been told to stay away from that crazy cow?"

Henry frowned, undaunted by her scolding. "I had to get on her. Lenny dared me."

Shaw chortled. Camilla's lips tipped upward in an indulgent smile.

Cat's ire rose. "Henry Jr., I ought to tan your hide. You could have been killed."

Henry scrunched his nose. "I don't like being called Henry."

"What do you mean?"

"Uncle Thomas calls me Hank. So does Uncle Stuart. That's what I want to be called."

"Well, too bad." Cat glared at the six-year-old. "Your name is Henry Jr., and that is what I will call you."

"You have to do as I say. Sissy says you're nothing more than a servant."

Shock weakened Cat's knees. She shot a glare at Camilla, whose face had suddenly reddened. "Is that so?"

"Oh, Cat, really. Don't get into a snit about it."

Shaw lifted Henry from the table. "C'mon, boy. Let's go see iffen we can find dat missin' tooth."

Cat turned on Camilla with fury. "How dare you tell him that I'm nothing more than a slave!"

"I never used the word slave." Lifting the bowl of bloody water, Camilla walked to the door and tossed the contents outside. She looked Cat squarely in the eye. "I believe I mentioned field hand." Camilla lifted her chin in unrepentant defiance.

Cat would have loved nothing better than to slap that arrogance right off her face. Instead, she gathered a breath and stared her down. Camilla could rail all she wanted, but the truth of the matter was that Cat ran things at Penbrook. The field hands, male and female, turned to her for instruction. So no matter how spiteful Camilla's words might be, in truth, she had no power to do anything.

"Perhaps I should take my son with me each day to the fields in order to keep him from your poorly executed upbringing. I will not have my son become a spoiled lord of the manor with no regard for the feelings of others." She stepped closer, standing inches from Camilla. "My son will never be like your pa."

"No one wants him to be like Pa," Camilla hissed. "And stop calling Hank your son."

"He is my son."

"Do you want him to lose all hope of inheriting Penbrook?"

"I warn you, Camilla, do not even threaten such a thing."

"I'm not the one threatening his future, Cat. Your reck-lessness is."

"What do you mean?"

"Don't you know what people are saying about you?"

Cat narrowed her gaze. "What are people saying?"

"That you're an unnatural woman. That you unsex your-self by wearing men's britches and strutting around in the fields like you're a man."

Laughter formed on Cat's lips. "Oh, Camilla, what do I care what they think about that? If I don't run things, who will care for Henry's inheritance?"

"You don't think I would? After all, I love him, too."

That much was true. As much as she was capable of lov-ing. But Camilla still held to the notion that one speck of Negro blood lowered a person's quality. No matter how min-iscule the African blood in her son's body, the taint was there in Camilla's mind.

"Do you love the part of him that I contributed?"

Camilla's face grew red.

"If you don't love all of him, then you don't love him at all." Cat turned on her heel and stomped out of the kitchen.

Camilla watched Cat storm out of the kitchen. For heaven's sake, she could get into a snit quicker than anyone Camilla knew. Or cared to know, for that matter. Of course Camilla loved her little brother. And thankfully, that African part of his blood made up such a small part of him that one couldn't see it. Even if you looked hard, there was simply no hint of Negro blood in the look of him.

Camilla wiped down the table and rinsed and put away the bowl. She set a pot of coffee to brew on the stove and sat at the table feeling the weight of loneliness.

The kitchen door swung open just as she was pouring herself a cup.

"Where's Cat?" Thomas stood, shaking, in the doorway.

Camilla shot to her feet. "What's wrong?"

He held out the telegram Cat had been reading before Henry's accident. "Where is she?"

"I don't know, Thomas. She was here earlier, but we had words, and she stormed off. Probably to the fields."

"She's not in the fields. I just came from there."

"Well, there are lots of them, aren't there? How would you know if you missed her?"

He scowled and scratched his head but didn't argue with her logic. "I suppose I'll have to wait until she returns to speak to her." He eyed the coffee. "Any more of that?"

"Of course." Camilla's heart dipped and soared at his boyish grin. "Please sit down, and I'll bring it to you."

"Thank you." He sat, eyeing the telegram once more.

"You're positively shaking, Thomas," Camilla said, setting down a steaming mug in front of him. "What's that about?"

"You don't know what's in this telegram?"

"Just that Captain Riley is going to visit at Christmas. Cat was about to tell me more when we heard Hank screaming." The first part of her statement was the truth, of course. The second was a bold lie. Cat hadn't seen fit to elaborate. But Camilla knew there was something more to Thomas's angst than simply Stuart coming for a visit.

Thomas's head jerked up. "Is Hank all right?"

Sitting across from him, Camilla spooned sugar into her coffee. "Oh, sure. He just fell off Claud and lost a tooth. There was a lot of blood, though."

Thomas shook his head. "That boy is fearless."

"Yes." Impatience nibbled at Camilla's insides. She had to get the conversation back to that telegram. "So, why are you so upset about Captain Riley coming for Christmas? We're all quite fond of him, even if he is a Yankee. Is that why you're so upset? I assumed you'd reconciled yourself to Stuart's presence long ago. To forbid him a place at dinner would be unforgivable after all he's done for us."

"I'm not talking about the visit. I mean what he has in mind afterward."

"I don't know what you mean."

He slid the telegram across the table. Camilla read it, her eyes going wide at the implication. "Riley wants to marry Cat and take her away?"

"It seems so."

In a bold move, Camilla reached out and covered Thomas's hand. "Why shouldn't she? He knows about her and doesn't mind that she's a Negro."

Thomas glared and jerked his hand away. "Cat isn't a Negro."

Stung, Camilla clasped her fingers and stared downward.

"She really is," she murmured. "You knew that years ago, when—"

Thomas shot from his chair, sending it crashing to the floor. "For the love of God, Camilla." He glared down at her. "Have some decency."

Shaking, Camilla rose slowly and faced him. "You dare to tell me to have decency? When you and she were found undressed in the hay?"

He raked his hand through his hair in a frustrated swipe. "It wasn't like that."

"Then why didn't you marry her, take her away?"

He frowned. "You know I wanted to. She was the one who refused."

Heat seared Camilla's cheeks at the memory of a secret only she carried. A secret she had every intention of taking to her grave.

"Well, that's all behind you. Cat made her choice. There's really nothing you can do about it."

He jerked his head up, his eyes blazing with a determination that made Camilla shudder. "Yes, there is something I can do about it. Something I should have done seven years ago." His boots thudded on the floor as he walked with purposeful strides across the kitchen.

"Thomas, wait!" Desperation drove Camilla to lower herself to running after a man. Something she swore she'd never do, even if it meant remaining a spinster forever. She reached out and grabbed his arm. "Don't make a fool of yourself over her. Hasn't she made fools enough of us?"

"Fools of us?" He shook his head, his eyes sparking with disgust. "She's saved us. I intend to convince her to marry me, if she'll have me."

"No! I won't allow it. I–I'll expose her for what she is."

He gave her a final look of disdain before leaving her standing, staring after him, her heart shattered into a million pieces.

1 9 4 8

The front door crashed open downstairs. Andy heard high-pitched laughter and the hiss of someone being shushed. He knew it had to be Ella. The foolish woman had obviously brought a man home. Buck would fire her in a heartbeat if he knew.

He set aside Miss Penbrook's diary and walked across the room. He opened the door just as Ella stumbled up the stairs, intoxicated. "What are you doing, Ella?" He stared past her to a man who didn't appear to have been drinking at all.

Ella sneered and waved her hand. "Go back to your books, Andy. You had your chance."

The man laughed and pressed his face against her ear. "He must be a fool."

"No, not a fool," Andy said. "Just decent enough not to take unfair advantage of a woman who has had too many drinks."

The man laughed. "You the same decent fella almost got yourself killed by Rafe a couple of weeks ago?"

Andy's ears burned. "Maybe I got some sense knocked into me. You think you might need the same thing?"

"Oh, shoot, Andy. Don't start acting all tough and manly. Leroy don't mean me no harm." She reached up and patted his cheek. "Do you, baby?"

"You know I don't mean you nothin' but good, beautiful woman."

Andy bristled. "Leroy, if you know Ella very well, you know she works for religious people who wouldn't want her to have a man in the house."

He laughed again. A laugh that was starting to grate on Andy's nerves. "I don't see no one around here but you."

"That's not the point. If Buck finds out about you, Ella will lose her job."

Ella gasped. "You think so?"

"You know it's true. Don't act like you don't."

She pulled away from Leroy and overcompensated, landing her squarely in Andy's arms. She pressed her head against his chest and sighed. "Oh, Andy. You trying to save me from getting canned? Thank you."

Leroy reached for her, but she yanked her arm away. "Go home, Leroy. I can't be losing my job."

"Woman, you're driving me crazy!" Leroy plunked his fedora on his head and stomped down the steps. "Don't expect me to keep coming around after this. I'm through with you this time. For good!"

"Good riddance," she said through a yawn.

Andy slid his arms behind her knees and swung her off her feet. She was half passed out, and he didn't relish trying to coax her down the hall to her room. This seemed easier.

He maneuvered around her to open the door. Carried her across the room, stooped, and struggled to pull down her covers. Finally, he laid her down, slipped off her shoes, and pulled the quilt to her shoulders.

With a sigh, she snuggled into her pillow.

When he reached the door, her soft voice called to him. He turned.

"Thank you, Andy. Ain't no one took care of me like

this since before my mama died."

"It's okay. Good night, Ella."

"Night." By her mumbled reply, Andy knew she'd most likely be asleep before he reached his own room.

CHICAGO

Lexie tossed on her bed until the bedclothes were wound tightly around her legs. She tugged and wiggled until they came free. Fresh tears slid down her face. She reached for her handkerchief on the nightstand and blew her nose.

Suddenly the tiny presence inside her protested the lack of food in her stomach. She slung off the wrinkled sheets and made a beeline for the bathroom, retching, dry heaving, then collapsing into a heap on the bathroom floor, sobbing her misery and loneliness.

After a time, she heard the creak of the door. Mama knelt beside her and gathered her into warm, comforting arms. A gentle hand caressed her head. "Oh, my baby girl."

"What am I going to do, Mama? Andy doesn't want me anymore."

"Did he say that?"

"All but."

"Well, 'all but' ain't saying, now, is it?" Mama adjusted so she faced Lexie. "I 'spect he don' want ya where ya might get hurt."

"So he says."

"Well now. Den ya jus' gots to trust him."

Lexie gave a short laugh and pulled away, standing. "Sure, Mama. I'll wait and trust him."

"Now, don' be disrespectful." She grunted. "Honey, help yo' mama up from dis here flo'." She heaved up from the floor and draped a flabby arm around Lexie's shoulders. "Come on. I's gonna hep ya back to yo' bed an' tuck ya in jus' like a little lamb."

Lexie allowed it. It was nice to be taken care of. If only Andy could find it in his heart to be protective toward her. Toward their baby. If only he still wanted her.

Georgia

Andy jolted awake. He sat bolt upright. Exasperated, he flung off the covers. That Ella. She was going to get herself fired. He opened the bedroom door. Rough hands grabbed him from either side of the door frame.

"I told you this wasn't over, nigger." The voice came from behind a white hood, but there was no mistaking the hate-filled eyes staring out from the holes. *Sam!* Hot fear seared through every nerve in Andy's body.

"Get him outside," Sam ordered the two men in white behind him.

They dragged Andy down the steps. There would be no saving him this time. He was dead for sure.

Protect Ella, God. She doesn't deserve to be hurt.

He was muscled outside. A dozen men, all dressed in white, let up a roar when he appeared. A flaming cross stood in the yard, burning part of Lottie's lawn. More rough hands seized him and tore Andy's shirt from his body. Two men bound his wrists and slung the end of the rope over a low-hanging branch of Lottie's favorite maple tree. Andy's arms were stretched above his head.

Relief that the rope wasn't around his neck quickly gave way to horror at the first snap of a bullwhip. Pain sliced through him as his skin ripped beneath the blow.

A scream tore from his lips before he could bite it back. With the second lash, he held it in. By the tenth, he was losing consciousness. How did his ancestors stand up under the abuse?

The crack of a gun stopped the beating. "You boys get on outta here."

"Mind your own business, Sheriff. This uppity colored needs a lesson, and we're giving him one."

"What's he done?"

Silence reigned.

"That's what I figured. If you're not gone in the next two minutes, I'm going to arrest every last one of you."

Slowly, mumbling, the Klan dispersed.

Andy felt the rope slacken, and he would have lost his footing had the sheriff not caught him. "Take it easy, boy. We'll get you to the hospital lickety-split."

"No," Andy gasped.

"Andy, don't be a mule." Ella's voice penetrated the fuzzy darkness. "You have to go to the hospital this time. I'm going to try to put a temporary dressing on your wounds. I'm sorry for the pain I'm going to have to cause you."

At the first ministering touch, Andy succumbed to darkness.

He awoke in the hospital, pain lacing his body, his mind screaming against the injustice.

"Well, look who's finally awake."

He turned his head toward the sound of Buck's voice. "Sorry for bringing this danger to your doorstep."

Buck nodded. "I guess ya can't help it."

"I'll leave as soon as I get out of here."

"No need for that kinda talk. Besides, the doc says yo'

gonna need a few days to rest an' make sure infection don' set in."

Pain defined his existence for three days. Medication kept him in and out of sleep during that time. Finally, on the fourth day after the whipping, he woke with some clarity and less pain.

He fussed incessantly to be allowed to go home. But his requests fell on the deaf ears of every nurse attending him. Finally, late that evening, a large, commanding black nurse brought him a set of clothing. "Get yourself ready to go."

"At night?"

"You want to get shot leaving the hospital?" She pushed out her lower lip and waddled to the door. "Leaving in the dark is your best chance of getting home safely."

Submitting to the logic, Andy waited for her to exit the room, then he dressed, eager to get out of the sterile environment.

He couldn't help the dread at the thought of what might happen to him next. So far he'd been beaten practically senseless—but he supposed he deserved that one—had almost been dragged down the road chained to the back of a truck, and now was whipped to within an inch of his life. He easily could have been killed all three times. Why was he still alive?

When he reached the back entrance of the hospital, a horse and wagon stood there waiting. He vaguely recognized the old-timer who had given him a ride his first day in Oak Junction.

" 'Evenin', young feller. Ole Jeb's here to take you home."

"I'm obliged." With great difficulty, Andy climbed into the seat.

The jostling wagon took him through parts of town he'd never seen. Nothing looked familiar, but Andy figured the old man was just trying to avoid being seen. When they left town, suspicion began to nip his mind.

"Why are we leaving town?"

"Jus' takin' ya where I's told."

"And where is that?"

"Miz Penbrook tol' me you jus' gonna get yo'self kilt if ya stay anywheres else. So Miz Delta done tole me, 'Ole Jeb, you go fetch that fool boy's things and don't you forget dem books. He gonna be needin' 'em.' So dat's jus' what I done."

"They moved me out to Miss Penbrook's without consulting me?"

"I reckon. And betwixt you an' me, it seem like de best thing."

"Why's that?"

"No one's gonna burn no crosses at Miz Penbrook's place. No black nor white. Prob'ly the only place you is gonna be safe until ya go back to dat Chi-ca-gy ya come from."

Andy let the man's assessment sink in. As long as he remained at Buck's, he would be putting them in danger. If what Jeb said was correct, staying at the Penbrook plantation was the smartest course of action.

They approached the enormous home under the light of a large moon. A startling sense of déjà vu shook him. He pushed the feeling aside and focused on the good fortune of staying at Penbrook. He would get answers much faster this way.

Still, unease tightened his gut. Did he really want to find answers? Or, as Miss Penbrook had mentioned the day he'd arrived, would knowledge be more of a chain around his neck?

From Cat's Diary

I overheard something today that could change everything. Thomas wanted to marry me all those years ago. I'm not sure why he believes I refused him. But I am positive Camilla knows. I have not allowed myself to be alone with Thomas, as he vowed to marry me. I heard the words, but the joy I expected to feel at such a declaration was absent from my heart. Oh, why? Why am I not beside myself with happiness? Isn't this what I've dreamed of for seven years? That Thomas would marry me and take me away from here to raise our son?

Camilla has threatened to reveal my true heritage. To tell anyone who will listen that I'm nothing more than a former slave. I heard her say so to Thomas. She hates me that much.

I must speak with her before I go. I wonder if I should confess to Thomas that little Henry is his son.

I'm so confused. The only thing I am absolutely sure of is that Henry Jr. must have what is rightfully his. I will not jeopardize his future for anything. Not even his father.

CHAPTER TWELVE

"What sort of fool are you, Sam?" Samuel Andrew Dane, young Sam's father, slammed his fist down hard on his desk, knocking over the photograph of Mary Ann, his late wife. "If you'd killed that boy, you'd have been arrested for murder. He isn't like the coloreds around here. He has connections in the North, and believe me, you'd never have gotten away with it."

"I know who he is, Father." His son glared at him, accusation shooting from his eyes. A sneer curled his lips. "What do you think will happen when your constituents find out you fathered a colored son?"

Samuel gathered a deep breath and sat back. "No one needs to know. And there's no need to harm Andy. He's done nothing."

"Andy." Sam shook his head and stared out the window behind the desk. "Both your sons named after you. You must be so proud of your virility. Did you know that colored gal was going to have your child?"

"Not at first. We didn't know for sure if he was mine or her husband's until a few days after his birth."

"Yes, the resemblance is uncanny. All the way down to the Dane cleft." He pointed to the dimple in his own chin. "You shame me, Father. And you shame every Dane man who fought for the Confederacy."

Samuel met his son's rage and disdain with a steady calm. Surprisingly steady. He'd always wondered how he might react if faced with the truth. "There's no shame in loving someone. Only in the sin we committed."

"Love? That is the sin. A white man was never meant to love a nigger. It's an abomination to God." He leaned across the desk, the look in his eye dangerous and filled with hatred. "And the only way to remove an abomination is through death."

"Listen to me, Sam. Andy's mother sent him away to protect him and us from this scandal. Miss Penbrook brought him back only to write her memoirs. The old lady will be dead before long, Andy will be back in Chicago, and no one will be the wiser. Rae never told a soul, other than Miss Penbrook, that Andy wasn't her husband's, although he figured it out. But he's dead, too, so he can't threaten our family honor."

Sam gave a short laugh. "Honor? What honor?" He strode with long, hard steps to the door.

"Son, give me your word that no harm will come to Andy from you or your Klan."

"Klan? I don't have any idea what you mean."

"Then let me put it to you this way. If any harm comes to Andy, there will be no mention of you in my will."

Sam's jaw dropped. "You would deprive me of my inheritance because of some nigger?"

"Yes."

"You disgust me."

"Be that as it may, I need your word."

Sam reached for the door and spoke through clenched teeth. "You have it."

Relief coursed through Samuel as he watched his son yank the door open and disappear on the other side.

He leaned back in his chair and closed his eyes. "Rae," he whispered, "our sin has come back to visit our children."

Andy sat painfully in the chair next to Miss Penbrook's bedside, listening with fascinated horror as the pieces fell into place at last. "So my father. . .wasn't Elijah Carmichael." He didn't ask it as a question, but rather stated it as a fact. A fact he had somehow known, though exactly how he'd known evaded his conscious mind. "I'm half white."

"That's right. And Elijah knew it. That's why he hated you so much." She peered closer with those eyes that seemed to see everything. "Do you remember the beatings he used to give you?"

Andy shook his head. "Not really."

She nodded. "Just as well. I don't suppose you remember much about your life before you went to be with the Rileys, do you?"

"No, ma'am. I only remember images of Mama crying and putting me on the train."

"She came to me for help. Elijah was drunk and threatening to kill you."

Andy swallowed hard. "It would appear I'm not well liked in the South."

"But the Rileys treated you well?"

A smile touched his lips. "I suppose I have you to thank for that."

"Put two and two together, did you?"

"Sort of. But who is Captain Stuart Riley?"

"Daniel's father. He died the year before you went to live with Daniel and Lois."

"They treated me like one of their own. Of course you are aware that I work for Daniel Riley's publication."

"The *Observer*. I know. I also know how hard you tried not to." She let out a laugh. "I admired you for wanting to find a position at a different paper instead of letting Daniel give you work."

"It was either that or never be able to take care of my wife." He gave a bitter shake of his head. "Yet look where I ended up."

"Daniel says you're the best writer and reporter he's ever worked with."

"That's very kind of him."

"It's more than kind. He wouldn't say so if it weren't true." Miss Penbrook's brow creased. "Why haven't you introduced him to your wife after all these years?"

"Mr. Riley told you that?"

She shook her head. "Lois did. She says it's like not knowing her own daughter-in-law."

"I visit on occasion."

"But you don't share your life with them."

"Doesn't show much gratitude on my part, does it?"

"Daniel and Lois don't want gratitude. They want love. They think you're the prodigal son."

Andy gave a short laugh. "I'm no one's son."

"What's that supposed to mean?"

He shrugged. How could he confide the fact that he had felt like an orphan since he was ten years old? No mother or father to hold him in the night. To love him, teach him, reassure him. Mr. and Mrs. Riley were wonderful people and had raised him in a loving home, but a black boy being raised by a white family, even in the North, didn't bode well. He knew he was different. Knew he didn't belong. And most people believed he was a servant boy.

Once they reached high school, even he and Jonas had drifted apart—Jonas to his sports and Andy to his academics. From that time on, he'd been utterly alone.

He looked back to Miss Penbrook. Her frail chest rose and fell in sleep.

So much for asking her whether Cat married Thomas or went to Stuart.

The diaries. . .

1 8 6 7

"I heard you talking to Thomas, Camilla." Cat seethed at the look of innocence on the woman's face. "So what are you saying? That I was imagining things? That Thomas didn't want to marry me? Perhaps I should go to him. I'm sure he'd be more than happy to explain it all to me."

Camilla scowled. "Fine. I'll tell you." She sipped her coffee and stared over the rim of her cup, a piece of the fine china she'd received from her mother after her death.

Cat shook off the memory of Madeline sipping from a similar cup. The woman's grace, dignity, and kindness were all things Camilla lacked. It took great effort to keep from slapping the cup out of her hand. Miss Maddy's last request still lingered in her mind. But that promise couldn't keep her from growing impatient at Camilla's hesitance. "Tell me."

"The day after the incident in the barn, Thomas found

me walking in the woods that separated our property from his uncle's. I suspect he was hoping you'd be there."

But she couldn't have been. Henry had chained her in the barn upon their arrival home. He'd stripped, beaten, and raped her. He'd kept her chained for days with no food, allowing only small amounts of water, until Madeline had threatened to disgrace him with a divorce.

She shuddered at the memories she had tried so hard to shove to the back of her mind. Without Madeline sneaking her food and water, she was sure she wouldn't have lived through those days. "What did Thomas say?"

"He asked me to speak to you for him. To meet him in the barn that night. He planned to steal you away to Canada, passing you off as a white girl so he could marry you."

"And you didn't tell him that your father had chained me in the barn like a dog?" Cat's bitterness grew with each word.

Camilla shook her head.

"I despise you."

"And I despise you." Her steely voice commanded Cat's attention. The two women were caught in a trancelike state, neither speaking nor moving, barely breathing.

Finally Camilla broke the silence. "Here's the way I see it. You have two men vying for you. I want one of them. So you must choose the other."

A short laugh spurted from Cat's mouth. "Oh, must I? And what makes you think I must?"

Camilla's full lips tilted in a humorless smile. "Because if you take Thomas away from me, I will tell everyone that Hank is your son. That will effectively cut him off from decent society."

Trembling with anger, Cat clenched her fists to keep

from scratching Camilla's eyes out. "I knew you were vindictive, Camilla, but I never thought you'd force a man who doesn't love you into marriage."

Camilla's eyes narrowed. "I have no intention of forcing him. But with you gone, he'll naturally turn to me. Don't you think?"

"I can see you've thought this out."

"I have. Quite carefully."

Cat fingered the rim of her cup. "Stuart doesn't want to marry me."

"Don't lie to me. Thomas found the telegram where you left it when Hank had his accident."

Cat shot her an outraged gaze. How dare they invade her privacy in such a manner? "Did you see any mention of marriage in the message?"

A frown creased Camilla's brow. "Well, no, now that you mention it. But he said he would be arranging for two tickets to Chicago after Christmas. I assumed he meant to take you home as his wife."

Cat released a bitter, cold laugh. "Well, you're wrong. Stuart is married already. To a wealthy woman who doesn't love him and cannot give him children."

A gasp escaped Camilla as the news penetrated her puritanical ideals. "Does he mean to divorce her in order to marry you?"

"No."

"Well, then, I don't understand why he is coming to visit."

"Oh, Camilla, really. Sometimes your innocence is difficult to believe. Stuart is planning to buy a lovely little home in which I will live as his mistress. Any children I may have will be given his name."

Camilla's eyes grew round and her mouth formed an O.

"So you see, whether you expose me here or I return to Chicago with Stuart, I will be scandalized."

Recovering, Camilla raised her brow and gave Cat a frank stare. "Yes, but if you go north and leave Hank to be raised by Thomas and me, he will inherit Penbrook, just as you want. Thomas will continue sharecropping the land. Penbrook will continue to grow."

Silence fell between them. Cat imagined life with Thomas and Henry but without Penbrook. She imagined life with Stuart, without Penbrook and Henry. Both options made her stomach churn.

"You've given me no choice but to refuse Thomas. However, that doesn't mean I have to accept Captain Riley's offer. I am quite happy to let things continue as they are."

Camilla's face twisted with anger.

Cat rose, squared her shoulders, and smiled to herself as she left the vile woman sitting alone. She would refuse Thomas. And she would not tell him that Henry Jr. was actually her son. . .and his.

She left the kitchen at loose ends. Normally, when she needed to think, she'd saddle a horse and head to the fields. The sight of cotton growing, at any stage, filled her with a sense of hope. But now the fields lay desolate, harvested, and that only depressed her. Still, a cool autumn wind blew through an open window, beckoning her outside. Standing on the porch, she closed her eyes and drank in the fresh, clean air, heavy with the scent of approaching rain.

"Storm's brewin'."

She didn't open her eyes at the sound of Shaw's voice. She

had grown accustomed to his appearing out of nowhere and no longer became startled. "It smells wonderful, doesn't it?"

"It surely do, Miss Cat."

Cat opened her eyes and looked at him. *Shaw.* The one person she knew loved her beyond a shadow of a doubt. His handsome, dark features were strong, filled with honesty and faithfulness. "Would you walk with me, Shaw?"

"Might get caught in the rain."

"I don't mind if you don't."

His thick, soft lips widened into a smile.

Cat's gaze rested there. "I like it when you smile, Shaw."

"Thank ya. It be nice when ya let yo'self smile, too."

"When I let myself smile?"

"C'mon. We best be gettin' to dat walk iffen ya don' want to git soakin' wet."

"Let's go." Shaw's steady strength fortified her, and she felt her optimism returning. "I, uh, heard from Captain Riley. He's coming for Christmas."

"Dat be right?"

"Yes." Cat stared at the towering oaks. "He's ready for me to go back to Chicago with him."

Shaw released a heavy breath and halted his steps. He reached out and pressed a massive hand to Cat's arm, turning her to face him. Her heart leaped at his touch. The same unsettling feeling of awareness that crept over her whenever his hand brushed hers.

"What ya thinkin' on doin' 'bout that feller?" He stared down at her with intensity. Not with eyes full of passion, like so many other men had. Shaw's expression bespoke. . .compassion.

He felt sorry for her? Outrage shot through her, but she

pushed it away as he silently waited for her to answer. How nice to know someone truly cared. "I don't know, Shaw. I can't decide."

In a bold move, he enveloped her hands in his. "Do de right thing."

Drawn in by his wonderful brown eyes, Cat couldn't look away. "What is right? Tell me."

"Stop lyin' to yo'self. Stop tryin' to be who ya ain't."

Cat stiffened. "What do you mean?"

"Ya knows what I mean."

"No, Shaw," Cat replied, yanking her hands away. "I don't know what you mean. How about if you enlighten me?"

Shaw stuffed his hands into his pockets and resumed walking down the lane.

Cat followed, taking two steps to every one of his. "Shaw, stop. Tell me what you mean." Silence met her. In frustration, she grabbed his arm. "Stop!" She walked around to face him. "Talk to me."

"Nobody can tell ya what ya already knows, darlin'." He cupped her cheek. "Ya can't live forever in a lie. Someday, somebody is gonna find ya out."

"You mean to tell me you think I should live as a slave instead of a white woman?"

His lips curved into an indulgent smile. "We's free, Miss Cat."

Cat refused to find the humor in his remark. "You know what I mean."

He released a sigh. "Yeah, I 'spect I do. Still, it ain't right what ya's plannin'. Goin' north to live in sin with a white man."

Cat gave a bitter laugh. "I suppose it would be holier if I

were to live the same way with a black man like you?"

A flash of hurt crossed his features, stealing away Cat's breath. He dropped her hands. "Miss Cat, ya go an' do 'zactly what ya wants to do."

Regret slammed into her gut. "I'm sorry, Shaw." She placed her hand on his muscled arm. "I had no right to say that. Please forgive me."

He turned to her. His skin looked dark as night against her hand. "I always do, Catherina."

Thunder rolled across the gray sky. Lightning followed, splitting the sky. "I 'spect ya better get on inside, befo' the storm gits bad." With one more long, melting look, he turned and strode away.

Cat watched his broad back. For one wild moment, she saw herself falling into his massive arms, laying her head against his chest, and allowing the weight of the world to shift to his shoulders, which were far stronger than hers.

As if reading her thoughts, he swept around. He stared, long, hard. Cat caught her breath. Everything in her wanted to go to him. Oh, there was so much she wanted to say. She knew he would understand the pain of those years as Henry's mistress, the struggle of caring for Miss Maddy and the household.

"Shaw!" she called out.

Slowly he started back to her, his eyes filled with questions. Shaw. . .she didn't even know his first name. Or his last, if Shaw was his first. Her stomach twisted. He had been a slave. He would never have anything more than what she offered him as a sharecropper on her son's land. If she went to him as a former slave, neither of them would have anything.

"Is somethin' de matter, Miss Cat?"

Swallowing, she shook her head. "I—I just wondered. . ."

"What?" He was so close she could have reached out and touched him. Rain splattered on her cheek, trailing downward like a tear as she forced a smile. "I just wondered what your last name is."

Instantly, his deferential expression returned. He smiled. "Only gots one name. Shaw."

"J—just Shaw?"

He moved a wet strand of hair from her forehead and tucked it behind her ear. Cat closed her eyes. "Just Shaw, Cat. Dat be all I kin ever be."

Reaching up, she covered his hand. Tears filled her eyes as she met his dark gaze. "Good-bye, Shaw," she whispered.

"Den ya's made yo' choice?"

She nodded. "I'm going to accept Captain Riley's proposition."

His eyes misted. "I's gonna be prayin' fo' ya ever' day fo' as long as I got bref in my body."

"Thank you." She pressed a kiss to his palm and walked away as tears came, quickly and unstoppable. By the time she reached the porch, sobs engulfed her small frame.

From Camilla's diary

"I'm going to kill him." Thomas's impassioned words filled Camilla with fear.

"Thomas. Think of the repercussions of harming a Yankee officer."

He sneered. "Riley's not in the army any longer."

"It doesn't matter." Cat's stone-cold voice broke through the tension filling the sitting room. "Thomas isn't killing anyone. This is my decision." She stared pointedly at Camilla. "As it was my choice seven years ago. I decide where I go and whom I go with. And I choose Stuart."

Thomas sank to the floor at Cat's feet and gripped her hands. "But he's asking you to be his mistress, Cat. What kind of a life is that? I'm offering to make you my wife."

The sight of Thomas on his knees before a common slave girl filled Camilla with rage. And the look of uncertainty filling Cat's face clenched her stomach. Cat would not change her mind. Camilla wouldn't allow it. "Thomas, for mercy's sake. Get up. Where is your pride? Cat is doing what she feels is best for her." And if she knew what was good for her, she wouldn't mess this up for Camilla.

Cat nodded. "That's right. You can't change my mind."

"But we love each other. We have since childhood."

"No, we don't. Oh, Thomas, you can't compare the passions of youth with the love a woman feels for a man." Her voice softened, and her face gentled to an expression Camilla had only seen when she looked at little Hank. Was it possible Cat truly did love Captain Riley?

" 'Scuse me."

Camilla looked toward the door. "What is it, Shaw?"

His gaze rested on Cat. "Cap'n Riley's comin' down da lane."

"Thank you, Shaw," Cat whispered.

He nodded and turned away.

Relief flooded Camilla at the news. Just a few more days and Cat would be gone for good.

Thomas stood. He squared his shoulders with dignity. "Go to your lover." The disdain in his voice left no doubt of his contempt.

Cat lifted a trembling hand and smoothed her hair back. "Excuse me, please."

Thomas turned away, refusing to watch her as she left the room to welcome Stuart Riley.

"I'm sorry, Thomas."

He jerked his head up and stared at her, eyes blazing. "Will you marry me, Camilla?"

She blinked as her breath caught in her throat.

Thomas closed the distance between them with just two long strides. He gripped her hands in his. "Marry me."

Joy shot through her. Her cheeks warmed with excitement. "Yes, Thomas. I'd be honored."

He crushed her to him and covered her mouth with his. His hard kiss was almost painful. "Get dressed. We'll go to the preacher right now."

"But what about a wedding with neighbors and a party?"

"Now, Camilla." His eyes warned her not to oppose him.

Camilla pressed her fingers to her throat. "Yes, Thomas."

1948

Andy stared at Miss Penbrook. "If you married Thomas, why do you publish under the name C. Penbrook?"

She sent him a toothless smile. "Why not just keep reading the diaries? They've served you pretty well so far."

"I want to hear it from you."

"I think you already know. Don't you?"

Andy searched the wrinkled face, the wizened brown eyes. *Wait a minute.* Camilla's eyes were blue. Suddenly the thought he hadn't quite been able to come to grips with made its way through his mind. "You're not Camilla, are you?"

She gave a soft sigh. "Ironic, isn't it? A woman born a

slave dies a Southern belle. What do you think people would think if they found out?"

Pain shot through his back, a reminder of what could happen to an "uppity colored," let alone a woman who had pretended for years, attended white functions, drank from their fountains, and eaten in their whites-only restaurants. "I wouldn't suggest you tell anyone at this late date."

"That's what memoirs are designed to do." Her gaze rested on the beam of light shining through her window. "I've lived my life in a lie. In death, I want the truth to be told."

"And you want me to tell it. Why? Why, Cat?"

She sucked in her breath. "No one's called me that in almost forty years. Not since Shaw passed on."

"You assumed Camilla's identity, didn't you?" He had visions of Camilla being murdered and buried in the backyard.

She shook her head. "Of course not. I took on the last name of Penbrook when I left Georgia." She laughed. "Camilla was fit to be tied. But I didn't care."

Andy's lips twitched. He stood to go. "You're quite a woman, Catherina."

"I was a foolish woman, Andy. I gave up love and decency, all because I resented who I was."

"Pardon me, ma'am, but I don't think so." A shrug lifted his shoulders. "I admire your spirit. Having white skin gave you a life you couldn't have had otherwise. You had no choice but to take advantage of it."

"I had a choice."

"But what was the alternative?"

She smiled. "Love."

"There's a lot to be said for love, I suppose."

Miss Penbrook turned her gaze to his. "What about

you? Why are you ashamed to introduce your wife to Daniel and Lois?"

"Ashamed? That's ridiculous."

"Don't deny it to me. You were raised white, and you want to be white."

"You're mistaken."

"Am I?"

"Yes," he said through clenched teeth.

"Then how come you don't visit your family down here? You weren't so young that you don't remember you had brothers and sisters."

Andy felt the blood drain from his face. He'd hoped to avoid discussing this topic with anyone. How was he to know the old hag was going to get so personal? "That's my business."

She nodded. "I suppose so. But your mama sent you away to give you a better life. Aren't you even curious as to how the others fared while you were brought up in a nice white home with plenty to eat, books to read, and a good job waiting for you after you finished your schooling?"

"No. I'm not. I didn't ask to be sent to the Rileys. I don't have to feel guilty for being given the benefit of a better life."

"Any more than I could help being born a slave in a white girl's body."

"That was different."

"Was it?"

"Yes."

Her lips, drawn over toothless gums, pursed as her face twisted in frustration. "Oh, go ahead and leave. I can tell you're about to bolt."

A frown creased Andy's brow. Had he pushed her too

far? "You want me to leave your home?"

"Of course not. I mean, leave the room. You know you want to get away from me."

Well, that much was the truth. "Good night, Miss Cat."

"Good night, my boy. Come see me tomorrow."

"I will."

FROM CAT'S DIARY
1868

> As promised, Captain Riley purchased a lovely house in the country for me. He has also secured a driver, a cook, and two maids. He visits me two nights a week and takes me to town. We attend dinners, parties, the theater. He is not ashamed of me. For the first time in my life, I am living as a woman of leisure and means.
>
> Camilla writes that she and Thomas are to have a child in a few months. She is having a difficult pregnancy and wishes me not to come for the harvest as I intended. She is afraid I might upset the household and cause her to miscarry.
>
> As summer pushes away the lovely spring blooms, I long for the sight of Penbrook and my darling son.
>
> I have taken to writing poetry to entertain myself, or perhaps it is by way of consoling my aching heart. Miss Maddy once said that writing down one's thoughts helps to sort through life's setbacks and joys. I have done this faithfully through the years and have found that taking the writing to a creative level brings me even more pleasure. I intend to share this with Stuart. Perhaps he will publish some short pieces in his paper.

-*Part Three: Darkness*-

They know not, neither will they understand;
they walk on in darkness.

PSALM 82:5

CHAPTER THIRTEEN
~CHICAGO, 1879

Cat pasted a smile on her lips as she looked about the tiresome group of gluttons and drunkards sitting around her dining room table. All of Stuart's friends whom he couldn't invite to his wife's precious table, he brought here to her home to entertain. Gamblers who enjoyed the racetrack as much as Stuart did. Upstarts and merchants who bought expensive ads in his paper.

Cat hated every one of them. From the loud, fat, painted wives and mistresses to the expensive-cigar-wielding, foul-mouthed, groping men.

But she and Stuart had made a bargain years ago when she'd tried to refuse their company.

"You want me to publish the poetry and short stories you write?"

"You know I do, Stuart."

"Then you play hostess to my clients and friends."

She hadn't had to think twice.

A smile tugged her lips at the memory. She and Stuart both knew how to get what they wanted.

From across the table, Stuart caught her eye. His face lit, and he lifted his glass to her, halting the dinner conversation.

"You're beautiful tonight, darling."

Affection for Stuart played across her heart. She lifted her glass to him. "Thank you, my dear."

He looked deeply into her eyes. Even after all their time together, he still stared at her with adoration. For the past twelve years, she'd never doubted his love and devotion. If his wife died, he wouldn't think twice about marrying her. Cat was glad his wife seemed to be in the best of health. Marriage didn't seem necessary, and she knew she was free to leave any time she chose. Which, she had to admit, had crossed her mind more than once over the past months.

Restlessness had overtaken the tranquil life she'd built for herself. She spent quiet days and nights alone, pouring out her words on stacks and stacks of paper. Five nights a week, she penned her poetry and stories.

At first she'd believed perhaps the restlessness would go away, as it had at other times. But it persisted. She missed Penbrook. She needed to go home. She knew that. But over the years, Camilla had found ways to keep her away. Her pregnancies and subsequent miscarriages. Six of them. She and Thomas were still childless. She faithfully sent photographs of Henry Jr. and updates about his successes.

Much to Cat's disappointment, Camilla and Thomas had sent Henry Jr. away to a boys' school in New York less than two years after she'd come to Chicago. She had finally stopped fighting them at Camilla's assurance that Henry would receive a better education in a Northern boys' school than he could ever get in a rundown school in the South—thus enabling him to better run Penbrook. Now he had graduated, and Cat had received word that he was back at Penbrook. At eighteen years of age, the next step in his education would be learning from Thomas and dear Shaw to run the plantation.

Cat's heart nearly burst with longing to be home, to watch her son transform from a boy into a man, capable of taking his rightful place as master of Penbrook. She looked up at Stuart. How would she ever convince him to let her go?

CHICAGO, 1948

Lexie's heart nearly burst from her chest as the operator placed her call to Oak Junction, Georgia. Would Andy reject her once again? She'd promised Mama that she wouldn't go alone without someone to meet her at the bus station. But that didn't mean she wouldn't keep trying to change his mind. It had been more than a week. Of course, she'd said she had no intention of ever calling him again, but what a woman said in a moment of rejection and what she meant weren't necessarily the same thing.

"Hello?" A woman's voice answered the phone.

"I'd like to speak with Andy Carmichael, please."

"He ain't here no more, honey."

Lexie's heart plummeted. "What do you mean? Has he left for home?"

"I don't know. He's been gone for a week. Never said so much as a good-bye and hasn't called since."

A week? Andy had plenty of time to get home, or at least contact her. She felt anger building again. "Thank you."

"You're welcome. Good luck. And when you see him, tell him Ella says hello."

Jealousy shot through Lexie as the line went dead. No doubt Andy had been up to his old tricks. His so-called concern for her safety had been nothing more than a desire to hang on to his newest lady. Just as she'd suspected in the first place.

Tears pricked her eyes. She ran up to her room, grabbed her jacket, hat, and purse, and stomped back down the steps. Mama stopped her just before she slammed through the door.

"Wait. Lex, honey. Where ya goin'?"

"To get a divorce!"

"Over my dead body, little girl."

"Mama, he ran around with another woman while he was in Georgia."

"I'm sorry, baby. I know how that must hurt ya. But don't ya think ya should talk to him before going off half-cocked to get some demon-possessed divorced."

"Demon-possessed? Oh, Mama. For goodness' sake, even Jesus said adultery justified divorce. How many times has Andy done this?"

"I don't know, baby girl. And neither do you. He ain't owned up to anything in a long time."

"Of course not. Would you expect him to admit it?"

Mama's ample shoulders lifted in a shrug. "He did the first time. And the second."

"I just don't know what to believe."

"All ya can do is turn this over to the Lord."

"I need to go for a walk."

A frown pushed Mama's brows together. "Ya ain't gonna go do somethin' awful like getting' some sinful divorce, are ya?"

"Not that I think it would be a sin in this case, but no. I'll wait to see Andy before I do anything like that. I just need to cool off."

"If it's cooling off you need, I can pour ya a nice glass of lemonade."

Lexie smiled and wrapped her arms around her mother. "Thanks, Mama. But I need to walk. Please don't worry."

Her concerned frown didn't ease as Lexie left her standing on the porch and took off down the street in the mild autumn air.

She walked until she knew what she had to do. If Andy wasn't coming to her, she would go to him. At least she would go to where he was sure to turn up. She went to the nearest bus station and sat on the bench until the bus headed downtown arrived.

An hour later, she walked through the front door of the *Observer* and stepped up to the reception desk. "Excuse me."

The red-haired woman behind the desk reminded Lexie of Lucille Ball. She looked Lexie up and down. "The agency send you over, sweetie?"

"No, ma'am."

"Didn't think so. They don't usually send your kind."

Heat rose to Lexie's cheeks. She bristled. "My kind?"

"Don't get all bent out of shape. I didn't mean anything by it. I don't care if you work here. We got us a colored reporter. Kind of the boss's pet, if you want the truth."

The redheaded woman's brash honesty was starting to grow on Lexie. She smiled. "That reporter wouldn't happen to be Andy Carmichael, would it?"

The redhead smacked her gum and curved her red lips into a grin. "Sure is. You his girlfriend?"

"No. I'm his wife."

"You don't say?" Her grin broadened. "Nice to meet you.

My name's Clara. I didn't know Andy even had a wife."

"Yes, he doesn't seem to remember it at the moment, either."

"Oh, one of those, eh? I'd send him packing in a heartbeat."

"I just might, Clara. But first I have to find him. Any chance he's been around here since he left Georgia?"

"I haven't seen him in weeks." The door opened, and Clara's expression slipped into deference. "Morning, Mr. Riley."

"Good morning, Clara. How are you today?"

"Fine, sir."

Mr. Riley had a kindly face despite his imposing height. He smiled at Lexie, his eyes gentle, and tipped his hat. "You must be the new girl. Your name?"

"No, sir." Lexie swallowed hard, fighting the tremors in her stomach.

His lips twitched. "You don't have a name?"

"Yes, sir, I do. But I'm not the new girl."

He sent her a wink. "My mistake. Clara, please bring a cup of coffee to my office and bring your pad. I need to send a letter." He turned toward the hallway.

"Yes, sir. Right away." Clara stood, sympathy written across her long face. "Sorry, honey. Looks like you're out of luck today. You got a number where I can reach you if I see him?"

Lexie sucked in a breath as she watched Mr. Riley disappear into an office at the end of the hall. "You might not know where he is, but I bet I know who does." Without waiting for permission, she bolted down the hall.

"Wait. Ma'am, you can't go down there."

Just try to stop me.

She burst into Mr. Riley's office before Clara reached her. He turned around, surprise raising his salt-and-pepper eyebrows. "Can I help you, young lady?"

Clara reached her, grabbing her by the shoulders. "I am so sorry, Mr. Riley. She followed before I could stop her."

Lexie pulled away from Clara. "Please, sir. I must speak with you."

"It's all right, Clara." He pointed to a chair across the desk from him. "Come, have a seat."

"Thank you." Lexie fought dizziness as she moved forward.

Mr. Riley glanced behind her. "How about a cup of coffee for Miss. . ."

"Mrs.," Lexie corrected. "Carmichael. And I wouldn't care for any coffee, thank you."

"Just some for me then." He dismissed the secretary with a glance.

"I apologize for barging in on you, sir, but I had to speak with you."

"Mrs. Carmichael. Any relation to Andy?"

"Yes, sir. I'm his wife."

Delight shone in Mr. Riley's eyes. "What a pleasure to meet you at last. Andy has kept you from us for so long, I feared you must be an abominable-looking woman."

Lexie's cheeks bloomed. "Andy never mentioned that his employer wanted to meet me."

The amusement dimmed from Mr. Riley's eyes. "How much has Andy told you about his upbringing?"

Lexie blinked at the sudden question. "Only that his parents sent him away when he was young, and he lived with a family in Chicago until he was grown."

"I see." Mr. Riley shook his head. "I don't suppose I should divulge information Andy hasn't seen fit to share, but I will."

"I'd appreciate it."

"Andy came to live with my wife and our four children when he was ten years old. We raised him like a son."

Lexie's eyes grew wide at the revelation. "Andy was raised in a white family?"

A chuckle formed on his lips. "That's right."

Betrayal burned through Lexie's heart. How could Andy have kept something so important from her for twelve years? "He must have been ashamed of me, not wanting to introduce me to his family." Tears burned her eyes and rolled down her cheeks.

Standing, Mr. Riley came around to her side of the desk. He pulled out a handkerchief and pressed it into her hand. "Here now. Take this." He knelt beside her chair. "How on earth could he ever be ashamed of such a lovely creature? More than likely he simply wanted to keep you all to himself. We have a large, imposing family."

"You're very kind."

"And you are very beautiful. It's easy to see why Andy fell in love with you."

At his compassionate words, Lexie burst into tears. "He doesn't want me anymore. We've been having trouble, and I wanted to come down to Georgia, but he said no. So I tried to call him to beg him again to let me come. But the woman at the rooming house said he's been gone for a week. That's why I came here, to ask if you've seen him."

He held her hand during the hysterical blather. "Sweetheart, Andy hasn't come back from Georgia yet.

He was hurt and moved to a safer place for the duration of his visit."

Alarm seized Lexie. "He was hurt? What happened?"

"Unfortunately, the South isn't always friendly to people of your color, Mrs. Carmichael."

"Please call me Lexie. Are you telling me that Andy was beaten up for being black?"

He gathered a breath. "I'm afraid he was. So you see, he was right to keep you away. He loves you too much to put you in harm's way."

"I have to see him. I have to go to him." She looked up. "Can you help me?"

"Now, Lexie, honey, I can't go against Andy's wishes in this. You might not be safe."

"But I have to tell him about the baby."

"You have a baby?"

Heat seared her cheeks. "Not yet."

His face brightened and a wide smile split his lips. "Andy's going to be a father?"

Laughter bubbled up inside Lexie at his excitement. "Yes, sir. In a few months."

"You realize what this means, don't you? I'm going to be a grandfather again."

Lexie's eyes widened, and she laughed out loud.

"What? You don't think I'll be a good grandpop to your young 'un? I have references, you know. Three of them."

"You're serious, aren't you?"

"Do you have any objections?"

"I sure don't. Not even one."

He patted her hand and stood. "We'll have to see about getting my boy back here as soon as possible."

GEORGIA

Andy tossed on his bed, unable to sleep. Tired of reading. He needed air. He tiptoed out of his small room that Delta had informed him was once Henry Penbrook's study. They had converted it into a bedroom around the turn of the century, she said, and it had remained that way ever since.

Under cover of night, he slipped through the enormous front door and looked across the field. He knew exactly where he was headed. And he knew how to get there without going to the road. At least if his memory served him well.

The cicadas called to one another as the smell of the freshly harvested fields filled his senses with the nostalgia of childhood memories. He followed the beaten footpath a mile and a half until he reached the spot where his parents' cabin had stood. It was still there. Or something was anyway. Twenty-six years was a long time to hang on to a memory when all you wanted to do was forget. Still, something inside compelled him to get closer. Did his family still live on this land? In the distance, he heard a cow's mournful cry.

He knew his mother and the man he'd thought to be his father were both long dead, but what of his four brothers and three sisters?

Movement behind him caught his attention. Before he could turn, he felt something press into his back. The business end of a rifle, from the feel of it.

"Don' move."

"Take it easy," he said, keeping his hands where they could be seen. "I don't mean any harm."

"That so? Then what you doin', sneakin' aroun' a man's house in the dark of night?"

"I lived here when I was a boy. I was just curious, I suppose."

"Name?"

"Andy Carmichael. My folks lived here when I was younger. I just thought I'd take a look. I didn't mean to trespass."

"Andy, huh?"

"That's right."

"I heard tell you was in these parts."

"News travels fast around here."

"It surely do. I's Jerome. Yo' big brother."

Cold sweat trailed down Andy's back. "Would you mind lowering your rifle?"

"I 'spect I can do that. Never can be too careful."

"I suppose not."

When the gun barrel was removed from his back, Andy turned and faced his brother. In the light of the lantern, Andy could see that the man wore dirty overalls. Typical of a poor colored man in the South. A man who poured sweat and blood into someone else's land just to buy his children one pair of shoes a year and barely enough food to fill his belly. Andy's chest felt heavy. Would this have been him?

"Well, you best come on inside. My Bessie was fit to be tied when she heared that cow bawling. She thought it be the Klan."

"I'd best be getting back. But please give your wife my apologies."

"You don' want to meet yo' family?"

"The middle of the night might not be the best time."

"My Bessie won' kere at all."

Andy's insides quaked. He had to get away from here.

This wasn't who he was. . .who he wanted to be. His head was beginning to spin with memories of beatings, pain. "I'm sorry, Jerome. I have to go." Turning, he stumbled back down the path to Penbrook.

He was still shaking when he reached his room. Stretching out on the bed, he closed his eyes, futilely trying to sleep. What had made him decide to go to the old cabin anyway? He'd had no intention of trying to look up relatives that he didn't even know anymore. The Rileys had raised him, and he felt more at home with their family than he ever could with dirt farmers and sharecroppers.

There but for the grace of God go I.

The saying wouldn't go away. His mind repeated it over and over. If his mother hadn't sent him away, he would have ended up precisely like Jerome and, most likely, his other brothers.

Still, in being sent away, he'd become something in between. He wasn't a black man in his soul. He couldn't be. He wasn't raised to be. It wasn't until he'd gone to work that he'd felt the weight of his heritage bearing down on him. The Rileys had been kind. . .no, more than kind. They had taken him into their hearts. Every last one of them. And he had always been made to feel as though he belonged. But he didn't belong. He was somewhere between white and black.

Exactly how Cat felt growing up as a white child until the reality of her heritage caught up with her.

Andy sat up in bed. The old woman, Miss Catherina Penbrook, had known his mother, had helped him escape an abusive stepfather. And now, all these years later, she had beckoned him to write her memoirs.

When Uncle Daniel had first called him into his office to inform him of the assignment, he'd refused to accept it because it meant stepping foot on Georgia soil. When Daniel explained that Miss Penbrook would allow no one else to speak with her, he'd relented and accepted.

Why weren't the pieces falling into place? There was still something missing. He switched on his light and riffled through the boxes until he found the next of Cat's diaries.

CHICAGO, 1879

How could I have been foolish enough to allow this to happen? I mustn't tell Stuart that I'm carrying his child. I will simply insist on a trip to Georgia. After all, it has been ten years since I've seen my home. Surely he will not deny me. I must visit Madame Flora. Her sons sharecrop the fields of Penbrook, though Shaw has never thought very highly of her. He calls her a witch, an abomination to God, and an evildoer.

But I've heard she has a way of helping a woman miscarry if she isn't too far along, and I need to avail myself of her services as soon as possible, before it's too late. I pray she can help me.

Chapter Fourteen
~ 1879

In the shadowy light of impending dusk, the sight of Penbrook brought tears to Cat's eyes. The hired buggy dipped
and swayed through the oak-canopied lane leading up to the
house. Even the initial irritation she'd felt when she found
no one waiting for her at the train station couldn't dampen
the joy swelling her heart at the prospect of seeing her
beloved son's inheritance prospering under his father's wise
management.

The driver pulled his buggy to a halt in front of the
steps. Cat accepted his help down. She glanced up at the
pillared plantation home and placed her hands on her hips.
There was not a sound from anywhere. Had they forgotten
she was coming? The cabbie heaved her trunk from the carriage and clanged it to the ground. "Ya got menfolks to be
a-carryin' dis here thing? It be too big for you."

"I'll be right back." She fixed him with a stern gaze.
"Don't you go anywhere until I come back, or you won't get
a cent."

"Yes'm."

Cat stomped up the steps. She opened the door easily,
with a twist of the knob. "Hello?" she called. No lamps or

candles burned to brighten the rooms against the graying sky. Apparently no one was home.

Cat returned to the porch, closing the door behind her. She scanned the horizon in all directions. The place had an eerie, abandoned feel to it that unsettled Cat. Even the sharecropper cabins on the edges of the north fields had been quiet during their approach. Empty fields, no children playing, no old men milling about their porches. Had their been some sort of exodus?

"Ma'am?"

Turning back to the driver, Cat began to untie her reticule. "I suppose I'll have to give you an extra two bits to carry the trunk inside for me. I can manage the smaller bags."

He shook his head. "Ma'am, I ain't gots time. I's already late to git Miss Lucy Tremaine from her music lesson. Her mama won' pay me iffen I's late again."

Narrowing her gaze, Cat studied the driver. "What is your name?"

"Joe-Joe, ma'am."

"All right, Joe-Joe. I'll give you an extra dollar."

"Dat's right kindly of ya, but I's afraid dat ain't de only reason. Iffen I don' pick up de missy on time, I's gonna lose my position wif dat family. Dey'll tell dey friends. An' I'll lose my position wif dem, too. Den I cain't feed my family."

Cat stomped the ground. "I'm sure it isn't as worrisome as all that."

His expression remained stoic, and he looked at the reticule in her hand.

Cat let out a huff. "Oh, all right. Can you at least carry them up the steps so they won't get damaged by the rain? I haven't the faintest idea when my family will return."

His face twisted in regret and indecision. She could tell he hated to disappoint her, but a man had to make a living. And he obviously made his living from his regular, satisfied customers.

"For mercy's sake. Never mind. Just leave them where you unloaded them."

"I's truly sorry, ma'am."

Cat released a sigh and reached into her bag. She drew out the fare plus an extra dollar. "Here," she said, sarcasm dripping from her lips. "I hope I haven't caused you to lose your standing with the oh-so-influential Tremaines, whoever they happen to be."

His eyes widened. "Oh no, ma'am. I cain't take dis."

Cat felt her heart soften. She gave him a gentle smile and curled his fingers around the money. "I'd be insulted if you didn't. Now, hurry before you're any later."

"Yes'm. Thankee kindly." She watched him go, amazed at how easily a mere twelve years up north had caused the plight of men such as that driver to fade from her mind. It was easy to push back unpleasantness when all you wanted to do was forget.

As the buggy rattled back up the lane, she looked down at her bags. What on earth was she going to do about them? Sudden exhaustion overcame her, and she sat heavily on her trunk. She buried her face in her hands. Unbidden, her mind conjured up the faces of her Negro servants in Chicago. Stuart had hired several to attend to things for her. He'd wanted to hire poor Irish. He'd thought the irony of a former slave being served by white women would be quite humorous, but Cat hadn't agreed. So he'd hired former slaves, free and ready to make a humble wage for an honest day's labor.

Still, Cat had to admit, the comparison between those Stuart hired for her and the Southern-born Negroes who never had the gumption to leave was vastly different. Her servants, for instance, performed the menial labor about the house and attended to household duties, but Stuart didn't treat them as inferiors. He allowed them their dignity and insisted they keep their heads erect and not shift their gazes to the ground in deference, as was so characteristic of the former slaves.

She supposed part of her affection for Stuart lay in his utter lack of prejudice against the black man. Or woman.

At the first droplets of rain, all thought left Cat except for the need to get her beautiful cherrywood trunk, a parting gift from Stuart, out of the rain. Seeing no other choice but to somehow get the thing inside, she grabbed hold of the hand strap on the end closest to the house and tugged.

By the time she got it to the bottom of the steps, her back ached and she was breathing heavily. A sob caught in her throat at the sheer impossibility of the task. It wasn't even something she could almost do. And she knew better than to try.

"Dat Miss Cat?" Shaw's familiar, warm voice came from the top of the steps.

She jerked her head up and looked at the dear face. In a heartbeat, she flew up the steps and flung herself into his massive arms. "Oh, Shaw. It's so good to see you. I thought everyone was gone."

"Dey's all at a barbecue on de river. De sharecroppers be celebratin' de harvest bein' done, and Mister Thomas done killed a pig for de occasion."

"Camilla is attending a barbecue given by the darkies?"

Shaw's eyes flashed at her use of the word. "Yes, Miss Cat," he said, lowering his gaze. "I 'spect I best be gettin' yo' trunk outta dis here rain."

Heat flushed Cat's cheeks, and regret shot through her heart. "I'm sorry, Shaw. I don't know why that came out."

He shrugged. "It be what's in yo' heart, Miss Cat."

"No. That's not true. Especially not about you. You know that."

He turned, his gaze penetrating. "Catherina, I knows dere's a fight inside o' ya. Like dis here war de white folks fought over us slaves. Ya gots to decide what side is gonna win."

Cat felt heat rise to her cheeks. Shaw knew that decision had been made for her twelve years ago. She was who she was. A white woman. A mistress to an influential man. She'd come to accept her place. But beneath Shaw's gaze, filled with love and longing, confusion clouded her brain. "Every time you try to reach deep inside my soul, it rains, Shaw. Do you think that means anything?"

He gave her a sad smile. "I don' hold de heavens in my hand, Miss Cat. Only God commands de rain." He reached out and took her white-gloved hand, pressing it to his chest. Cat could feel the strong, steady beat of his heart. How she would love to lay her head against his shoulder. What would it be like to be loved by this man? But one look into his passion-filled eyes and she knew Shaw wasn't thinking romance. His passion was for his God.

"Oh, Catherina, why won't ya bow to His holy name? I pray ever' day dat He will bring ya de peace dat only He can. But He can't do dat while ya hold yo' sin so tight.

You gots to let it go. It won' be so hard once ya set yo' mind on repentin'."

Panic rose and lodged in her throat. Why couldn't he be like other men? Why couldn't he want her in a way she could understand? A way she could satisfy and be done with? But no, not Shaw. He wanted her to find peace that came with religion.

"Cat?" Shaw frowned. "Can't ya give up de fightin' and let God shine His light into de darkness of your soul?"

Anger poured through Cat. He thought her dark?

She sputtered, but he pressed work-hardened fingers to her lips. "Anybody can be white as a lamb on de outside but jus' as dark as night on de inside. My outside be dark, but inside, God's light shines, makin' me His. Ain't no white nor Negro inside the soul of mankind. Not where God lives."

She highly doubted it. Besides, her trunk was getting soaked and her stomach was beginning to feel queasy. A side effect of her little secret. The secret she would soon be rid of if all went well. She cleared her throat and pasted on a smile.

"I don't know what you mean, Shaw. For mercy's sake, you run on and on, while I'm standing here in the rain getting soaked to the skin. Is that any way to treat an old friend?"

"No, Miss Cat." Shaw's face was suddenly void of emotion. He hurried down the steps and hoisted the trunk effortlessly across his back.

"Is my room still available, or has Camilla stripped it bare and set fire to it to rid the house of my foul presence?"

An indulgent smile tipped his lips. "It be 'zactly like it was when ya went away."

"Lovely. Will you please take my things up there?"

"It'd be my pleasure."

Before he could do as she asked, a young maid entered the foyer from the hall leading to the kitchen. "Oh, Shaw. Thank de Lawd dat be you."

"Everything be all right, Annie?"

The young woman's cheeks darkened. "Yes. I jus' thought it might be bad people comin' in when de missus and mister be away from de house. I jus' got spooked a little, dat's all."

Cat bristled at the girl's reference to Camilla as the missus. She bristled further over the girl's failure to notice her and behave in a respectful manner, and she felt a sense of outrage at the way the girl fawned all over Shaw. It was obvious the man couldn't just stand on the step all day with a heavy trunk on his back.

Without even a proper introduction, she fixed the girl with a steady gaze. "Well, Annie, as you can plainly see, we are not bad people out to rape and pillage."

The girl's eyes widened. "Yes, ma'am."

"It's 'miss,' and I am sure you have work to attend to while the family is away. Or do you shirk your duties unless there is someone watching you every minute?"

"Now, Miss Cat. Ain't no need to fuss at de gal. She be a good, hardworkin' young thang."

"Thank ya, Shaw." The pretty face, beaming with adoration, was more than Cat could take.

"Well, then, if you've time to stand around and blather all day, perhaps you need a few more duties."

"Oh, no, miss. I's goin' back to de kitchen to scrub de flo'—agin."

"Fine. Then perhaps poor Shaw may continue up the

steps before he falls over from the weight of my trunk, which he kindly agreed to carry upstairs to my room."

For the first time, the foolish girl seemed to notice Shaw's burden. "Oh, my. I's sorry, Shaw. I's just rattlin' away like some magpie, and here ya is totin' dat heavy thing."

He smiled. "It ain't so bad, Annie. Don' ya go worryin' yo'self." But a grunt combined with the sweat beading on his brow belied the comment.

"Please continue up the steps, Shaw. There's no point in injuring yourself trying to be brave."

"Yes, miss."

Cat followed behind him. "And stop calling me miss. How many times have we discussed that?"

"I don' rightly know, miss."

"Stop that!" She walked around him. "Here, let me get the door for you."

"Thank you, m—" Breathing heavily, Shaw entered the room. "Thank you."

Cat took in the sight of her old, familiar room. It needed a good airing out. Apparently Camilla hadn't even bothered to open a window. She went to the doors leading to the balcony and unlatched the lock. She grabbed the knobs and pushed, expecting to release the doors and feel a rush of fresh air. Instead, the doors resisted. She jiggled and yanked, and still they wouldn't budge. Just as she was getting frustrated, she felt Shaw behind her. Warm, strong. *Oh, Shaw.*

"Step aside, Catherina," he said. His voice was low and husky, and Cat knew he, too, was moved. If she turned, she'd be in his arms. She couldn't resist. To her disappointment, his arms stayed at his sides. Still, his chest rose and fell, his tension palpable.

"Shaw?"

"Don', Miss Cat. It ain't right. I can't have ya like dat. And ya knows how things be betwixt me an' de Lawd."

Feeling the weight of defeat, Cat moved aside and let him open the doors. How could a woman compete against an invisible God?

"Shaw, is Madame Flora still living on the land?"

Air, thick and moist, breezed in as the doors finally gave way. Shaw turned, his dark brow puckered, eyes narrowed. "Why ya wantin' to know dat?"

Cat had no intention of allowing him to read into her soul this time. She turned her back and pretended to swipe at the dust on her bureau. "Oh, I just wondered. You know how I always liked her."

"Yeah, and I remember she be a servant of the debil. Dat's all dey is to it, Miss Cat. An' ya best be stayin' away from dat wickedness."

"So, I gather she is indeed still living on the land?"

Shaw scowled and released a frustrated breath. He gave a stubborn lift of his chin. "I ain't tellin' ya one way or de other."

"You just did. Now, if you'll excuse me, I'm very tired from my day. Will you please send that simpleminded little maid up here to help me change the bedding and freshen up the room a bit?"

"Annie ain't simpleminded, Cat. She's right smart." His smug grin grated on Cat's fragile ego.

Jealousy flowed like molten lava through Cat's veins. She sniffed. "Well, maybe you don't know she's simpleminded because you're even more simple than she is."

1 9 4 8

Andy's lips twitched at Cat's obvious jealousy over the young maid. He closed the diary and leaned back against the pillow, lacing his hands behind his head. He stared at the ceiling and allowed his thoughts to take shape.

Learning that Miss Penbrook was actually Catherina had infused Andy with the makings of a fantastic book. Miss Penbrook had fallen in love with a black man while living with a white man. Did she honestly want all of that coming out in a book after her death? It seemed the old lady was finally ready to shed her false image.

But why bother at this late stage? Everyone who mattered was gone. Or so he assumed. Then again, perhaps not.

His eyes grew heavy as he pondered the possibility that some of the younger people in the diaries might still be alive.

The next thing he knew, a hard knock pulled him from sleep. Sunlight streamed in through the window, and he squinted against the glare as he sat up and called a greeting.

Delta opened the door. She frowned at his disheveled appearance. "You sleep in your clothes, boy?"

"I fell asleep reading. Something I can do for you?"

"You gots a call on the telephone."

"This early?"

She gave him a look of disdain. "It be nigh onto eleven o'clock. You's sleepin' the day away."

"I worked late," he replied with a sheepish grin. "Do you happen to know who is calling?"

"Mr. Riley from Chicago."

"Uncle Daniel?"

"Uncle?"

Andy's face warmed. "I'm coming."

On the way to the kitchen, where the only phone in the house sat on a small table, Andy tried to come up with a convincing argument why he should stay in Georgia a little longer.

"Hello, Uncle Daniel."

"Andy! Wonderful to hear your voice."

"Yes, sir. You, too."

"How's the research going? Are you getting much help from Miss Penbrook?"

"More than I expected. I am also in possession of several volumes of diaries from Miss Penbrook and two other women who lived in the house where she was raised."

"That's good, Andy. Real good."

"Yes, it is. I'm almost ready to pack things up and come back to write the book. But I need a few more days at least. There are some loose ends to tie up."

"Things about Miss Penbrook, or is this personal?"

"Part of it's personal," he admitted. "I'm remembering some things about my life before I went to live with you and Aunt Lois. I'd like the opportunity to look into it a little."

"Well, there's a small issue here at home that you're going to need to attend to as soon as possible. So let's say I give you one more week."

"That should do it, sir." Andy frowned. "But what's the problem back there?"

"I'll let Lexie explain that."

"My wife?"

"Yes. A beautiful young woman and sweet as they come. You chose well."

Pride lifted Andy's heart at the praise. Still. . . "How did the two of you meet?"

A chuckle filtered through the phone line. "Let's just say you have a determined woman on your hands."

Andy laughed out loud as Daniel told him about Lexie barging into his office. He hadn't seen the spunky side of his wife in years. Not since she'd lost the last baby five years ago.

"Is Lex okay, Uncle Daniel? Anything serious I need to know about?"

"It can wait a week." The gentle certainty in Daniel's voice reassured Andy. "Just finish up what you need to do there and then come back to your wife."

"It might not be that easy. She hasn't exactly been begging."

"That's between the two of you. But there's no denying Lexie's love for you, son. And your love for her. That's enough of a start."

A giddy sense of glee shot through Andy. "You think she still loves me?"

"I'm positive. She told me so."

"Then maybe I haven't completely ruined my marriage. Thank you for calling."

"You're welcome. Oh, and for the record, Lexie has agreed to stay with us until you return so we can get to know her. Do you have any objections?"

"None at all." Actually, the news gave him a sense of relief. At least he knew she was safe and away from Robert. "Is she there now?"

"She's lying down resting."

"In the middle of the day?" Alarm seized him. Lexie had the energy of three people. The only times she'd slept during the day were during illness and pregnancies. "Is Lexie ill? I can come home right away."

He hesitated, which sent Andy into a near panic. "She was a touch under the weather earlier, but nothing a little rest won't take care of."

Andy forced himself to relax. He had to believe his uncle. After all, the God-fearing man wouldn't lie. "All right. Give her my love, will you?"

Delta entered the kitchen just as he was replacing the receiver. "Got a call from Buck a little while ago."

A sense of loss filled Andy when he thought of Buck and Lottie and their children. He had never been one to form attachments very quickly. But this special family had shot straight into his heart. "How are they?"

"Fine. Sent you an invite for supper."

The offer was tempting. He almost agreed right away but thought better of it. "I'd best not. With Sam Dane and that Klan after me, I think I ought to stay put."

A frown creased Delta's brow. "Ya think Buck'd let some white-hooded coward harm ya? Rafe's comin' by to git ya. Seven o'clock. Sharp."

Andy nodded. "All right then. I'd be happy to join them for supper."

"Fine. I'll ring over there and let 'em know."

"Thank you."

"How's Miss Penbrook's story comin' along?"

"The research is coming together nicely."

Delta hesitated, drew a breath, and said softly, "Ya wouldn't make her out to be somethin' wicked, would ya?"

So Delta was aware of her employer's true identity. Andy wondered how many others knew and kept silent. After his own run-in with Southern hospitality, he wasn't too keen on the idea of setting Miss Penbrook up for public speculation.

He squeezed her shoulder. "No, ma'am. I will not do anything to impugn her integrity."

"There you go with that fancy talk." She scowled. "You know I ain't got no idea what that means."

Andy smiled fondly at the housekeeper. "I'll protect her good name."

"That's all I'm askin'."

"How is she today? Any chance I'll be able to talk to her?"

Delta shook her head. "I'm afraid she ain't doin' too well. The doctor said she's about to knock on St. Peter's gate." A great sigh lifted her shoulders.

"I'm sorry."

Her expression softened as she caught his gaze. "Maybe she'll be up to visitin' with ya tomorrow."

Andy nodded. "I hope so." In the meantime, he had the diaries and almost a full day to work.

FROM CAT'S DIARY

Camilla and Thomas arrived home late from the bar-becue, along with my son. Young Henry seemed happy to see me, but I could tell he didn't really remember me. My heart aches at the thought that I am nothing more to him than an old memory. Perhaps Thomas and Camilla have mentioned me over the years. But gauging from his offhanded hello and hasty retreat to his bedroom, I am sure he has no idea that if not for me, this land would be nothing more than cheap farmland, just like most of the plantations in rural Georgia.

Camilla appears older than her years. She did not even pretend to be pleased to see me. Thomas's eyes lit up, though, and when he embraced me, he held me longer than necessary. Camilla left the room and did not return. The atmosphere is quite oppressive between them. Thomas does not appear to be at all happy. I am sorry for them both.

Still, whether they are happy or not, Henry is thriving. He's grown into a handsome young man with many of Thomas's characteristics and features. I am amazed that Camilla has not figured out that her husband is Henry Jr.'s true father.

Tomorrow I will search out Madame Flora. I pray she has the ability to relieve me of my problem.

I only hope Shaw never discovers what I'm planning to do.

-Part Four: Light-

He shall bring forth thy righteousness as the light.

PSALM 37:6

CHAPTER FIFTEEN
~FROM CAT'S DIARY, 1879

It seemed to Cat that all she'd done, from the moment her eyes opened this morning, was smile. Oh, it was good to be home. Camilla's frail excuse for not sending someone to meet her at the train station fell on disbelieving ears—Thomas's and Cat's. But Camilla insisted the letter specified dates in the following week.

Thomas had saddled two horses and whisked Cat away to tour the fields, now empty but for the occasional stray bulb of cotton. "Oh, Thomas. You've done marvelous things with this land. I'm so grateful."

He drew a deep breath and stared across the fields with a pensive gaze.

"What is it?" Cat asked.

A shrug lifted his shoulders. "I always thought I'd have land of my own some day. If the war hadn't come, I'd have inherited my father's lands. But the Yankees stole that from me."

"You know you're welcome here for as long as you live."

"I do know that. But this land will always be Hank's, as it should be. It already is, for all intents and purposes. All the legal documents have been drawn up, and ownership has transferred to him."

"Why don't you get Henry to deed a plot of land to you and Camilla? It's only right, after all. Camilla's father originally willed her a tidy sum. But of course the war cleaned out all his assets except the plantation. By rights, she should get part of Penbrook as compensation."

He shook his head. "I couldn't take Hank's land. I'm considering something, though. Camilla has no idea, but I've been saving all these years, Cat. I've put away enough to buy enough cattle and horses to start my own ranch."

"Cattle? But Thomas, you can't allow cattle to graze in these parts. You'll be run out of Georgia on a rail."

Tenderness softened his expression. "I'm talking about going to Texas, where my sister and her husband live. Mother moved there during the war. I stayed because of you. I should have gone after you left Penbrook, but I couldn't leave Camilla alone to look after things. Now, with Hank ready to take on the plantation, I have my chance. I want to make a fresh start before I'm too old. My brother-in-law has found some good land for me. I—I sent a draft to buy it."

"And how does Camilla feel about this?" When he hesitated, Cat let out a gasp. "Surely you're not saying you would leave her?"

Thomas's eyes hardened. "She's my wife and is welcome to join me. But I don't expect she will."

"Don't be silly. Of course she'll go with you, if that's what you truly want to do. Camilla would follow you to the ends of the earth. She's loved you since she was fifteen years old."

"And I've loved you that long."

Sadness clutched Cat's heart at the love in his eyes. "Thomas, that was nineteen years ago. We were children filled with passion."

He moved his horse next to hers and reached out to take her hand. "I still love you. God help me, even now, after everything."

Once, those words would have caused her heart to sing. Now they left her emotionless.

"You don't love me," he said softly. "I know that. But I can't help myself."

"What about your wife?" After years of glowing reports from Camilla of the happiness she and Thomas shared, Cat couldn't even imagine that Thomas wasn't in love with her.

"She hasn't been a true wife in many years. She's lost too much." He spoke with regret. "At one time, I thought we could be happy. But one baby after another in the grave and she's become a bitter, angry woman. She blames me."

Cat pulled her hand away and gave a nonchalant wave. "We've all suffered loss. It's no excuse to be a shrew."

"Perhaps not. But after losing our last child, she just can't bear the thought of losing another."

Understanding dawned. "And it's easier not to take a chance that she might become with child again."

"Yes. We haven't shared a bed in quite a few years." He leaned toward her again.

She saw the passion in his eyes and knew it wouldn't take much to encourage him to take his solace in her. But that would never happen. Any love she'd felt for Thomas had dissipated years ago.

"You should try harder to woo Camilla, Thomas. Any woman will respond to a man who treats her with gentleness and love."

He looked deeply into her eyes. "Even you?"

A smile touched her lips. "As long as that man isn't married to someone else."

Thomas twisted his lips into a sneer. "Oh, is that so? From what I've seen, you have a preference for the ones who are married."

Cat's ire rose at the ill-mannered comment. "Only one. And you are not that man. Now, if you'll excuse me, I'd rather tour the rest of the fields alone."

Without awaiting an answer, she nudged her horse forward. She ignored his calls, relieved when he didn't pursue her. This argument was just the excuse she needed to follow the path through the woods to Madame Flora's alone and unwatched.

Assured that Thomas hadn't followed, she allowed the horse to slow to a walk. Last night's downpour had given the land an earthy fragrance that filled Cat's senses. The rain had given way to a light shower, whispering to her as though singing a lullaby. She felt refreshed and happy.

But as she approached the clearing in the woods, which she would have to cross to reach the old medicine woman's cabin, she felt the first twinge of doubt. Could she really get rid of the life inside her? Flesh of her flesh? Bone of her bone?

Her thoughts went back to the first time her mother had laid little Henry in her arms. Despite the circumstances surrounding his conception and the months of hating the growing child within her—Henry's child of rape—Cat had taken one look at his tiny mouth firmly clutched to her breast, and all the hatred had left, replaced by the fiercest love imaginable.

She pulled on the reins and stared at the trail of sunlight shining through the thinning foliage. If she could love a child she had believed to be a product of Henry's cruel and savage abuse, couldn't she love a child fathered by a man who loved her and for whom she felt admiration and genuine affection?

Stuart yearned for her to become pregnant. Every month for the past twelve years, he expressed his hope. He'd finally begun to believe that he was incapable of fathering children. With an enormous amount of relief, Cat had eventually come to accept that explanation, as well. In the beginning, she might have welcomed children, but now she knew the ramifications.

There weren't too many secrets in the circles in which Stuart moved. People would know the child was his, borne of his mistress and not his wife. Her child would be looked down upon. Ridiculed and ostracized by polite society for something over which neither of them had any control—the circumstances of one's birth.

Fortified by that final thought, Cat nudged her horse forward once more. This sacrifice was for her child. It was the best course of action.

Just as she was about to leave the woods, she heard laughter and the sound of snapping twigs. Movement caught the corner of her eye. A flash of a blue dress followed by a pursuing man. "Stop! Who's there?"

Silence filled the woods. Even the insects and birds ceased calling to their mates. "Come out, or I'm coming after you. I have a gun," she lied.

"Lawd." The female voice trembled with alarm.

"Don't shoot, Miss Cat."

A few yards away, she heard the crack of a twig as her son came into view. "Henry Jr., what on earth are you doing?"

He turned to the trees and reached out. "It's okay," he

said softly. "You won't get into trouble."

Cat felt her world spin as young Annie, the housemaid, stepped out, her black hand firmly clasped in Henry's. "What are you two doing?" Cat dismounted, planting one hand firmly on her hip. Her face twisted into a scowl, matching the rage building inside her.

"This is—" Henry began, but Cat gave him no chance to continue.

"I know who the little harlot is." Cat stared her down. "Last night she was making eyes at Shaw. Today she's doing God-knows-what with you in the woods."

Annie's eyes grew wide, and she stopped short, wrenching her hand from Henry's grasp.

"Miss Cat," Henry said. "Please don't talk that way to Annie. I love her."

"Love!" Cat exploded. "Don't be a fool."

All the years of sacrifice. Not pursuing Thomas when she knew he had fathered her baby. Working her fingers to the bone to see that Penbrook prospered. Leaving Penbrook, and Shaw, and becoming a white man's whore so that Camilla could marry Thomas and give Henry a good life. All the sacrifices she'd made so that her son's future would be assured. And now he wanted to throw it away on a black whore? She wouldn't allow it.

"This girl only wants to get your white baby in her belly so she can extort money from you and lighten her bloodline. She knows you'd never marry someone like her."

Tears flooded Annie's big brown eyes. Without a word, she turned and fled toward the house.

Angry sparks flew from Henry's eyes. His face twisted in fury. "I love her, Cat. You have no right to say such things!"

"No right?" Outrage overrode reason, and she blurted out her deepest secret. "I have every right, young man. I am your mother!"

Henry's face paled, then went red. "That's a lie. My mother and father were Madeline and Henry Penbrook. My mama died when I was a baby."

Cat's heart raced. How could she have revealed the truth in such a manner? But now that it was out, she could no more have tucked it back into the shadows than she could have denied her love for her son. Her voice softened. "Miss Maddy loved you like a son. But I'm the one who carried you, bore you, and nursed you. You are my flesh and blood, Henry Jr."

"It's a lie. My mother succumbed to an illness, and my father was killed when Sherman marched through Georgia. You were nothing more than a slave in our household who stayed on for hire after the war."

Pain twisted Cat's heart. "That isn't true." Her voice caught in her throat. "I know this is confusing. We couldn't tell you the truth when you were a child. But now that you are grown. . . Perhaps I still shouldn't have told you. But you have to know what I gave up so that you could inherit this land."

"You're a liar." The cold, low tone sent a shiver up Cat's spine.

"Ask Camilla if you don't believe me."

He gave her another long, hard glare, then turned and crashed through the woods toward the house.

Cat pressed her head against the mare's neck. Had she made a mistake? She debated whether or not to return to the house with Henry and make sure Camilla told him the truth, but she knew Camilla would ultimately confess. The years had not been kind to her. She had grown frail, and her will seemed to have fled. She'd never have the gumption to lie about it, not when Henry confronted her.

She gave the mare a gentle nudge forward and continued on to Madame Flora's cabin.

The woman stood regally on her front step as Cat approached. Cat had always been fascinated with the former slave, who was of French and African descent. Her amber-colored eyes bore through Cat, seeking, probing. "So, you've come."

Unease and a touch of embarrassment crept through Cat. The woman was obviously expecting someone else. "I'm sorry. I hope this isn't a bad time. My name is Catherina. I knew you twelve years ago, before I left Penbrook."

"I remember you. And I've been expecting you today. Madame Flora always knows when a young woman needs her help."

Cat fought her amusement. "Really?" The sarcasm was hard to veil.

The woman arched one eyebrow as her gaze darkened. "You do not believe in my powers of second sight?"

"Let's just say I'm not a believer in much, and certainly not in something I can't see. Besides, I didn't come here for a fortune. I am well aware of my future. I'm more interested in your power to help a woman out of a fix."

"I have the potions cooking. Come back tonight by the light of the moon, and I will remove that which you wish removed."

"But you don't even know why I've come."

"I know." Her snakelike eyes commanded Cat's attention, and she felt drawn into the hypnotic gaze. Shaw's words came back to her. *Witch. Wicked. Works of the devil. Evil.*

"H–how long will it take?"

"If you are not too far along, you will drink the potion and expel the blood and tissue within a few hours. If the child has had enough time to form and grow larger than the size of my palm, I will have to help your body deliver."

Cat pushed back the image of a hand-size baby with tiny fingers and toes. "How much is this going to cost me?"

"Can you put a price on your happiness?"

A short, bitter laugh emanated from Cat's throat. "I'm sure you've figured out a way."

Madame Flora gave a toothless grin and named her price. Cat balked at the ridiculous amount. "No one around here can pay that much. What do you charge the sharecroppers' daughters?"

"My price is my price. Some can afford the full amount; others cannot. For those who cannot, we find a way for them to make up the difference. You, my dear, can afford the full price."

"Fine," Cat grumbled. "It's highway robbery, but I suppose I have no other choice." She reached into her bag and pulled out a few bills. "Here's half. You'll get the rest when I'm satisfied that I am free of my little. . .problem."

1 9 4 8

Rafe's old truck rolled to a stop in front of Buck's rooming house. Andy frowned at the large gathering on Buck and Lottie's porch and yard. "I guess they're having a party. I hope I'm not imposing."

Rafe laughed and killed the motor. "Lottie always has room for one more. Come on."

Andy turned to his newfound ally. "You're staying?"

He shrugged. "Like I said, always room for one more. Even someone like me."

Andy and Rafe made their way toward the porch. A path formed and people stared. "You'd think they'd never seen a white man before," Andy said, irritation sliding through him at the rudeness of these guests.

A chuckle rumbled in Rafe's chest. "These people are used to me. You're the one they're staring at."

Heat warmed Andy's neck. "Oh."

Buck greeted them. He slapped Andy on the back. "Good to see you back in one piece." He gave Rafe a pointed look. "Again."

"No sense in bringing up bad memories. Andy and I have made our peace, and all that's forgotten."

"Glad to hear it. Family is family, and there ain't no room for fightin'."

Andy frowned at the statement. Was Buck getting confused?

Rafe laughed and clapped him on the shoulder. "I'm going to find Ruthie."

Andy turned back to Buck. "How are Lottie and the children doing?"

"As fine as can be. Let's go find Lottie. She been wantin' to speak with ya."

"I'd love to catch up with her, too."

Laughter from the kitchen reached them before the men were even close to the room. Buck rolled his eyes. "Women."

Rafe winked. "Happy women, Buck. I love the sound of happy women."

Andy thought of Lexie. How long had it been since he'd heard the melodious ringing of her laughter? Months? Years?

As they entered the kitchen, which was filled with a dozen women of various ages and sizes, Andy felt utterly alone.

Lottie emerged from the middle of the group and rushed to him. Taking him by surprise, she flung her arms about him and held on. Bewildered, Andy looked over her shoulder at a grinning Buck.

"It's okay. You can hug her back."

Andy's arms encircled her loosely and gave her a cursory pat. She let him go and held him at arm's length, beaming. Andy was glad she'd missed him, but he felt a little unworthy of the happiness shining from her eyes.

"Tell him, Buck," she said, "or I'm going to burst with the news."

"I thought the family was wantin' to wait until we was all together."

She shook her head. "I'm not waiting another second."

Buck released a sigh. "Woman, you as impatient as a chile." He draped his arm around her and drew her close to his side.

"Tell me what?" Andy asked. "What's going on here?"

"Well, the reason for this gatherin' an' all is 'cause Lottie here. . .well, she be your little sister."

Andy's mind refused to take in the information. "Can you repeat that, please?"

Lottie threw herself into his arms again. "I'm your sister, Andy. After you showed up at Jerome's place last night, we figured it was time to tell you the truth."

"I didn't have a sister named Lottie."

"Andy, I'm Charlotte. Remember how we used to run up to Miss Penbrook's house and pick mulberries from her trees and then bring them back to Mama? She baked the best pies."

Stripped of words, Andy stared at the woman, two years his junior, whom he'd been closer to than anyone in the world for the first eight years of her life. But how could this woman, this mother of six children, be his little Charlotte? Then it gripped him. The reason she brought on memories of his mother. He reached out and touched her face. The action brought quick tears to her already shining eyes.

"You look like Mama," he whispered.

An older woman stepped forward. "I'm Tawny. Does you remember me?"

Andy embraced his older sister.

"I'm Bessie." The woman dipped her head and refused to look him in the eye. "You was at my cabin last night. I'm married to yo' brother Jerome."

"Sorry about scaring you, ma'am."

"Ya already met my Ruthie." She nodded at the other side of the room.

Andy turned his gaze at the familiar name. Ruthie stood nestled in Rafe's protective embrace. Gathering a deep breath, he closed the distance between them. "I hope you'll forgive my behavior at the club that night. Rafe is a good man. And it's obvious you two love each other. I was out of line."

Ruthie's expression softened to a beautiful smile. She gave him a quick hug. "Sure, I forgive you." Her smile broadened to a grin. "Uncle Andy." The room erupted in laughter.

Andy spent the next four hours getting reacquainted with his brothers and sisters, meeting spouses, nieces, and nephews. Even cousins. He looked around. His family, like all families, comprised a mix of successful and unsuccessful.

One brother owned a barbecue restaurant that was frequented by blacks and whites alike. "I gots a reputation for the finest barbecue in four counties."

"Yes," his wife said, backhanding him lightly on the chest. "And a bigger reputation for braggin' about it."

Jerome seemed to be the poorest among them. He still sharecropped the land owned by Miss Penbrook. He shrugged. "I's saved me about half o' what it's gonna take to buy Mama and Daddy's land. But I don't know what's gonna happen when the old lady passes on." He turned to Andy. "She look like she might hang on awhile?"

Andy's heart went out to him, but he knew the old lady was fading fast. No way would she live long enough for Jerome to save up half the money it would take to buy the land their parents had sharecropped.

"The doctor isn't giving her much time, I'm afraid."

Jerome's expression sank. "I figgered it was gettin' close to her time."

Bessie sniffed. "Maybe she's plannin' to leave it to ya. That'd be the decent thing to do."

Ephraim, the oldest of the five children, shifted on the porch. "The only decent thing that old woman ever did for the likes of us was sendin' Andy here away so Pappy didn't kill him for being half white."

The animosity in Ephraim's tone sent a tremor through Andy.

"Ephraim, you've been drinking again." Lottie scowled and planted her hands on her hips. "I thought you promised no more of that. You know you can't stop before you get dog-faced drunk. For shame."

Ephraim patted her shoulder. "Shame, shame, shame. I'm a shame to the family." He staggered toward Andy. "I'm not the only one in the family to shame us. Our mother laid down with a white man and spawned a bastard. That be a lot more shameful than drinkin' a little bit ever' now and agin." He spun around toward Ruthie and Rafe. "And our own little Ruthie is followin' in her grandmammy's steps, ain't she? Lying down with a white man. How long before she spawns a half-white child, too?"

"Careful, Mr. Carmichael." Rafe's warning tone spoke of control and under-the-surface anger. "I can't have anyone insulting Ruthie. Not even her uncle."

Buck stepped in and took Ephraim's arm. "Come inside with me," he said softly. "I'll pour you a cup of Lottie's strong, hot coffee."

"What're we gonna do, Buck?" Ephraim leaned heavily on the other man. "They're breedin' the color right out of us. Before long, we ain't gonna be black no more. We's gonna be as white as the old lady."

"Shh. No, we ain't. We's who God made us. Black, white. It don' matter what's on the outside. Only what's on the inside."

Andy watched Buck successfully remove Ephraim from the porch.

"I'm sorry, Andy," Lottie whispered.

Tawny took his arm. "I was old enough to know somethin' was goin' on when Mama was seein' your pappy. It was the only time in my childhood that I remember Mama being truly happy. She was in love. Later, after Pappy died, she'd tell me things about how they met and that he woulda married her iffen she wasn't already married to Pappy. She swore he loved her, too, but she never gave his name."

Andy stared at his sister. "You don't know who my father is?"

A frown creased her brow. "No. Mama took it to her grave."

But she didn't. Andy knew the name of the man who had sired him. He knew his white half brother, too. Even Sam's friends seemed to know.

The choices warred within him. On one hand, he wanted to share the name, give some sort of proof that he did, in fact, have a father. But on the other hand, he knew that his mother and Miss Penbrook must have had a reason for keeping it hidden.

Family members began leaving soon after. Amid "nice to meet yas" and "Don't be a stranger," Andy felt accepted by this large and loving family of his. Still, when Rafe gave him the nod that it was time to go, Andy couldn't help but feel relieved. Fifty family members and new revelations were too overwhelming to take in such a large dose.

Lottie came forward to say good-bye. Andy's heart softened. Such a sweet woman. He'd been drawn to her goodness before he'd known of their connection. Now he felt a surge of genuine brotherly love. He allowed her embrace.

"The family never felt whole without you, Andy."

As Rafe's truck rumbled along the road leading to Penbrook, Andy tuned out Rafe and Ruthie's recap of the evening. The amazing events of the day were beginning to catch up with him, and his breathing was coming faster. He'd hated this part of his heritage for so long. He hadn't understood why they'd sent him away. As a member of the Riley household, he'd learned to strive for success. He'd grown up in a wealthy home and never lacked for anything. Living in Georgia for the first ten years of his life, he'd never had decent clothes and food was scarce. He'd come to believe that being white was better than being black.

Even though he couldn't change his skin color, he could control his behavior. And that's what he'd done. Tried to blend in as much as possible. He finally understood why his skin was so much lighter than his brothers and sisters.

Rafe dropped him off at Miss Penbrook's. "I'll be back to pick you up for church on Sunday."

"No, thanks. That's not necessary. I don't go to church."

"You have to go this week. Clara's youngest boy is getting baptized. Besides, your family wants to introduce the prodigal son."

His grin stayed with Andy as he walked up the steps, somehow knowing he was going to be in church come Sunday morning.

※

Ruthie saw them first. She didn't scream; she couldn't. The roadblock of vehicles forced Rafe to stop the truck. Headlights illuminated the white robes and hoods. Ruthie slipped her fingers into Rafe's hand, but for the first time since they'd fallen in love, she didn't feel safe. Rafe would not be able to protect her this time. Tears filled her eyes as he turned to her, heedless of the approach of men on either side of the truck. He took her face in his hands and thumbed away the tears from her cheeks. Then his lips met hers in one last kiss.

※

Samuel Dane answered the knock at the door.

Rafe and Gabe's father, Sheriff John, stood on his porch,

wielding his shotgun. "Where is he?"

"What's the problem, John?"

The sheriff pushed his way into the house, weeping. "They got my boy."

"Who?"

"The Klan. And don't pretend you don't know Sam's the ringleader. Sure as he whipped that Yankee colored, he killed my son tonight."

Bile rose to Samuel's throat. "What are you talking about?"

"The bastards tossed a brick through the jail window with a note telling me where to find them."

Samuel's legs weakened. "Where to find who?"

John ignored Samuel's question. "I found the two of them." He groaned with grief. "In Penbrook's north field. Both of them hanging." He retreated to the porch just in time and vomited all over the steps.

Samuel's mouth went dry. "Two of them? Who else?" *Dear Lord, please, not Andy.*

"Rafe and his little colored gal."

Relief mingled with grief over his friend's loss. "John, if my son had anything to do with this, I'll find out."

"Just tell me where he is, and I'll take care of it myself."

"You can't do that. Vigilante justice is lowering yourself to their level. Let the legal system run its course."

A low sound tore from John's throat. One that could have been hysterical laughter or perhaps a sob. "You know what kind of justice the courts of Georgia will have for a colored gal and the white man who loved her so blindly that he refused to carry on with her discreetly? I understand you want to protect your son. But I couldn't protect mine, and I won't let you protect yours from what he's got coming to him." He pointed the barrel of the shotgun at Samuel's chest. "Now, where is he?"

"If I knew, I'd tell you. But I haven't seen him all evening."

John's grief-stricken gaze locked with his. "I believe you, Samuel. I don't hold you responsible for the animal Sam's become. And I'm sorry that I'm going to have to kill your son. But I have no choice."

The sheriff made a half turn, and Samuel grabbed the shotgun. "Sorry, John. I can't let you go off half-cocked to find my son and kill him in cold blood." He struggled to wrench the gun free from Samuel's arms.

"That's what he did to my boy!" the irate man screamed, gripping the weapon tightly. "Killed him in cold blood. An eye for an eye."

"No. Not an eye for an eye. You have to let a jury decide." Sweat beaded on Samuel's brow as he fought for his son's life. He understood a father's desire for revenge. But what if Sam were innocent?

The sound of gunfire exploded in the room, and the sheriff dropped to the ground. Samuel stood in disoriented silence, trying to wrap his mind around the fact that his friend was lying on the ground with a bullet through his head. It couldn't have come from the shotgun.

"Thank you, Father."

Samuel glanced up to find Sam putting away his pistol. "I'll say that I came into the room and found you in a struggle for your life. I had no choice but to shoot."

Samuel looked at the young man he'd raised. His son. But a man he no longer recognized. "How could you have killed three innocent people tonight?"

Samuel poured himself a drink. "I'm truly hurt that you

didn't thank me for saving your life, Father."

Was he deliberately avoiding the issue of whether he had killed Rafe and his girl? "I was winning the struggle. In another minute, the gun would have been in my hands. There was no need to kill John."

"We both know there was a very good reason. He would have shot me the second he laid eyes on me. Who would you have rather seen die tonight, Father? John or your own flesh and blood?"

"Neither one of you had to die."

Sam lifted his glass of whiskey in a toast, then gulped it down. "Better give the deputies a call and let them know the sheriff's position has been vacated." He strode toward the door.

"What about Ruthie and Rafe? Did the Klan get to them?"

"Father, I've told you before. I don't know anything about a Klan."

Samuel watched him go. Tears burned his eyes at the monster his son had become.

Chapter Sixteen
~Georgia, 1879

Cat arrived back at Penbrook knowing she would have to answer for blurting out the truth to Henry. Half the truth anyway. Only she knew the full truth. Out of fear for Henry's future, she'd kept hidden the fact that Thomas was indeed a father. If Camilla had known, she might not have allowed the land to go to Henry. Now it was too late. It had already been legally transferred.

She found Camilla, Henry, and Thomas in the parlor, deep in discussion.

By the ashen look on Camilla's face and the anger on Thomas's and Henry's, it was obvious Camilla had confessed.

With grim determination, Cat stepped into the room.

Thomas lifted his eyes to hers. "Cat? Is it true? Is Hank your son?"

She nodded. "Yes, he is."

"My father raped you?"

Henry's outburst brought a gasp from Camilla's lips. "Hank, please," she said. "Don't be vulgar."

He kept his tortured gaze fixed on Cat. "Camilla, I'm sorry to offend you. But I'm trying to understand the circumstances of my birth. If my father's wife wasn't my mother, and Cat was a slave in the house simply because she had a small amount of Negro blood, then I can only conclude she was forced by my father."

Camilla let out a huff and answered Henry before Cat could find her voice around a lump in her throat. "Oh, all right. Yes. The whole household knew that my father was a monster. He forced Cat to give you up to my mother because she couldn't have any more children. She could never bear him a son to carry on the Penbrook line." Her eyes focused on the floor. "Isn't it ironic that I should inherit her unfortunate malady?"

Thomas sent her a look filled with disgust. "Please, Camilla. This is not about you. Let's focus on helping Hank adjust to this news."

Camilla nodded and stared, red-faced, at her hands. "I—I apologize."

Cat's heart went out to her. She went to Camilla's side. Wordlessly, she sat beside her on the sofa and covered her hand. Camilla's eyes were wide when she caught Cat's gaze. She clasped Cat's hand between hers in a painful grip, as though drawing strength.

Henry's eyes were filled with confusion, remorse, and anger. He stared at Cat. "You're truly my mother?"

"Yes."

"And I was. . .conceived in rape?"

Tears stung Cat's eyes. "I'm so sorry."

Henry came and knelt before her. "You're sorry? You've done everything to protect me, to give me more than you had. You have nothing to be sorry for." His eyes filled with tears. "My father was a monster. Is that why I ache for Annie? Did I inherit a lust for Negro women?"

Camilla gasped again but kept her mouth closed.

"Hank," Thomas spoke up. "You're nothing like your father."

"Tell them." Camilla's whisper was barely audible. She turned her gaze upon Cat. "Tell them." Camilla's eyes pleaded. "End your son's suffering and guilt over my father's sin."

Cat met Camilla's wide gaze, trying to understand. "I don't know what you want me to say."

"Look at them. Together. Side by side. Why do you think I sent poor Hank away to school? The resemblance was growing every day. It was becoming obvious."

Shock jolted through Cat. "You knew?"

Camilla's head moved in a barely discernable nod. "I figured it out when he was about eight years old."

"What are you two talking about?" Thomas stared from one to the other.

Drawing a shaky breath, Cat met Henry's gaze. "You don't have to worry about inheriting any evil qualities from Henry Penbrook. He isn't your father."

Henry stood and paced the floor, silently digesting the newest information. He released a half sigh, half groan. "I don't understand."

Cat stood and went to her son. She placed her hand on his shoulder. "Thomas is your father."

Thomas's face blanched. "What?"

"It was you. Not Henry."

"You mean, that one time, in the barn?"

Cat nodded, feeling her cheeks warm at the memory.

In a beat, Thomas closed the distance between them. He grabbed her by her arms, shaking her, tears filling his eyes.

"Why didn't you tell me?"

"I'm sorry, Thomas. Your father knew. He figured it out before I did that Christmas before you joined the army. But he convinced me that you would give up everything for me. And that it would be bad for you to do so."

He pressed his forehead to hers. "I would have taken you away, married you."

Cat reached up and caressed his hair. "I know," she whispered. "But it wasn't meant to be. We must think of our son now." She pulled away and turned to Henry.

He stared back, his eyes filled with confusion and pain. "I don't know what to believe anymore." He turned and left the room.

Thomas stared at Camilla. "You knew this and didn't tell me? All these years, I could have been raising my own son, and you sent him away?"

"I was afraid you would go to Cat."

His eyes blazed with anger. He would have melted Camilla to nothing with that look if she'd had the gumption to look him in the eye. He spoke through clenched teeth. "You've never been more right. I would have gone to her. I would divorce you and marry her today if she'd have me." He turned and followed his son.

"He's just upset, Camilla." Cat's heart raced within her breast. Panic rose. Everything she'd worked for in order to build her son's life was beginning to crumble. What would happen to his inheritance now? Would Camilla expose them and claim Penbrook?

Gathering a calming breath, she turned to Camilla. "He'll be all right once he calms down."

Camilla's shoulders rose and fell. "No, he won't. He

hated me before any of this came out. He'll hate me all the more now."

Camilla fell silent and remained so for long enough that Cat finally left her and retired to her room. Carrying her child heightened the fatigue she felt from riding today—an activity she hadn't engaged in much during her years in Chicago. She wrote a brief letter to Stuart, informing him of her safe arrival and letting him know that she would return within the month. By the time she slipped the letter inside an envelope and set it on her desk to be taken into town the following day, exhaustion had swept over her. She was only too glad to loosen her corset, stretch out on her bed, and give in to the blessed darkness of sleep.

When she awoke, dusk had fallen. She dressed, pushing back the thought of what she had to do in the next few hours. Tomorrow, when her little problem was over, she could focus on her son, figure out what step to take next in order to ensure a wonderful future. She stole through the dusky night and saddled the mare she'd used earlier.

"Miss Cat?" Shaw's voice echoed in the dark barn.

Cat started at the interruption. "Heavens, Shaw. Can't you announce yourself before sneaking up on a person? You gave me a fright."

"You ain't fixin' to go fer a ride with the dark settin' in, are ya? Ya shouldn' be out by yo'self anyways."

"That's for me to decide, not you."

"I ain't lettin' ya go off ridin' all alone." He started to saddle his horse.

"I won't be alone." She gave him a pointed look. "It just so happens I'm meeting someone. A man." The lie rolled off her tongue with shameful ease. Still, with Shaw sniffing around, she'd never be able to accomplish her mission to-night. Better to let him believe she had a private liaison than to know what she really had in mind.

"Who ya gonna be meetin'?"

"That's my business."

Shaking his head, he continued saddling his horse.

"You can't go with me."

"Unless ya tell me who you's meetin', I's goin', and det be final, Miss Cat."

"But you can't!"

He fixed her with a long, steady look that clearly re-vealed his determination.

"Oh, all right. I'm meeting Thomas."

"Thomas?" Hurt flickered in Shaw's eyes as he stopped saddling the horse.

"Yes. Are you happy now that I've been forced to break my confidence?"

"Ya mean, you's meetin' him in sin against God and de wife of his youth?"

Cat's stomach dropped at the hushed, sickened tone in his voice. She swallowed hard. "That's right. And you had your chance, so you have no call to object."

"Oh, my precious Cat. When ya gonna surrender yo' heart to almighty God? Don' ya know dat His love is what you been cravin'? Not Mister Thomas, not even ol' Shaw."

Cat's heart nearly beat from her chest. The awe in his voice when he spoke of God drew her in, almost making her believe.

He reached out. "Come back to de house. Don' meet wif Mister Thomas. Don't add dis sin to yo' name."

If only it were that easy. She mounted the horse and

nudged it forward. When she reached Shaw, he looked up at her, pain and regret clouding his face. "I'm sorry to be such a disappointment to you. But God forgot about me a long time ago." Against her will, a sob caught in her throat. "Please don't follow me."

She took off in the opposite direction of Madame Flora's cabin so Shaw wouldn't get suspicious if he watched her ride away. She rode along for a time, not taking any chances. Finally satisfied that he wasn't following, she turned the horse and doubled back. She followed a worn path through the woods and beyond.

Eerie silence greeted her when she reached the cabin. She dismounted and tied up the horse in front.

Swallowing back a sudden rush of fear, she knocked on the flimsy plank door. It swung open. "Hello?"

"Come in," Madame Flora's low, husky voice beckoned. The woman was dressed in a shapeless, dark red and purple robe. A matching turban encircled her head. She handed Cat a cup of steaming brown liquid. "Drink."

"What is it?"

"Herbs to relax you and expel the contents of your womb."

Cat sniffed the cup. She made a face at the pungent odor. "This is necessary?"

"I assure you, it is. Drink quickly. The hour is almost upon us."

"What hour?"

"We must be ready at the stroke of midnight."

The woman was crazy. Still, Cat knew she had no choice. She shuddered and gulped the foul-tasting contents of the cup.

Madame Flora's lips curved into a one-sided smile. "That's it. Now, undress and lie on the table."

Alarm seized Cat as she glanced at the table. On a towel sat a sharp, hooked instrument, a knife, gauze, and a bowl. Her head began to spin. "What did you give me?"

"Shh. Don't worry." Her soothing tone sounded far away. "If you do not miscarry fully, I'll help you along. Now, hurry and undress before you fall asleep." The woman came at her, face distorted, then moved away. Cat blinked hard. Fear spiked through her. *Oh, God. Shaw was right. This is an evil place.*

Run. Resist the devil.

"I need to go. I can't. . . . Don't use those things on my baby. It'll hurt him."

"Don't be a fool. What you are carrying is not a baby. It cannot feel. Perhaps the medicine will cause you to miscarry on your own. Otherwise, I'll have to scrape out your insides, or you will get an infection."

Barely able to concentrate on what the woman said, Cat tried to focus enough to make out the door. The herbs were killing her baby! *No! God, please. I don't want to kill my baby.*

But it was too late. Her stomach rebelled, and she began to retch.

When her stomach was empty, Cat felt herself being led back to the table. She was powerless to resist. Tears slid from her eyes as her clothing was removed. Madame Flora spoke softly, soothingly, but Cat couldn't make out the words. They sounded foreign. Otherworldly.

Summoning as much strength as she could, she opened her eyes. Madame Flora had transformed into a beast. Her great claws moved back and forth across Cat's abdomen. Her words grew louder. A scream formed in Cat's throat, but she hadn't the strength to give it sound.

Help me, God. Please.

Resist the devil.

Cat gathered every ounce of courage she could muster. "No! I resist the devil." She knew she barely made a sound. Miraculously, the mumbling ceased. Before she could even breathe a sigh of relief, it started again. Tears burned her eyes. She didn't have the strength to continue resisting.

Her heart cried out for help once more. An angry roar reached her ears just before she lost consciousness.

1 9 4 8

A shudder crept through Andy as he lay on his bed reading Miss Penbrook's diary. Life was so fragile. He wondered why God gave babies to folks who didn't value their lives and refused to grant children to people like him and Lexie who longed for children and would celebrate every day as parents.

He thought of his own birth. A mistake by all rights. But thank God for the Rileys, who had taken him in and turned everything around for him. What if Lexie and he could find a child who needed a home?

Excitement filled him. With the diary still in hand, he wandered to the kitchen and snatched up the telephone receiver. He put in the call and waited for the operator to announce the connection. "Hello? Aunt Lois? It's Andy."

"Andy? For mercy's sake, son. Do you realize the time? Is everything all right?"

"Yes, ma'am. I'm sorry to disturb you this late. But I'd

like to speak with Lexie if I could. It's urgent."

"Of course. I'll go wake her."

The thought of Lexie being awakened in the middle of the night when she was ill brought quick reason to Andy's mind. "Wait. Maybe you'd best let her sleep. It's not so urgent that I can't wait until morning."

"That's probably for the best. How are things shaping up for your book about Miss Penbrook?"

He gave a short laugh. "I'm discovering as much about myself as I am her. But she definitely led a full life."

"She certainly did."

"I—I met some people tonight."

"Oh? Who?"

He smiled. "A wagonload of my family. Brothers and sisters, nieces and nephews. They're all over the place down here."

She let out a quiet laugh. "How do you feel about that?"

"I understand some things that I didn't before. I know why I was sent away. Knowing that it was for my protection makes it easier to forgive my mother."

"I'm so glad. I've prayed for years that God would help you understand. I knew He would make a way. Do you remember anything about your brothers and sisters?"

"My memory is a little blurry, but the pieces are fitting together."

"Family's important. Don't forget that."

"Yes, ma'am. You're right. All these years, I've felt like I didn't have a family. As much as I love you and Uncle Daniel, it wasn't the same as having flesh-and-blood family close by."

"I understand. You're not finished with the diaries, are you?"

"Not quite. There's not a lot left, though."

"You finish those books and get home to your family, sweet boy. We love you and miss you."

"I will."

Andy said good-bye and hung up. He glanced at the diary still in his hand, and a sense of urgency shot through him. To be done with these. To finish what he came to do and go home. Reconcile with his wife, maybe even start attending church again. He and Lexie had plenty of time to talk about adopting children. He would love any children they brought into their home as much as Uncle Daniel and Aunt Lois had loved him and raised him as their own.

He sat at the kitchen table and opened the diary once more.

1 8 7 9

Relief flooded Cat when the doctor announced her well, with no sign of miscarriage as far as he could tell. "But I'd advise you to get plenty of rest."

Camilla thanked the doctor and walked him out.

Shaw peeked around the corner of Cat's bedroom door and gave a tap.

Tears flooded Cat's eyes, and she reached for her friend. "Thank you for saving my baby. And most likely me."

"Weren't me alone. De Lawd done sent me to ya."

"I prayed. For the first time since I was a child."

"Dat's a good thing, Miss Cat."

A knock at the door broke off any response Cat might have made. She smiled at her son. A tentative, wary smile. "Come in, Henry." How would he react to knowing she was going to have another baby?

"You feeling okay?"

"I will be soon. Thank you for asking."

He nodded, then cleared his throat nervously.

"Mercy, Henry Jr., what is it?"

"Hank. Please."

Cat looked him in the eye. The eyes of a man, not a child. "Hank," she said, smiling with pride at her son. "You obviously want to say something."

"Now might not be the best time to mention this, but. . ."

"What is it?" Dread nipped at Cat's insides like an unruly puppy.

"I just wanted to let you know that I'm leaving Penbrook. Tonight. Annie's coming with me. I have signed away my rights to Penbrook to Camilla."

"No! Henry, don't throw away your life."

"You mean for a Negro?"

"You know that's what I mean."

"Why shouldn't I marry her? I have Negro blood, as well, and I have no rights to Penbrook."

"I did not sacrifice your entire childhood and my chance to marry your father so you could grow up and throw away every opportunity I've given you. Sleep with her if you must, but do not marry her."

Henry stepped close and bent, kissing her on the cheek. "Good-bye. . .Mother."

Cat threw back the coverlet and padded after him into the hallway. She grabbed his arm. "Please. Please don't do this."

Thomas emerged from his room. "Leave the boy alone, Cat. For God's sake."

"Thomas, please speak to him. Don't let him throw away his future."

Thomas pointed to the bottom of the stairs, where Annie waited. "Take a good look at her. That is our son's future." He leaned in close to her ear. Cat smelled liquor on his breath. "You gave away our happiness for absolutely nothing."

Tears streamed down Cat's cheeks as she released Henry's arm and turned back toward her room. Somehow she knew she'd never see her son again. It all seemed so pointless. She stretched out across the bed and placed her hand on her still-flat stomach. Maybe this baby would be her second chance to do something right.

1 9 4 8

Dawn stretched along the horizon by the time Andy made his way back to his bedroom. He'd been in bed only a few minutes when Delta knocked on his door and announced that Miss Penbrook was asking for him.

"All right, I'm coming," he said, a wide yawn tugging at his mouth.

Delta's lip pushed out in disapproval. "Boy, you gots to learn when's for sleepin' and when's for doin'."

"I'll get back to night sleeping soon enough. I'm almost done with the diaries."

Delta handed him a mug of steaming coffee, which he gratefully accepted. "Just don' spill it on nothin'," she groused.

Andy slipped his arm around her. "You know, you shouldn't be so grouchy with me. We're practically family."

She let out a loud harrumph. "So they finally told ya, huh?"

"Yes, ma'am."

"I reckon you think you's too good for the likes of them."

"Nope." He winked at her and hurried to the stairs.

When he reached Miss Penbrook's door, he knocked loud enough so she could hear. At her bidding, he entered. "Good morning. Miss Delta said you'd like to see me."

"Yes. I'm feeling a little better today."

"I'm glad to hear that. Would you like me to open your blinds, ma'am? The sun is rising perfectly just outside your window."

"How thoughtful." Her frail voice worried him.

He opened the blinds. "Would you like me to prop you up so you can get a better view?"

"Why all the niceness all of a sudden?"

"I don't know. Just in a good mood."

She sniffed. "Wish I had something to be in a good mood about. I don't want to be one hundred years old." She stared at the pink and orange painting rising from the eastern horizon. "I wanted so much more for my life." She turned her gaze to him. "What about you? Has life fulfilled your expectations?"

Andy couldn't hold back his grin. "You know it hasn't. Is that question your way of getting me to open up?"

"Don't be smart. Tell me about your dinner with the family."

"Not much gets by you, does it?"

"Well, Delta is Buck's aunt." She scowled at him. "What do you think? Are you happy to be reacquainted with them, or are you too uppity to mingle with your own kind?"

"I enjoyed it. Are you surprised?"

"No." She reached up and patted his cheek, then dropped her hand as though the sheer act of moving her arm was too much for her. She closed her eyes and gathered in a slow, laborious breath. "I'm not long for this earth,

Andy. Before I die, I need to know, what are you going to do with the diaries?"

"What do you mean?"

"Are you going to write my story?"

"I don't need to write it. You already have. In pages and pages of journals."

"They're disjointed. I need someone to piece together the truth."

"Are you sure you want me to reveal so much about you to the world? You've kept your secret this long. Why come out with it now?"

"I trust you, Andy. You'll know the right thing to do when the time comes."

"Do you feel up to answering a few questions?"

"For a little while."

"Some of the diaries are missing. If my guess is right, they're from the ten years you spent in Chicago with Stuart Riley."

She nodded. "You would be correct. Those aren't for you."

Jealousy pinched him, but he knew better than to try to press Miss Penbrook when she didn't want to be pressed.

"All right then. Tell me about the new baby."

1882

Cat sat on the bench next to Shaw and gave an exasperated huff. She stretched out her arms toward the child on his shoulder. "It's my turn to hold him. He's my baby, isn't he?"

A frown creased Shaw's brow. "Dis here chile be de Lawd's chile, and don' ya be forgettin' it. He saved yo' baby boy."

"I know, I know. I was there, remember? But I did have

to carry and birth him, so he's mine, too. Don't you think God might share him with his mother?"

She smiled down at her precious, sleeping two-month-old son. Perfect in every way. The herb hadn't been designed for anything other than to alter Cat's mind and weaken her so that Madame Flora could perform the abortion without resistance. But Cat had heard a voice telling her to resist. It could only have been God. "I know God saved my baby, Shaw."

"I knows it, too. An' I 'spected ya to show a bit o' thanks and serve Him now. But ya jus' go on and on, thinkin' it be okay to run yo' own life. I knows ya done sent Cap'n Riley a letter and ya plan to take dis here boy back and set him smack dab in de middle of a life o' sin betwixt his mama an' his pappy."

"So what if I am? What business is that of yours?"

Stuart was due to arrive on Tuesday's train. Cat had three days to ready herself and the baby.

"God saved dat chile from the mouf o' de lion for a reason, Miss Cat, an' ya gots to make sure an' teach him right."

Cat snatched her baby from Shaw's arms and cuddled him close. She shuddered at the memory of Madame Flora and her plan to use Cat's abortion as a blood sacrifice in order to heighten her dark powers.

When Cat had believed her to have transformed into a beast, she had merely donned a grotesque mask with the face and mane of a lion as part of her ritual.

Even in Cat's semiconscious state of mind, she'd been aware of exactly when the battle was over. Shaw had come against the devil in the name of the Lord. He'd commanded Madame Flora to leave Penbrook land and never return.

And they hadn't seen her since. Rumor had it she had taken up residence in the next county over and had resumed her practice.

"Comp'ny's comin'." Shaw stood as a wagon rattled up the oak-lined path.

"I wonder who would be coming out today." She peered closer, but the sun's glare prevented a clear picture. She stood and carried the baby to the steps for a better view. A parasol peeked out over the seat of the hired buggy. The driver for hire waved as the buggy swayed and rattled closer.

"Hello, Joe-Joe," she called. "How are you?"

"Doin' good, Miss Cat."

"How are the children and Dora?"

"We's about to add another 'un to the family." He beamed with pride.

"Congratulations. And how is Miss Lucy Tremaine?"

"Well, Miss Cat, she be gettin' a mite fat, I's afraid."

Laughter exploded from Cat. "Good for her!"

He pulled the reins, and the buggy halted. "I brung ya a visitor."

The lacy parasol shifted as the passenger stood and accepted Joe-Joe's help down the steps. When Cat recognized the woman, her stomach plummeted. "Shaw," she whispered, "take the baby."

"What's wrong, Miss Cat?" he asked as he did her bidding.

"That's Mrs. Riley."

"Who?"

The woman stepped forward as though she owned every inch of the land. She held her head with dignity, and her posture bespoke quality. She addressed Shaw. "As she said, I am Mrs. Riley. Her lover's wife." She turned her gaze to the bundle Shaw held in his arms. Her expression softened. "He favors my husband a great deal."

Cat finally found her voice. "I think so, too. May I ask why you are here, Mrs. Riley? I know it is not to congratulate me on the birth of my son."

"How astute. May I hold the child while your servant carries my bags into the house?"

"Shaw is not a servant. He is a friend."

"I see. In that case," she said to Shaw, "may I ask a favor of you, sir? My bags are going to be left on the ground by that hired cabbie who assures me that unloading luggage is not included in the ridiculous fare I paid for the privilege of riding in a buggy that I rather feared might not make it in one piece."

"It'd be my pleasure, ma'am." Shaw handed the baby to Stuart's wife without so much as a glance asking Cat's permission.

"Thank you." Mrs. Riley looked down at the sleeping boy, and a look of awe smoothed the wrinkles around her eyes. "He's wonderful, isn't he?" she said softly.

"I think so."

"May I sit with him?"

"Yes, on the bench."

As she sat, Cat faced her, leaning back against a pillar. "Would you like to explain your presence now, Mrs. Riley?"

The woman gave a sigh and looked up into Cat's eyes. Every nerve in Cat's body fought to keep from running away in shame. Summoning her strength, she steeled herself for a battery of verbal abuse.

"You are beautiful and very strong." She smiled sadly. "I can see why Stuart fell in love with you."

"Thank you" hardly seemed appropriate, so Cat said nothing.

"He will be coming in a couple of days to meet his child." She glanced down at the baby. "His son."

"Does he know you're here?"

"No, he doesn't."

Shaw carried the bags up the steps and stood. "Should I take dese into de house?"

"No." The harshness in Cat's tone resonated across the porch.

"Leave them on the porch." Mrs. Stuart smiled. "Thank you for your kindness. Perhaps you will be good enough to be my escort to a hotel or a rooming house later?"

"If it look like it be necessary," Shaw said, his reprimanding gaze on Cat.

She jerked her chin upward. "Thank you, Shaw. Please leave us alone now."

A deep scowl marred his face. He turned to Mrs. Riley. "I be in de barn iffen ya be needin' me, ma'am." He tipped his hat to Stuart's wife, then headed off. Cat felt the weight of betrayal deeply.

"I have a proposition for you, Catherina Penbrook."

"I'm not interested in any proposition you might have to offer."

"Then allow me to give you some information. My husband and I have drawn close once more as husband and wife."

Laughter found its way to Cat's throat. "Come now, you don't really expect me to believe that."

"Regardless, it is the truth. God has a way of restoring even the most broken of lives, and that's what He's done for us."

"God?" Cat began to tremble. "What's He got to do with Stuart and me?"

"Absolutely nothing," she said bluntly. "He does, however, honor marriage, and He has everything to do with my husband returning to me, heart, soul, and body."

"If what you say is true, why would Stuart be coming to take me back to Chicago with our son?"

"I'll tell you. He intends to offer you the life you led before, only he will not live with you or become involved with you on any kind of romantic level. You will live in your house with the child you bore him, and he will be free to visit any time. The child will have his name, and you will be well provided for. When your boy is old enough for school, he will be sent away so that he isn't treated poorly for the sins of his parents. You and Stuart will visit him separately over the years so that no one questions whether or not you are married to his father."

The idea appealed to Cat more than Mrs. Riley could have imagined. Except for the thought of her son being sent away and being all alone at a boys' school.

"That's what Stuart has in mind?"

She nodded.

"But why would he send you before him?"

"Stuart doesn't know I've come."

"Isn't deceit a sin? Shame on you. And here you and Stuart are starting over with God's blessing." Sarcasm twisted her lips.

"Be that as it may, I've come to plead my case with you before you speak to my husband."

"Oh? And what case might that be?" Cat folded her arms and watched as Mrs. Riley held her son against her shoulder.

"Frankly, I'd like you to allow Stuart to bring the baby back alone."

"I beg your pardon?"

"Surely you can see how much better it would be for any child to be raised in a home with two parents who are married and in love?"

"Give me my son," Cat said through gritted teeth. She yanked the baby away. The quick motion startled him, and he let out a howl.

"Please, listen to reason. If Stuart brings you to Chicago, how long do you think it will be before he succumbs to temptation?"

"Ha! So that's it. You're afraid I'll take him away again."

"Yes. Partly."

Her honestly silenced any insults Cat might have thrown.

"Oh, Cat. I've seen you with my husband from time to time, you know." She smiled. "You have never once had the glow of a woman in love. And you wouldn't have stayed away so long if you loved him."

"There are different kinds of love. I care for Stuart a great deal."

"I know. But not the way I do."

Jealousy burned white hot. Maybe she didn't love Stuart the way this woman did, but she had loved. Still loved. *Shaw*. Nevertheless, the woman's soft words filled her with shame. And shame fueled her anger. "Why should I do as you ask? I could simply keep my son here at Penbrook. Tell everyone his father died."

"Would you have your child live a lie? What if he eventually were to learn the truth? He'd never forgive you."

The thought of doing the same thing to her second child

that she'd done to Henry Jr. caused panic to shoot up from her stomach and choke nearly all the air from her throat.

Apparently taking her silence for consideration, Mrs. Riley spoke again, "I am willing to make it worth your while to do as I ask."

Cat jerked her head and caught the woman's gaze. "You want to buy my boy from me?"

"No. I want you to give him to his father to raise and allow me to adopt him as mine. If you do that for me, I will do something for you."

Curiosity got the better of Cat. She frowned. "What?"

Mrs. Riley rose and walked to her bags. She opened one satchel and pulled out a book.

Cat maneuvered the baby in order to take the book. When she saw the title on the cover, her jaw went slack.

The Poems and Prose of C. Penbrook.

She looked up at the woman. "You're saying you will publish my works if I give you my son?" A fierce love for her child rose within her, and she dropped the book on the porch.

Mrs. Riley retrieved the volume. "No. I know you love your son and wouldn't give him up for something so trivial. However, sending him away will create an empty place in your heart. Writing for publication will keep you occupied. Unless my father misses his guess, and he rarely does, these will be quite popular sellers."

"Mrs. Riley, I'm sorry you came down here for nothing. I can't give up my son. I'll fetch Shaw to drive you to a rooming house."

Disappointment washed across her features, but she lifted her head graciously. "I understand."

Cat snuggled the baby close to her heart as she hurried down the steps and toward the barn. Tears formed in her eyes and dripped on the downy head. "Shaw!" Her lips trembled the name.

He came to her without hesitation and gathered her close. "What dat woman want, honey? She upset you?"

"She wants me to give up my baby so that she and Stuart can raise him." She poured out the whole story, including the arrangement Mrs. Riley wanted to make.

"Do you think God saved the baby so I could let Stuart and his wife raise him?"

He rested his chin on her head and stroked her hair. "I's not de one to be askin'."

"I suppose not." Cat pulled away. "Mrs. Riley is ready to go into town. And please don't tell me I should have invited her to stay at Penbrook."

"I won't." He started to leave, then turned back. "Follow yo' heart, Miss Cat. Ya heard God's voice once in a time of trouble. Listen again, an' He'll tell ya what His will be fo' dat boy."

For three days, Cat wrestled with God. By the time Joe-Joe delivered Stuart to Penbrook's door, she knew what she had to do.

Camilla ushered him into the parlor, appearing genuinely happy to see him.

His face lit with pleasure when he saw Cat. "You are as lovely as the day we met, my dear."

"And you are a liar." She chuckled along with him. "It's good to see you, Stuart."

"And you." His eyes trailed over her, and Cat realized Mrs. Riley had been right. Stuart might want to do things properly, but she would be more temptation than he could resist.

"Camilla, will you please give me a few minutes alone with Stuart?"

"Of course."

Cat waited for her to leave, then stood and faced her baby's father. "Stuart, I've made a decision. I will not be returning to Chicago with you."

He hurried to her side. "Cat, please reconsider. I need to be in my son's life."

"Until he's five, and then you'd send him away to boarding school. What kind of life would that be for him?"

Stuart's gaze darkened. "How did you know?"

"Your wife was here a few days ago."

"Sarah?"

"Yes. She told me of your offer to take care of me and to send our son away to school. She also told me that the two of you have renewed your love for each other and that I would have no place in your life other than the fact that I am your son's mother."

Stuart's face grew red. "It has to be that way. I've committed my life to Christ and living right."

"I understand. And believe me, I'm pleased for you. But I can't accept the life you're offering."

Defeat clouded his eyes. "May I see him?"

"Yes, of course. Come with me."

Cat led him to the nursery. Their son's wide-eyed, contented face greeted them. "Well, looky there. I thought you were asleep, young man." The baby twisted his lips into a tentative smile at the sound of his mother's voice.

"He's my son." Stuart's awe-filled tone sent a tremor to

Cat's heart. She knew her decision was the right one. She lifted the baby and held him close, kissing the downy head. Then she placed him in his father's arms.

"I am giving him to you, Stuart. To you and Sarah."

"Y–you're. . .what?"

"I don't want him to be raised the way you suggested. That's no life for a boy. Your wife is a lovely woman. She loves you, and I'm certain she'll raise him the way God wants him raised."

Stuart cradled him close. "What's his name?"

"Daniel. Because, as Shaw said, God pulled him from the lion's mouth."

1 9 4 8
Andy stared at the old lady in disbelief. "Daniel Riley, the man who raised me, is your son?"

She nodded.

"Does he know?"

"He learned of it when he was grown. His father told him. Believe it or not, I became friends with Stuart's wife and visited often. She raised him remarkably well."

"That's how you knew you could trust him when my mother came to you for help on my behalf."

"I knew Daniel would love you and treat you as one of his own. He's always been special."

"What happened with Henry Jr.?"

Miss Penbrook closed her eyes. "Another time."

Andy left the room, his mind buzzing with excitement despite his lack of sleep. He felt sure he would get the rest of his answers today, and tomorrow he could be on his way home to his wife.

He went in search of Delta to let her know Miss Penbrook was alone but sleeping. He found the housekeeper at
the kitchen table, her face buried in the crook of her arm.
Her sobs filled the room.

Andy crouched down next to her chair. "Miss Delta,
what's wrong?"

The woman raised her tear-soaked face. She looked at
him with such anguish that Andy felt it himself. "They've
killed our little Ruthie."

"What?"

"Last night. They was waiting for 'em. Down at the
crossroads. Hung 'em both."

"Rafe, too?" Andy's head began to spin.

"Dear God," Delta moaned. "Why?"

Chapter Seventeen

Andy retreated to his room, unable to breathe, unable to think, his mind swirling in a black mist. *It could have been me. It could have been me.*

Panic seized him. He had to get away from this god-forsaken place before the Klan came back to finish the job. He couldn't remove the mental image of the two of them hanging side by side. It played over and over, like a scratched record.

He started packing his clothes with every intention of leaving Georgia immediately, story or no story.

Delta burst through the door. "Buck was right."

"About what?" he asked without stopping.

"He said you'd be hightailin' it outta here."

"Good for him. He was right." Andy tossed the last of his clothing into the suitcase and snapped it shut. "I have a wife back home who needs me. And I don't intend to become an evening of sport to a group of white cowards too afraid to show their faces."

"Buck also said you'd feel guilty." Delta's gentle tone fed Andy's raw emotions.

Tears formed in his eyes. "The man responsible for this is Sam Dane. He hates Rafe and Ruthie because of what happened between my mother and his father. If he'd never met me, the anger wouldn't be so fresh. Rafe and Ruthie would have had a little more time to make their plans to run away together."

"Now, you's gonna stop this right now. The way that fool Rafe was flauntin' his love for Ruthie, you'd have thought he wanted to be a target. Or he thought he couldn't be a target because his pa's the sheriff and his brother is a member of the Klan."

"For such a secret society, an awful lot of people know who's who."

Andy's fear mingled with contempt. For the Klan. For the blacks who hung their heads in fear and shame. For the whites who honestly believed they were justified in killing a person for having the wrong-colored skin. He was leaving this ignorant, mixed-up society and going home where he belonged, and he'd never return as long as whites reigned supreme. He grabbed his bag and headed for the door.

Delta blocked his exit. "Just like that? You is gonna leave?"

"That's right."

"What about Miz Penbrook?"

"I have enough to write her story."

"No, you ain't. The las' part is the most important. It's what she's been waitin' on."

"Waiting?"

"Waitin' to die. If you leaves, she gonna lose all heart."

Andy lowered his bag and dropped to the bed. He leaned forward, resting his forearms on his knees. "All right. One more day. But that's it. After that, I'm out of here."

1 8 8 0

Camilla stood on the porch and stared at her husband,

without emotion, as he told her he was leaving her.

"There's nothing left for me here now that my son is gone."

Taking the sharp edge of his words without feeling the cut, Camilla knew she would survive whatever the future brought to her.

"I'm going to join my sister and her family in Texas. Perhaps have a chance at a real life."

"When will you leave?"

"As soon as the rest of my arrangements are made. In the meantime, I have procured a room above the saloon. I won't be back to Penbrook."

"I suppose you'll be wanting a divorce."

"I already have Mr. Sutter looking into it."

Camilla heaved a sigh. "I once believed that the worst thing that could happen to a woman was living her life without a husband and children." She glanced up and captured his gaze. "I imagine being divorced with no children will probably be worse."

"You brought it on yourself. Nothing about our marriage was true."

"My love for you was real."

Thomas stared at her silently. "I'm afraid any affection I felt for you has long since been snuffed out."

"And I for you, unfortunately." She gave a tentative, sad smile. "I wish you well, Thomas."

She watched him ride away, then turned back to the house. Cat hadn't left her room in the week since Stuart had taken her son. Shaw brought her food, tried to make her eat. But Cat's sorrow would not be consoled.

Camilla knew she was probably the last person Cat wanted to speak to. Still, she climbed the steps and knocked on Cat's door. When no answer came, she twisted the knob and went inside.

Cat lay on the bed staring out the window as though in a trance. "Shaw thinks I have to have light," she said, her voice flat. "That perhaps the sun shining through my window will lift my spirits and make me forget that I've borne two sons and neither are mine."

Camilla lifted the coverlet and climbed into the bed. "Thomas is divorcing me and leaving for Texas. He's gone for good."

Cat reached across the bed and clasped her hand. "We're alone again."

"At least we have Shaw to look after us."

"Yes, Shaw."

"You love him, you know."

"I know. But it can never be."

"I suppose not. What will become of us, Cat?"

"We'll survive. Together. Just like we promised Miss Maddy."

"Like sisters?"

"Yes."

Camilla swallowed hard. "I'm afraid."

"Of what?"

"My head hurts constantly. My vision blurs from time to time."

A gasp escaped Cat's throat.

Camilla felt gratified that she cared. "I suppose I'll die the way Mother did."

"Oh, Camilla. We'll send you to doctors. Big-city doctors. Miss Maddy didn't have the choice. But you do."

"No. I've seen too many already. They probe and

prod, but no one has a cure."

A tear slid down Cat's cheek. "I'll take care of you. The same way I cared for your ma."

Camilla tightened her grip on Cat's hand. She supposed this was how her mother must have felt when she was dying and Cat was the only person she had to hold on to. Now that Camilla understood, shame filled her at the memory of her behavior back then. Without Cat, Penbrook plantation would have died in the aftermath of the war. Whatever Cat may have done wrong, she had also done so much right.

"Thank you," she whispered. "For everything."

Cat's fingers curled around hers, and Camilla knew she understood.

FROM CAT'S DIARY

Cat crawled out of bed while Camilla snored softly, her cheek resting against the fluffy feather pillow. She walked to the bureau mirror and smoothed back her hair. She knew the time had come for her to pull herself together. Camilla would need every ounce of strength Cat could give her. She stared down at the woman who had been both enemy and friend since they were barely more than babies. Sadness welled up within her. She allowed a few tears to slip down her cheek. Poor Camilla.

1948

Andy spent two days reading, taking notes, referencing and cross-referencing. Comparing Camilla's entries to Cat's.

Camilla had no more entries after Thomas left. And Cat's were sketchy at best. The years seemed to slip by un-noticed until five years later.

1 8 8 5

> *Camilla left me today. I know she's in a better place and*
> *is no longer in pain. I thank the Lord for this. But I*
> *shall miss her terribly.*

1 8 8 6

> *Stuart sends word that our son is quite popular among*
> *his schoolmates and shows promising aptitude for his*
> *studies. They've invited me for the holidays.*

The next few years were filled with short entries detailing
Daniel's life. He and Cat had a special rapport even before
he discovered she was his mother, which grew even stronger
afterward.

1 8 9 7

> *Word arrived from Canada. Henry Jr. has succumbed to*
> *pneumonia. He was buried last week. Annie is coming*
> *back to Georgia with their little girl, Rae. I'm sure her*
> *parents are overjoyed their daughter is coming home. I*
> *ache that I shall never see my son's face again this side of*
> *heaven.*

During entries such as this one, Andy was able to sur-
mise that Cat had finally made peace with God. Somehow
it gratified him to know this. His own peace with God was
fragile at best. Still, he knew something inside his heart had
changed. Softened.

1 9 0 1

Cat sat at the kitchen table sipping a cup of tea. Once she'd
preferred the bitter taste of coffee, but over the years, her

stomach had become sensitive and she found tea more to her liking.

Her Bible lay open to the Psalms. She read aloud the words she had come to know by heart: "I will praise thee; for I am fearfully and wonderfully made." That scripture always reminded her that God had created her with a purpose in mind. To be sure, she had gone about things in a way He'd never intended. Even now, when she was all alone and older than she'd ever thought she'd become, she had to believe that God somehow had a plan for the rest of her days.

A quiet knock drew her from her musings. She looked toward the back door. "Come in." Shaw filled the doorway. Gentle affection lifted Cat's heart at the sight of him. "Good morning, Shaw," she said. "I have your coffee ready on the stove."

She started to rise, but he waved her back to her seat. "I'll git it."

"How's the harvest coming along?"

He sat across from her and spooned sugar into his cup. "Fine. I think dis gonna be da best year in a long time."

"That's good news."

His eyes perused her face with affection and familiarity. "God done blessed dis land, Catherina."

"Yes, He has." She looked at the aging man sitting before her and, not for the first time, imagined that he shared this house with her. Shared her life. Was free to take her into his arms. Though time had softened the passion between them, it had deepened their friendship. And their love.

A sigh escaped her lips. Shaw reached across the table and covered her hand.

"Would it really matter now if you and I got married?"

she asked. "After all, what could people do to us at our ages?"

She didn't expect him to reply. They'd discussed this more than once over the past decade, but it invariably came down to one reality. "You gots to think about yo' grand-baby," he always said.

Rae's sweet face came to her mind. Not really a baby anymore, the ten-year-old girl was the spitting image of little Henry.

She peered into his dark eyes. "Do you really think the day will come when white folks around these parts will allow a colored to own land? I'd like to will all of Penbrook to Henry's daughter."

"Only de Lawd knows fo' sho'. But ain't no way she gonna hab dat chance iffen you and me git hitched."

She lowered her gaze to their entwined fingers. "I know you're right." But that didn't lessen the hurt.

At least she could still have morning coffee and prayer time with Shaw. They'd shared their lives as close friends over the years since she returned to Penbrook for good. Closer than most husbands and wives, but not able to go for walks together, hand in hand, arm in arm. They would share their lives in this manner, she imagined, until one of them died.

1 9 0 5

> *I don't know what Annie is thinking to allow my grand-daughter to marry at fifteen. But it's done now. Her husband, Elijah, is a drunkard and a sloth. But I have given them a cabin lest my darling Henry's daughter be left in the cold. Henry would never approve. If only he were here to look after his little girl.*

1 9 1 0

How can a human feel such pain and still remain alive?
My darling Shaw has succumbed to a lung infection.
He is in the hands of Jesus now. I rejoice for him, but I
weep for my own loneliness. How long must I live with-
out him? I am not a young woman anymore. I've had
my share of the good and the bad life can afford. Shaw
was the largest part of the good. I shall count the days
until we are reunited in heaven.

1 9 1 2

Rae's third baby is born. It is only too obvious the boy is
not Elijah's. I've had to bribe the fool to keep his mouth
shut and raise little Andy as his own. He will not harm
Rae or her new son if he wants any more money from
me.

1 9 1 7

Daniel tried to join the army, but he is terribly near-
sighted, and they didn't want him. Praise be to God.

Andy stopped reading. His eyes scanned over what he'd
read. Rae. Elijah. Andy. Miss Penbrook's diaries had suddenly begun detailing his own life.

1 9 1 8

Andy is the light of my life. He comes to my door often.
I'm teaching him to read. He's the brightest child I've
ever seen.

Andy's heart pounded inside his chest.

1922

> *I have no choice. I must send Andy away, or Elijah will kill him in a fit of rage. Daniel and Lois have readily agreed to take him in. My granddaughter wept bitterly and clung to the boy when I told her what must be done. But she knows it is the only way to save him. His life will be spared. And he will have a future that is worth more than tending fields.*
>
> *Who knows if perhaps my little Andy is the very reason God delivered Daniel from the mouth of the lion?*

Overwhelmed, Andy leaned back in his chair and let the fact sink in that Miss Penbrook was his great-grandmother. Henry Jr., his grandfather. All of his sketchy memories of childhood seemed clearer now. He remembered Miss Penbrook giving him cookies and lemonade, listening to his stories, and applauding his genius. The memories came back with more clarity now that he knew who the old woman in his mind happened to be.

He had question upon question to ask her. But more than anything, he wanted to gather the frail old woman, his great-grandmother, in his arms and squeeze out all the hurt she'd endured in her lifetime.

He shot to his feet and raced down the hall to her room. Stopping before her door, he composed himself. His light tap elicited no response, so he opened the door and slipped inside.

The old lady lay facing the window. Bathed in light, her face shone.

Andy caught his breath at the expression of rapture on her face. "Miss Penbrook?"

She remained still. Andy stepped closer. Tears sprang to his eyes. She stared but didn't see. Now he understood the smile on her lips. Miss Penbrook had seen the face of Jesus.

He took her cold hand and pressed it to his lips. "Thank you, my great-grandmother Catherina."

Laying her hand back on her chest, he called for Delta.

Andy left the room, his mind still spinning from the discovery that he had a full heritage. Black and white, rich and poor. Young and old.

THREE DAYS LATER

The burial took place in the little cemetery at the edge of the woods behind Penbrook House. In a letter of instruction, Miss Penbrook had handpicked each of the mourners she wanted to attend her funeral. She was laid to rest next to Shaw in the old slave cemetery.

At the old woman's request, Andy gave the eulogy. Now he understood the reason for the diaries. He stood at the graveside and took in the sight of his large family.

"On a hot Georgia day in 1852, a woman named Naomi stood on the auction block. They were selling her, apart from her baby. In a moment of desperation, she snatched her four-year-old daughter and tried to run away. A woman named Madeline Penbrook saw the tragedy playing out before her and dared to change the lives of a slave woman and a little girl named Catherina."

EPILOGUE

Andy smiled down at his daughter as she squirmed against his chest and made cooing baby noises. He knew she wouldn't be satisfied with him for long. But for now, he relished the warmth of her little body, the soft scent of her recent bath.

"Let's let Mama sleep for a few more minutes, little one."

At the sound of his voice, the baby stopped squirming and stared back at him with curious assessment. Wild love swelled his chest every time he looked at his baby girl.

"Cat's awake?" Lexie's sleepy tone spoke from the bed.

Andy smiled and nodded. "Only for a few minutes."

"Why didn't you wake me?"

The baby let out a hungry wail. Andy chuckled. "We were just about to."

He walked to the bed and laid his beautiful daughter in his wife's arms. "Catherina Carmichael, you are loved." He sat on the edge of the bed and marveled at the sight of the two females in his life.

He stroked the baby's satiny head as she latched on to her mother's breast. The decision to name the baby after Cat had been an easy one. He and Lexie had agreed that in many ways the elderly woman had saved their marriage. To be sure,

Andy's trip south had been life changing. In the aftermath, he'd reconnected with his wife. Had reconnected with the Rileys. And most important, had reconnected with God.

Though Andy had returned to Chicago after his great-grandmother's funeral, his thoughts often turned to Georgia. Along with several thousand dollars, Cat had willed him the Penbrook diaries, minus those she'd set aside for Jonas. The inheritance had been more than he ever dreamed he might receive.

Andy hadn't been surprised that Cat had willed Penbrook to Daniel Riley. Indeed, Andy would have been afraid to accept if she'd willed it to him. Especially after his run-ins with the Klan; specifically, his half brother Sam.

A year after Rafe's and Ruthie's deaths, no one had been arrested for their murder. Andy had strongly suggested that his Southern family pursue justice. But in spite of their bitterness, no one was brave enough to follow through. Perhaps they would some day. But for now, fear kept them quiet and a murderer stayed free.

Andy thanked God for sparing him. He knew he'd never take his life for granted again. He welcomed the second chance to be the husband, and now father, that he'd always wanted to be.

A soft snore captured Andy's attention. Lexie had fallen asleep with Cat at her breast. His lips pulled into a smile at his wide-eyed daughter. Now with a fully belly, Cat obviously wasn't ready to go back to sleep. She stared up at him with beautiful brown eyes. Her lips puckered, and she cooed as though longing to share all the love in her heart. Enchanted, he lifted her in his arms and walked across the room to the rocking chair.

In this baby, he saw all that was good about the world. The innocence of a child who had never known bigotry, who would never have to hide who she was.

Andy prayed that Cat's soul would stay as pure and unfettered as it was this day. Only God knew Cat's future, but Andy intended to do all he could to see that she lived, loved, hoped, dreamed—had every opportunity to be all she was created to be. Unlike her predecessor, his Catherina had been born free. And with God's grace, Andy would see to it that she remained free.

TRACEY BATEMAN

Tracey Bateman serves as president of American Christian Fiction Writers and has over a dozen stories in print. Her life is filled with chaos and fun due to comical kids and a supportive husband. When not writing, she spends time with family and friends, reads her favorite authors, and sings on the praise team of a rapidly growing contemporary church, where the focus is on raising the standard for God. She has adopted this philosophy in her own life and strives for excellence in every area. She believes all things are possible and encourages everyone to dream big. Tracey lives with her husband and four children in Missouri. For more information, visit www.traceybateman.com.

If you enjoyed

The COLOR of the SOUL

then read

FREEDOM of the SOUL

next in

The Penbrook Diaries

by Tracey Bateman

ISBN 1-59789-221-1

Coming in October 2006

Available wherever Christian books are sold.

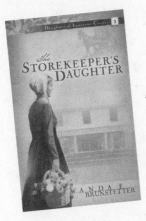

Heirs of Anton

by Susan K. Downs and Susan May Warren

Heirs of Anton: Ekaterina

When an unusual package arrives in the mail, Ekaterina "Kat" Moore boards a plane to Russia, her ancestral home, to seek some answers—and perhaps find love.
1-59310-161-9

Heirs of Anton: Nadia

Former CIA spy Nadia Moore is sneaking into Russia to save her husband from a gulag execution. But can she resurrect the love she thought had died?
1-59310-163-5

Heirs of Anton: Marina

When Russia is invaded by Hitler, Marina finds herself alone and pregnant. If she does—or doesn't—fight for the motherland, what will be her child's future?
1-59310-350-6

Heirs of Anton: Oksana

Oksana harbors a state secret so dangerous she dares not share it with the man she loves. Will Anton's fledgling courage destroy her future?
1-59310-349-2

Also available from
BARBOUR PUBLISHING, INC.